# THE
# SCORPION
# TALES

# THE
# SCORPION
# TALES

## SUDHIR NAIR

### PARTRIDGE
A Penguin Random House Company

**To order additional copies of this book, contact**
Partridge India
000 800 10062 62
orders.india@partridgepublishing.com

www.partridgepublishing.com/india

# CONTENTS

# Contents

To

Amog and Bhuvi
**You are everything to me.**

# Acknowledgements

At 45 when I decided to write my first collection of short stories, I was aware that I have neither any formal training in writing nor the backing of any literary figure. All I had was this burning desire to tell a few stories and a set of people who had unshakable faith in me.

Dad, thank you for giving me the greatest gift I possess—my imagination. You have always inspired me.

Mom, your sense of humor is infectious. I am sure wherever you are, you are making people laugh with your jokes.

My immediate family Madhu, Ganesh, Priya, and Sunita, thanks for all the love and affection.

My friends (especially from Round Table), for all the encouragement and motivation—if I don't mention some of them, I will not do justice to this book.

Jeetu—you always manage to get the best out of me. Thanks for all the encouragement and support. Most importantly, thanks for believing in me. You are truly awesome.

Satish, Biju, Mohan, Patty and the Krishnans—thanks for all the honest feedback.

The kids—Adi, Abhi, Amatya, Aishu, Akshita, and Samhita—thanks for just loving me as I am.

Amog, thanks for the unconditional love and for making me so proud with all that you do.

I save the best for last: my best friend Bhuvi, thanks for the patience of vetting each page, making a hundred corrections every time I changed the manuscript. Thanks for discussing every plot, for questioning my characters' every motive (and thankfully never my own motives), and most importantly, for never losing faith in me through all those roller coaster rides of ours.

Everything I do, I do it for you.

# THE PHANTOM PHONE

I t all seemed so unreal.

Christopher was not a guy who pulled a fast one just for laughs. His integrity was unquestionable, as was his sobriety. Yet, on that day as he told us what bordered on the incredulous, we wondered if he was pulling a fast one on us.

'Stella is dead,' he said gravely.

'What?' I asked, not sure if I had heard him right.

'Stella . . . is . . . dead,' he said even more slowly, almost as if his speech was slurred.

It was a Sunday afternoon, and the four of us—Akhil, Shiv, Mohan, and I—had just returned to Shiv's home after playing a cricket match. Having won the twenty-overs-a-side match, we were in quite high spirits. Not mine actually, because I did not get a chance to bat or bowl in the game. For one full session of the match, I had been banished to a sweeper position by my captain. I understood why they named the position thus, especially since I did not have the support of a long off or a third man, and was expected to fetch the ball every time the ball crossed the thirty-yard circle on my side.

Shiv had pulled out a deck of UNO cards and started to deal out a hand. I was too tired to play and was lying on the couch ready to doze off when Christie, short for Christopher, turned up looking quite dazed.

There was a sense of disbelief amidst us after we heard the news, even more so because we had met Stella the previous evening. The occasion had been a birthday party of one of Christopher's cousins which we had gatecrashed, primarily to chat up a few girls and, in the bargain, also gorge on the delicious buffet spread. Money was hard to come by and any parties, invited or uninvited, were most welcome.

'Are you serious?' Mohan asked a stupid question.

'You think I would joke about this?' Christie asked, clearly rattled.

'But . . . we just met her yesterday and she was fine.' This time Akhil butted in. I was too shocked to say anything. 'She was laughing and cracking jokes,' Akhil added.

'How?' Shiv asked. Shiv was typically that—not someone who wasted words. *If you can communicate something in one word, why say four?*

'I am not sure,' Christie answered, pausing.

'Accident?' Shiv asked.

'It is rather bizarre. I am not sure I can word it properly,' Christie mumbled. After a long pause, he added, 'I don't think you guys are going to believe me. I wouldn't blame you. I couldn't believe the bloody thing myself when I first heard it.'

Clearly, there was an interesting story in it, which got my attention. We all remained silent and waited for Christie to speak.

'This happened the other day, I don't remember exactly when,' Christie started. 'Clearly, I did not give much credence to her story when she told me the first time—'

'What happened?' I asked, trying to bring Christie's focus back to the business at hand.

Christie was clearly irritated at my interruption.

'Will you wait for me to finish?' he asked, glaring at me. 'Stella told me that she was trying to call up a friend of hers. Because she did not have any balance left on her mobile phone, she called from a payphone near her home.'

'Okay, all right, continue,' Mohan interjected as if the smaller details were not important.

'The payphone part is important,' Christie remarked, understanding Mohan's standpoint. 'You will soon know why.'

'Point taken,' Mohan conceded.

'Like I was saying, Stella was trying to call up a friend of hers from a payphone. I understand that Stella dialed the number a couple of times, but the call wouldn't get through. On the fourth or fifth attempt, even before she could hear the phone ring on the other end, someone answered the call. Stella told me that she felt as if it had been waiting for the phone to ring.'

'It?' Shiv asked.

'Yes—*it*,' Christie replied. 'You will understand why I deliberately used the word *it* soon.'

I saw everyone's eyes light up. My own eyebrow was reaching for my hairline.

'Stella immediately understood that the voice she heard was not that of her friend, but that of an old woman. It was frail and weak. She realized that she had got through to the wrong number. She asked the lady which number the call had landed on and was taken aback at the lady's rudeness.'

'Why, what did the old lady say?' Akhil asked.

13

'Seems like she told Stella to check the damn number before she dialed, or something to that effect.'

'Oh,' Mohan gasped.

'Exactly,' Christie continued. 'Stella disconnected the line and redialed. For the second time that day, she got connected to the same wrong number. The same voice answered the call and discovering it was Stella again, rudely asked Stella if she was blind. Stella supposedly apologized. However, the lady let loose a barrage of obscenities and Stella was clearly ruffled.'

'And then?' I asked, not clear where this was heading.

'You know Stella well. She is not one to lose her temper that easily,' Christie said.

We all shook our heads. We often referred to Stella as the counselor. She had amazing listening skills and patience.

'However, Stella told me that she had no idea what got into her and she found herself screaming at the top of her lungs,' Christie said. 'What Stella told me next was weird. She said that the old lady started laughing.'

'Laughing?' I asked, confused. 'Why would she laugh?'

'Precisely what I asked Stella. Obviously Stella did not have an answer. But listen to this and this is where it really gets crazy, man. Stella swore that the laugh ended in the deep-throated chuckle of a man.' Christie shuddered, recalling his conversation with his dead cousin.

I felt a chill go down my spine. I looked around and everyone in the room was looking at each other in shocked amazement. Everyone except Shiv. Shiv did not believe in the paranormal. He scoffed and called it mumbo jumbo and ghost crap.

'Continue,' Shiv said, disguising a scornful smile. If the whole conversation had not been about something as serious as Stella's untimely death, I suspect he would have cracked a joke or dismissed us as crackpots.

'Stella said that a man then started speaking to her,' Christie continued from where he left off. 'He warned Stella that she would die within a week.'

'How?' Akhil asked, his eyes almost popping out of his skull.

'I don't remember exactly,' Christie said. 'Something about catching a flu or fever and dying. Some nonsense. Like I said, I did not give this strange talk any more importance than it deserved. However, I knew that Stella was very disturbed. In fact, I thought she was okay when I met her yesterday. She did not refer to the conversation. I thought she had forgotten all about it.'

'Then how did she die?' I asked.

'No idea,' Christie said, still trying to come to terms with his cousin's death. 'When my uncle went to her room, she was found lying dead on her bed. She had complained of feeling feverish yesterday night after the party and so went to bed as soon as she got home. But this morning . . .' Christie left it at that.

'Now what?' Akhil asked after a few moments of silence.

'I don't know.' Christie sounded despondent. 'I had suggested a post-mortem, but Uncle was not too happy with my idea. I guess I will keep you posted if we have any updates. Will you be attending the service?'

'Of course we would,' I said and looked around for support. The others just sat around looking at the floor. Shiv obviously was deep in thought.

'Christie, do you happen to have the number that Stella dialed?' Shiv queried.

'Yes. I do,' he said and dug into his pocket. 'Like I said, I did not take the issue seriously, but Stella insisted that I keep this,' he said, rummaging through a wad of paper bills he had pulled out of his pocket.

'What is it?' Shiv asked.

'I told you she called from a payphone near her house. This is the receipt,' he said, handing over a slip to Shiv. 'Why do you ask?'

'Nothing really. Just inquisitive,' Shiv said dismissively, keeping the slip in his pocket. 'Can I keep this with me?'

'Sure,' Christie replied.

'What about the funeral?' Mohan asked.

'I suggest you guys keep off it,' Christie suggested. 'Just come for the 7th day service, that will do.'

None of us disagreed.

'I need to leave. Just dropped in to inform you,' Christie said, getting up.

One after the other, we got up and hugged Christie.

'Take care, man,' I told Christie, walking him to the door.

After Christie left, we all sat silently, not knowing what to say. It was an uncomfortable silence until Shiv pulled the slip out of his pocket. We all gathered around him to take a peek. There were two bills printed on the slip. Each mentioned details of the phone number, date and time of call, and the time clocked for each call. I noticed that the first call was for ten seconds. Within a minute Stella seemed to have redialed. The second call was for one minute and fifty-six seconds.

'There is still so much that science can't answer for.' Mohan was the first to speak.

'Bull crap,' Shiv said, obviously annoyed.

'Don't say that,' Mohan retorted. 'The proof is in your hands.'

16

'This? Proof?' Shiv thundered.

'Yes, it is,' Mohan defended himself. 'Look at the phone number. It is most ominous.'

'What is so fishy about the number 81366630?' Akhil asked.

'Look at it closely,' Mohan replied. 'Now, if you break it up into smaller parts, you will notice that to start with, 8 is considered as the unluckiest amongst single digits. So is the next number, 13. The next three digits are 666 and that's supposed to be the number of the devil. This is followed by 3. There is a saying that 3 a.m. is the devil's hour as it is exactly the opposite of 3 p.m., traditionally taken to be the hour when Jesus died.'

'Whoever feeds you this rubbish?' Shiv asked, clearly angry with where the conversation was headed.

'I saw it in a movie called *The Exorcism of Emily Rose*,' Mohan said somewhat sheepishly.

Shiv just nodded his head in disbelief. 'People like you will believe any crap and that is why our country still believes in god-men, astrologers, and palmists.'

Mohan was clearly taken aback by the personal attack.

'So you tell me, oh wise one, how did Stella die then?' he asked sarcastically.

'Uh-oh,' I intervened. 'Let's not start a fight here.'

'Ask him to explain what happened,' Mohan reiterated.

'You want to know what happened. I will tell you what happened,' Shiv said forcefully. 'Stella just plain psyched herself to death. That is what happened.'

'Great,' Mohan said, still smarting from the earlier personal attack. 'It is as simple as that. Just because Mr. Know-it-all says so. Can you also explain how she got the wrong number twice, or is that a mere coincidence?'

'Mohan, I am sorry about having shouted at you earlier. It is just that all this superstition stuff irritates me, especially when it comes from an educated guy like you,' Shiv said, sounding truly apologetic.

'Apology accepted, but you still need to answer my question. If Stella dialed her friend's number, how did the call land at that spooky place, wherever it is, not once, but twice?' Mohan said, not wanting to let go.

'I think I can actually explain your point. Remember what Christie told us? He said Stella dialed the number a couple of times, but the call wouldn't get through. That probably means that there was a problem with her friend's number. Would you agree?'

A couple of us nodded, but I was still unclear about what Shiv was saying.

'Good. Now I want you to visualize what might have happened. Close your eyes', Shiv said, 'and just visualize what I am saying.'

I closed my eyes and started to focus on Shiv's voice.

'Stella dials the number the first time. She does not get the number. She presses the redial button three or four times. She gets the same response. She cradles the receiver back, picks it up, and this time, punches the number fresh into the phone. She gets a wrong number. She punches the number fresh into the phone once again and gets the same number.'

'But how can she get the wrong number twice?' Mohan asked again.

Shiv turned to me and asked, 'What happens when you dial the dispatch section from your intercom every time?'

'I get the proofreader Ram,' I laughed, understanding where he was headed. 'That is because the dispatch section number is 4668 and Ram's number is 4558. The 5 and 6 always get mixed up.'

'Possible?' Shiv asked, turning to Mohan.

Mohan obviously didn't want to give in. He thought about it for a while and finally said, 'Possible. But I am not fully convinced.'

'The only way I can convince you, as I see it, is by getting a real ghost and making it declare that ghosts do not exist,' Shiv said.

We all laughed. Mohan was, however, unimpressed.

'Let me put all your doubts to rest,' Shiv said and picked up his cordless phone from the base station. He dialed the number 81366630, in a way we could all see, and put it on speakerphone and increased the volume to maximum. We heard the faint blips and we were all startled when suddenly the voice of a woman came through. 'Please check the number you are dialing.'

After the initial shock had passed, we fell on the floor laughing and imitated each other's startled expressions.

More than anything, I was happy there was a rational explanation to what had happened. And even though there was a nagging doubt somewhere in my mind, I decided to ignore it.

The whole week was a particularly busy one with our editorial team at office deciding to come out with a special edition on mobile phones and tablets. The advertising team was running around like a headless chicken, trying to garner as much advertising support as possible for the four-pager.

We had attended the seventh day service for Stella, but we did not indulge in any detailed conversation about the circumstances of her death. The incident was soon forgotten and almost erased from our memories. This story wouldn't have been written either, but for a series of incidents that followed that weekend.

As a matter of routine, the five of us would usually meet at a local pub on Friday evenings to discuss just about anything, from the IPL auctions to which media executive was sleeping around with which client. The plans for the rendezvous were usually made on Friday during lunch at the office. Shiv, Mohan, and I reached the office canteen and waited for Akhil to join us.

Akhil entered the canteen a few minutes later accompanied by Anita. Anita, 32 and still single, was the secretary to our marketing director. One look at Anita and you wouldn't question why she was still single. Not that Anita had not tried every trick in the trade to ensnare some unsuspecting victim in a cybercafé or a chat room. But most often, they took their first look at her and made a quiet getaway.

Anita was a very resourceful worker though, and one of her assets was her voice. On the phone, she came across as a flirtatious pretty young thing who could be sitting on your lap and talking to you. We fell back on her every time we wanted an appointment fixed with a slippery or reluctant client.

That day, though we were not surprised to see her, we were surely intrigued that Akhil had brought her straight to our table. I hoped that she wasn't planning to join our evening pub-hopping group.

'You should hear what Anita has to say,' Akhil said, smiling gleefully.

I was hoping that she had some inside information on our increments. What she said was far from that.

'I got this number from one of my friends, yeah,' she started. That was another thing about Anita. When she talked to you, she always ended with a 'yeah'. Surprising, I had never heard her say 'yeah' when she talked on the phone.

'Which number?' Shiv asked.

'That 81366630, yeah,' she replied while we all gave each other knowing glances. 'A guy picked up the phone and talked to me, yeah.'

'What?' Mohan blurted out. 'You actually talked to someone on that number?'

'Yeah, yeah!' she said, quite surprised that we didn't believe her.

'What did this guy say?' Shiv asked.

'I was trying the number because I wanted to know what it was all about, yeah. One of my friends told me that the person who picks up the phone can predict your future, yeah,' Anita said in amazement, and her hands were covering her cheeks.

*'Wow,'* I thought, *'now it has become an astrology hotline. Shiv was right. People will believe anything.'*

'Around 10 p.m. last night I got through the number, yeah. A guy picked up the phone and I asked him if it was 81366630 and he even confirmed it, yeah!' Anita continued from where she had left off.

'You called from a mobile phone?' I asked.

'No, from my residence landline, yeah,' Anita replied.

'Did you get the number on the first attempt?' Shiv countered.

'No, yeah. I had been trying since 8 p.m. and was about to give up when I suddenly connected,' Anita replied, marveling at her own persistence.

'And?' Shiv encouraged.

'Well, this guy confirmed the number and I was sooo excited, yeah,' Anita said, her excitement visible on her face. 'I asked about my future, yeah, and told him things like I was unmarried and waiting for Mr. Right.'

'Wonnnderfool,' Shiv added rather sarcastically. 'Did you give him your home address too, and tell him you live alone and all that?'

'No, yeah,' Anita replied. 'I am not so dumb, okay. Anyway, I asked him to tell me about my future and he refused. I kept pestering him and he said he knew that I was wearing something dark, because of which he couldn't see into the future, yeah.'

'And were you wearing a dark dress?' Mohan asked.

'I wasn't, yeah. In fact, I checked up everything and I was wearing nothing dark and I told him so. He asked me to recheck and I discovered that I had on a dark band to tie up my hair, yeah!'

'Wow,' Akhil said. 'How could he have known?'

'That is what surprises me, yeah. Anyway, after I had removed the band, I asked if he was willing to tell me my future, yeah, and he said that he could. He told me that something was bothering me and that he would give me a clear picture if I met him at Hotel Horizon today, yeah. He said he would meet me as an ordinary man and that I should go alone—'

'How would he recognize you?' I asked.

'He said he would, yeah. Initially, I said I wouldn't be able to meet him today and that I could only go there the day after. He agreed, but I was too excited and I agreed to meet him today itself.'

'And do you plan to go?' Shiv asked.

'Of course, yeah,' she said. She noticed the sullen expression on Shiv's face and asked, 'I shouldn't?'

'Of course not, you stupid woman,' Shiv blurted out in frustration. 'Don't you see he is a bloody fraud?' He turned to us in frustration. We looked at each other. 'Can't you guys see it?' he asked.

'No,' I said. 'For example, how did he know Anita was wearing something dark?'

'Very simple,' Shiv answered. 'At any given moment of time, we are all wearing something dark. Especially a girl likes to dress up in more colors,' he reasoned.

Anita surely was happy to hear her being referred to as a girl. She nodded her head vigorously.

'You are wearing a black shoe, Akhil is wearing a dark tie, I am wearing a shirt with black stripes, and Mohan is in all probability wearing dark-colored underpants,' Shiv said.

I looked at Mohan, who had a 'How did Shiv know I am wearing dark underpants?' expression.

'Are you?' I asked Mohan on the side and, before he could answer, added, 'Wearing underpants at all?'

He just nodded. 'Of course I am wearing underpants. But how the hell did Shiv find out?' he asked me.

I started to look at Shiv as if he had just transformed into Sherlock Holmes.

'Wow,' I said in admiration.

'There is nothing *wow* about it,' he said. 'Listen to the wordplay here and you will understand. That guy isn't saying "black". He is using the word "dark". The chances of someone wearing black are much less. But the minute you say "dark", you have increased your chances of a hit to 50 per cent.'

I found Shiv's comments logical and convincing.

'But', Mohan asked, 'how did this guy know there was something troubling Anita?'

'Look, at any given moment of time, there is something troubling all of us. Anita asked him about the future. Now if you were not troubled by something about the future, why would you ask about the future?'

'I would ask if I was plain inquisitive,' Mohan answered.

'Point taken. But our lady had given away too much like her marital status, her age, her weight, and God knows what else,' Shiv said, gesturing wildly.

'I didn't tell him my weight, yeah' Anita protested, but nobody bothered to respond.

'I have one last question for you, Shiv, and that is, how do you think he would have recognized Anita this evening?' I asked.

'I am glad you asked me that,' Shiv replied. 'It should be easy because you won't have many single women visiting Horizon tonight. Add to that his knowledge of her age, etc., etc.'

We were all fairly impressed with Shiv's reasoning. He did seem to have an answer for everything.

'That means I stay away from that place today, yeah?' Anita said sadly. Something told me she didn't mind hooking up with a fraud at this juncture of her life.

'Yes, ma'am,' Shiv said.

After Anita left, Akhil remarked, 'I almost thought we had a nice little adventure on our hands.'

'We still do,' Shiv said, 'because *we* are going to Hotel Horizon tonight.'

'We are? But you asked her not to go,' I said.

'Dude, if she landed there with us, and the guy got one look at her, trust me, he wouldn't ever come back all his life. He would run all the way from here to Timbuktu,' Shiv laughed.

That night the four of us proceeded to Hotel Horizon in Akhil's car.

Once we reached there, it quickly became apparent why Hotel Horizon was picked as the rendezvous point. There were hardly any cars in the parking lot, which gave us an idea of the crowd inside the hotel. Hotel Horizon used to house a popular pub called Na some time back, which was run by a third party. After a police raid, it became clear that Na was the short form of narcotics. The pub quietly shut down. The only other popular joint in the building, which also had two hundred fully air-conditioned rooms, was a lounge bar called the Call of the Wild.

I often wondered whoever came up with such strange names. The Call of the Wild? That too for a lounge bar. Seriously?

The lounge bar was decently lit up with a few bar stools put up near the bar counter, apart from cubicle-like seating arranged in three rows. The music was quite loud and the lights were brighter than you would expect in a lounge bar. Most of the tables, as expected, were empty. There were a few customers sitting at random tables. In all, looking at it from a weekend perspective, I deduced that it would not be long before the bar got a call from the wild and shut down.

Shiv selected a table close to the entrance with a good view of the bar counter.

'Our target will sit there,' he said, pointing to the counter, 'he will walk in, survey the room from the entrance. When he doesn't spot his prey, he will walk over to the bar, order a drink, and sit on one of the bar stools, waiting for her to show up. You can be sure that he will be dressed to kill.'

'How can you be so sure?' I asked.

'I am not,' he replied, smiling. 'I could be dead wrong. I am just hypothesizing.'

We waited for a few minutes and very soon our person of interest appeared. He was around five feet eight inches in height and of medium build. He wore a GAP T-shirt and had shades hanging from the front pocket. He had been generous with the gel on his hair and less than generous with the razor on his cheeks. He sported what looked like three-day-old stubble, and what made it worse was that it was in patches. Just as Shiv had described, he stood near the entrance, surveyed the room, and walked to the bar counter.

'Now what?' I asked.

'Now we make sure it is him,' Shiv said.

'And how do we do that?' Mohan asked.

'Wait for him to give something away, and if I am not mistaken, he will give us what we are looking for just about now,' Shiv said.

A single lady walked into the lounge bar and I quickly turned to look at our person of Interest. He got up from his seat expectantly and hesitated for a moment before deciding to move towards the lady. I looked back at the lady; she waved to someone at one of the tables and gave out a loud howl of laughter. I at once looked back at our fraudster and he sat back in his bar stool and looked around to see if anyone had noticed his moment of embarrassment. His eyes met mine for an instant and I looked away.

'Let's go,' Shiv said and quickly got up and moved towards the man. The man saw us approaching and for a moment seemed confused to see a group of four men walking briskly towards him. He quickly looked away and busied himself with a coaster placed on the bar counter.

We quietly surrounded the man and Shiv slipped his hand around the man's neck tightly. Curious watchers would have thought two friends were having an intimate chat.

I heard Shiv say, 'Anita sent us.'

'Who's Anita?' the man responded, trying to shrug away Shiv's hand. His initial expression was aggressive and then, seeing that the strength of numbers was on our side, mellowed down.

'I don't know any Anita,' he said. Obviously he was new to such situations and had no idea on how to handle them. I had expected a real smooth operator. This was a disappointment.

Shiv smiled and whispered something in his ear. I couldn't hear Shiv over the blaring music. However, the response was quick since I saw the man call the bartender and hand over a couple of notes hurriedly.

Shiv turned to me and said, 'You and Mohan wait here. Akhil comes with me.'

'Why can't we come?' I asked Shiv, disappointed.

'We don't want to attract unnecessary attention,' Shiv responded.

It was obvious as to why Shiv chose Akhil over us. Akhil was a six–foot, bearded, fierce-looking giant. Mohan, on the other hand, was five feet six, and a couple of inches shorter than me. Me? That is another story altogether.

We waited at our table and, after waiting for a good ten minutes, ordered two bottles of Budweiser to kill time. Half an hour and a couple more of Budweisers later, Akhil and Shiv showed up.

'What happened?' I asked, all keyed up.

'Like we thought,' Akhil said, reaching for my bottle and drinking from it, 'the guy is a fraud.'

'And?' Mohan asked.

'Looks like this phone thingy has gone viral,' Akhil said. 'His phone number is 81266630. Evidently he keeps getting calls from excited idiots who want to check this story out. Once in a while he calls gullible people and fleeces money out of them or, as he puts it, wants to strike up a friendship with willing women.'

'He admitted to as much?' I asked.

'More or less,' Shiv chipped in, 'he was not very cooperative, but then Akhil had to rough him up a bit.'

'And you handed him over to the police?' Mohan asked.

'No. We had to let him go,' Shiv answered.

'Let him go? But why?' I asked.

'Evidence, sweetheart,' Shiv smiled. 'We have no evidence to take him to the cops. All we could do was to take an assurance from him that he wouldn't scam anyone else.'

'What stops him?' I asked.

'Nothing,' Shiv replied, 'but after his encounter with Akhil, I doubt he will be eager to try his act very soon.'

We sat in a moment of silence, listening to the music. There was still something that was nagging me, something I was missing out on.

'It worries me', Shiv said, thoughtful, 'that there are so many idiots who fall for this thing. We should do something.'

'What can we do?' Akhil asked, continuing to drink from my bottle. I so wished he had sat next to Mohan.

'Mohan, your cousin works in our office as a journalist, right?' he asked.

'Yes,' Mohan confirmed.

'Can you call her tomorrow? We will try and get a news article written in the newspaper. Hopefully that will act as a deterrent,' Shiv said.

'But tomorrow is a holiday,' I reminded him.

'Not for journalists,' he said, 'and as for you?' He asked me, 'Would you prefer to sleep at home or be a part of an adventure?'

The way he said it, there was no doubt where I would be the next morning.

The next morning, Mohan's cousin Sneha met us in the canteen. I was meeting her for the first time and I already disliked her. Maybe, it was the way she talked, reminding me of Scooby-Doo. Or maybe it was because she was Mohan's cousin. I couldn't be sure.

'I heard about this story and was in fact planning to run a small article in tomorrow's city edition,' she said.

'I have already done some research on the subject,' she said, cleaning her spectacles. 'The phone number was actually disconnected a few months back according to the service provider. But, I managed to get the address where it was installed.' She paused for us to break into applause. We didn't, so she continued, 'It is just a couple of kilometers from here and I was planning to go down there and see if I could get some more inside information.'

The way she said 'inside information' almost seemed to me like she was planning on visiting either the CIA or Pentagon. I reminded myself that I was unjustly getting prejudiced against her.

'We will join you,' Mohan volunteered.

We decided to drive down to the address on our bikes. Since there were five of us, we had to take three bikes. Shiv hopped on to Akhil's bike; Sneha obviously felt more comfortable with Mohan, which was fine by me. I didn't want to make small talk with her. She definitely was not my type. I rode on my bike alone.

After going through a few long, winding roads which took us uphill, we reached our destination. I was surprised to see that the place had started to resemble a picnic spot. Almost a hundred people had gathered outside the house and it was obvious that it didn't take the skill of a Sneha to rustle up the address from the service provider.

The house looked really spooky to me. It was a double-storied building with a large courtyard running all around the house. The house had not been maintained well and was begging for a coat of paint to restore it back to some semblance of decency. There was a large banyan tree in the courtyard and, with all those aerial roots hanging down, looked like something that could be passed off as a prop in a horror film. The walls of the building were covered with moss and there was a peculiar smell around the house, the smell of cheap liquor.

An old caretaker was around, and when he got somewhat close to us, I readily identified the source of the peculiar smell. Thankfully, he didn't look like one of those characters from a horror movie. He must have been pushing 70, I guess, and was wearing a battered khaki uniform. He was making a half-hearted attempt to shoo away the crowd that had gathered around the building. Secretly he seemed to be enjoying the attention the building had suddenly garnered. Sneha decided to walk ahead and have a chat with the caretaker. We decided to stay back.

'No point hanging around here now,' Shiv remarked, looking at the crowd.

'There is definitely something in there,' Mohan said quite ominously. We were watching the building from across the road.

'Don't go down that lane now,' Shiv warned.

'You are obviously not tuned to understand these kinds of things,' Mohan started.

'Tuned?' Shiv asked. 'Is it a radio station to tune into?' Shiv's voice was soaked in sarcasm. One thing with Shiv was his sarcasm. It could really get to you when he spoke in that irksome tone, and I could see Mohan getting quite red in the face.

'Guys, chill. We are in a public place,' I reminded them, trying to calm things down. It wasn't working, however.

'This idiot will never understand,' Mohan said, moving away.

'It must be the summer heat,' I said to Shiv in an attempt to try and cool things down.

I thought Mohan was out of earshot, but unfortunately Mohan heard my uncharitable remark and stood sulking. Nobody talked to anyone for what seemed like a long time. We watched Sneha talking to the old caretaker as if watching a sunset on the beach. Sneha snapped a couple of pictures of the building on her mobile with the watchman standing in front of the building. She came back smiling.

'He is ready to talk,' she said.

I was suddenly reminded of the strange smell and not particularly enamored by the idea of being in close proximity to the old man.

'I will wait here,' I offered.

Nobody else offered to wait with me. I busied myself looking around the building. I entered the gate and walked to the far corner of the compound as far away as possible from the building. I could see the caretaker's quarters from where I stood. The caretaker stood outside his quarters with the others, engaged in an animated conversation. I resumed my investigation and noticed that the compound had not been swept of the dry leaves for ages. The compound wall was around six feet high facing the roadside, but on the opposite side, it was hardly four feet high. I found that strange and walked to take a peek over the wall. I readily understood the reason as the home was built on a precipice. There were huge granite rocks at the bottom which looked like pebbles from up here. I estimated the drop to be over seventy feet on this side, and a fall would result in certain death. No burglar would risk the climb on this side of the compound. I quickly moved away from the wall.

I looked around aimlessly, trying to find something that could be a definitive clue to help crack this case. *'Elementary, Watson. It was the caretaker who murdered the owner of the building,'* I imagined myself saying to Shiv as the others looked at me with abject admiration. Too bad I didn't have the observation skills of a Sherlock Holmes. Nor did I have his guts, and so I continued to stay as far away from the building as I could.

After a few minutes, the others returned. Nothing was spoken as everyone walked towards our respective bikes. This time around Shiv decided to ride with me on my bike.

He brought me up to speed on the drive back to the office. My helmet, the wind, and the traffic ensured I did not get to hear him fully and the information was quite disjointed.

'Lots of people have come since morning. There seemed to be nothing wrong with the place except for the owner's daughter who was mentally sick. There was a phone with the exact same number, but it was disconnected. The phone has not been heard ringing for over a month now. The house was owned by a non-resident Indian. The owner's daughter was staying in the house until a month back. Presently the property is up for sale and so on and so forth . . .'

After I stopped the bike at the office, I turned to Shiv and asked, 'What did you mean when you said the owner's daughter was mentally sick?'

'She went bonkers,' Shiv said and continued, 'got up one day raving mad and running around the house tearing her clothes. I know that will be fodder for Mohan to preach about paranormal stuff.'

'And where is she now?' I asked.

'Getting treated somewhere in the US,' Shiv said.

'Now what?' I asked.

'I think Mohan needs a shocker that will get him out of this voodoo stuff. I am thinking of something,' Shiv said.

'What do you have in mind?' I asked.

'Just wait and watch,' Shiv said, winking his eye but not giving anything away.

We saw Akhil parking his bike and walking towards us. Very soon Mohan reached us and bid goodbye to Sneha. She just waved goodbye to us from a distance and walked away.

'What next?' Akhil asked as Mohan walked towards us.

'I suggest we visit the house again tonight,' Shiv said. 'This time we will enter the house.'

'Are you nuts?' Mohan asked.

'I think you are chicken, Mohan,' Shiv said smiling. 'That is the reason you hide behind this mumbo jumbo. Yes, I know it. You are a chicken.'

I could see through Shiv's game plan. This was the lesson he was talking about.

Mohan probably saw through it too. He surprised us with his next statement.

'I am game,' he said. 'What time do we meet and where?'

Shiv was momentarily taken aback. He probably hadn't expected Mohan to succumb to his plan so soon.

'Right in front of the house at 11 p.m.,' Shiv said.

'Done,' Mohan said.

'Done,' Akhil said.

The three of them looked at me.

'Done,' I said reluctantly. What the hell was I thinking?

I was in no hurry to reach the house before the others did. In fact, I started from my home only after I got a confirmation SMS from Shiv, Akhil, and Mohan that they had started for the destination. I drove leisurely and found all the three waiting for me when I reached the site.

'What took you so long?' Shiv barked.

'Traffic,' I lied.

'At this hour?' Shiv inquired. I just smiled and let it pass.

'The caretaker is asleep and won't disturb us. I reached here an hour back and bought him a bottle of rum. Said it was a token of appreciation for letting us talk to him earlier in the day,' Shiv said, laughing. 'By now, he would be snoring so loud that all ghosts in the house would have been driven away.'

I prayed it was true. We approached the gate and opened it. I expected to hear a long squeak like the ones you hear in horror movies. Nothing like that happened. The compound was pitch dark and so was the building. The only source of light was a street light, a good fifty feet away from the building. Unfortunately the huge tree in front of the building blocked it out.

Shiv took the lead and seemed absolutely unfazed by the task at hand. Akhil seemed at ease too. Mohan surely didn't seem too comfortable. In every horror movie, you have a group of smart-asses who go into weird and eerie places to investigate strange sounds without a flamethrower or even a machine gun. I used to groan and curse them, wondering why they were walking into danger, and invariably they used to get eaten by an alien or hacked to death by a zombie. And here I was walking into a spooky building with three other half-wits. How did I get talked into this? I had a real bad premonition about the whole activity.

'Do you all have your mobile phones?' Shiv asked as a last-minute check.

'Why mobile phones?' I asked out of curiosity.

'Light,' Shiv replied.

We walked the short distance from the gate to the building silently. The truth is I was too scared to say anything. If there was something evil in the building, I didn't want to attract any unwanted attention. We walked to the front door and found it locked.

'The door is locked, let's go back,' I whispered to Shiv.

Shiv ignored me and started to walk around the house to check if there were any other entrances. The others followed him. I didn't want to be left behind alone and so I ran to catch up with them. We found one more door at the back, but that one was locked too.

'The only possible way in is from the balcony,' Shiv said. 'I can see a door there.'

'How do we reach the balcony?' Akhil asked. I sure hoped he was not serious.

'The tree,' Shiv pointed out. 'Which one of you is good at climbing trees?' he asked.

I looked at the tree to check how the feat could be achieved. There was indeed a branch that curved towards the balcony, but it did not seem like it could take my weight. Not that I was keen to volunteer. In fact, nobody volunteered. Nobody wanted to be the first one in the house.

'Cowards,' Shiv laughed. 'I will go first.'

Shiv was the most athletic amongst us and there was no doubt that if anyone could reach the top, it would have to be him. He started climbing the tree and seemed to be pretty good at it. He did slip a couple of times but seemed to be quite sure of the route almost as if he had done this before. He did pause a couple of times to adjust his backpack. As he reached the edge of the branch, he balanced himself precariously, to place one foot gingerly on the balcony wall. I estimated that the whole journey from the bottom to the balcony must have been covered in less than two minutes. I seriously doubted that I could even reach halfway in that time.

'Guys, I am here,' we heard Shiv call out. 'Let me look around a bit.'

He reappeared at the balcony after what seemed to be a long time but was actually only a couple of minutes.

'Look what I found,' he said, holding up a ladder for us to see. 'You guys can come up with the ladder.'

As if I was dying to.

He lowered the ladder real slowly, not making unnecessary noises which would have attracted any attention. Surprisingly the ladder seemed just the right height to reach the balcony. I offered to go up first, mainly because I didn't want to be the last. I climbed up the ladder, all the while keeping an eye on the banyan tree. I didn't want one of the branches to reach out to me and grab me. As I reached the top, Shiv helped pull me up the balcony wall. I turned around to see Mohan had already reached halfway up the ladder. Akhil soon followed. I turned on the assistive light app on my phone and the light was bright enough for me to see that the balcony floor was dusty. I could feel the dust tickle my nostrils and I let out a loud sneeze.

'Shhhhh,' I heard Shiv say. Mohan quickly covered his mouth with his hands to muffle a sneeze.

I focused the light around and noticed a lone open door, which led us into what must have been a bedroom. We walked in and found that there was no furniture in the room.

There was another open door inside, which in turn led us into a large hall which had multiple doors leading to different rooms.

'I can't find the phone anywhere,' Shiv said, trying to look around in the dim light that emanated out of his phone display screen. 'If we find the phone dead, we can conclusively prove that no hanky-panky exists here.'

We all dispersed to different sides of the room to search for the phone. I ensured that I stayed close to Mohan.

'This door here leads to the stairway,' Shiv said. 'It seems to be locked from the outside.'

Though my phone did have a fairly powerful light, I still found it difficult to see very clearly. Luckily, there was no furniture in the hall either for us to trip on and fall over.

That is when I first heard a sound, a low gurgling sound.

'Quiet,' I said. 'Do you hear that?' I asked.

The sound only got louder and had by now turned into a strange hissing sound. We all froze with fear.

All of a sudden, a door which was a few feet away from me opened with a loud bang. I turned my phone to focus the light at the door. There was a bluish bright light coming from the room and I was able to see some sort of smoke or mist emanating inside the room. As my eyes struggled to adjust to the light, I was stuck with plain dread, as I saw the smoke take on the form of an old woman.

I was yet to recover from the panic attack when something else incredible happened. Shiv, who was closest to the door, got pulled into the room, and within a couple of seconds, the door banged shut from the inside. I heard a muffled scream from inside. The entire incident had occurred in less than a minute.

I panicked. I ran towards the balcony only to find both Akhil and Mohan already there scrambling to reach the ladder. Mohan managed to get onto the ladder first. Akhil tried to reach for it next, but I pushed him aside and got onto the ladder. Halfway down the ladder, I saw Mohan running out of the gate. The bloody fool even stopped to try and close the gate behind him in a bid to slow down whatever he imagined was chasing him. In one quick motion, he had got onto his bike and zoomed away. All this happened even as I was still halfway up the ladder.

I did not bother to climb down all the way. Somewhere in the middle, I decided it was better to jump. I couldn't see how far the ground was as I took the plunge and landed on my hands and knees. Bruised, I did not wait for Akhil either and ran towards my bike. I remember fetching my key from my pocket, starting the bike, and racing away. It must have been a good couple of minutes later that I heard my mobile ringing. It was Akhil.

'Where are you?' he asked and didn't wait for me to answer. 'Drive down to my home, both of you,' he said. That is when I realized that Mohan must have been on call conference.

'Okay,' I heard Mohan say. I could still feel his heart throbbing through the phone. Much like mine, I should admit.

'Okay,' I mumbled. There were a thousand questions I wanted to ask, but the line had already gone dead. I turned the bike towards Akhil's home. He was a bachelor and stayed alone in an independent bungalow. When I reached there, both Akhil and Mohan were already inside his home.

'Where is Shiv?' I asked.

'No idea,' Akhil said, extremely edgy, 'his mobile is switched off.'

'What do we do?' I asked.

'Let us go the police station,' Mohan suggested.

'We can't do that,' Akhil quickly intervened. 'What will we say?'

Evidently none of our brains were working.

We all sat in silence for a few minutes, not knowing what to say or do.

'I have called Christie and asked him to come,' Akhil said after a while.

Almost on cue, the doorbell rang. I was hopeful that it was Shiv. We all ran to the door. It was Christie.

'What happened?' Christie asked.

For the next few minutes, we all narrated our horror story to him.

'We should never have messed around with the spirits,' Mohan said on the verge of tears.

'Will you stop it?' Akhil said. 'Think of what we should do.'

I wanted to kick myself for not having heeded my premonition. If only I had been sensible and asserted myself, we wouldn't have been in the situation we found ourselves in. No point in blaming myself alone—it was a collective decision, a very stupid one at that.

'I always warned you guys that there are spirits, and you should not mess around with them.' Mohan was almost bawling by now. 'That house looked haunted from the word go.'

'Then why did you agree to go?' Akhil asked.

'I agreed to go to prove that I was not scared,' Mohan said, fighting back tears.

'Why did you run if you are not scared?' Akhil asked.

'You ran first,' Mohan shouted back at Akhil.

'And you pushed me away from the ladder so that you could reach your bike first,' Akhil said, almost stifling a laugh.

That seemed strange to me.

'Hold it', I said and turned to Akhil. 'What is the game?'

'What game?' Mohan asked, puzzled.

'There is something happening here that you and I don't know about,' I said to Mohan. 'These guys are playing a practical joke on us.'

Akhil and Christie tried to look serious as if they had no idea what I was talking about. Mohan had no bloody idea what I was saying.

'Guys, this is damn bloody serious,' I shouted at Akhil. 'If this is a joke, you guys have taken it too far.'

'Okay, okay. Chill,' Akhil said.

'You are right, it is a joke and you guys fell for it,' Shiv said, entering the house from outside. 'But trust me, this joke was not targeted at you,' he said, looking at me. 'In fact I warned you earlier that I planned to pull one on Mohan.'

I was lost in mixed feelings. While I was so damn pleased to see Shiv alive, I was already thinking of ways to kill him for scaring the daylights out of me.

'You third-rate scum of the earth,' I said, fuming.

Mohan was still in a state of shock. He stood glaring at Shiv.

'Apologies, guys,' Shiv said, 'I just wanted you guys to understand that there is no such thing as ghosts and that fear would make you not only believe in these things but also behave irrationally.'

It took Shiv and Akhil an hour to get Mohan out of his shell. We laughed recounting how each one of us had behaved in those few minutes. Akhil put up a show on how I had shoved him aside to get onto the ladder first and how I had jumped halfway down the ladder.

'So you were in on it all along?' I asked Akhil.

He just smiled and nodded. 'Christie was not aware though. I only told him on the way back from the house. I told him that Shiv and I were playing a prank and to just play along.'

'I don't understand the special effects that we saw back there,' Mohan spoke finally.

'Let me explain,' Shiv offered. 'I had to set it up in such a way that it looked convincing. The truth is, after you accepted the challenge, Akhil and I went back to the house. We purchased a bottle of rum for the caretaker on the way because his cooperation was essential for our plan to succeed. Obviously, once the caretaker was with us, we put the plan into action. We first wanted to set up the act on the ground floor but discovered that there was no power available on the ground floor. It was available only on the first floor and power was essential for my plan to succeed.'

'Bloody hell,' I said, shocked, 'you mean there was power available on the first floor?'

'Yes,' Akhil laughed, 'but as Shiv said, for our plan to work, we had to get you to the first floor. Our initial plan was to lure you through the staircase to the first floor. However, the caretaker refused to keep the door open on the ground floor because all the furniture is kept there. We understood that and requested him to keep the balcony door on the first floor open. We actually had to buy the caretaker an extra bottle for that.'

'Then Akhil had a genuine doubt,' Shiv said. 'What if you guys refused to climb the tree to come to the first floor? So we talked to the caretaker and got the ladder arranged on the first floor. That way, you guys would not be able to excuse yourselves.'

'Smart thinking,' I said, 'that way hauling ourselves up must have added to your excitement, not to mention the way we bolted out of there. What about what we saw in the hall up there? How did you manage that?'

'Did you guys notice me carry this backpack?' Shiv asked, pointing to the backpack lying near the couch. We nodded.

'The backpack had some very basic items,' he said. 'Here, let me show you.'

He opened the backpack and pulled out a pocket flashlight, a steamer, and some gum tape.

'This here is a steamer you can buy in any pharmacy store,' he said. 'People use it for inhalation when they have a stuffy nose and this here is a clever contraption,' he said, pointing to the torch.

'Notice what I have done here?' he said and pointed to the glass side of the torch.

'What is that?' I asked.

'It is a film, a negative from an old camera roll. You don't get to see them now with all the digital cameras. I have slipped the negative in between the glass and the bulb,' he said, 'The negative has a picture of my old grandmom. Let me demonstrate the effects of my contraption to you,' he said.

He walked into one of the bedrooms, followed by us. He set the steamer down and poured water into it until it was full. He plugged it in and switched off the lights of the room. He switched on the flashlight, but I couldn't see the dramatic effect that I had seen earlier.

'Just hold on,' he said. 'The steam needs to build up in the room. The steam will then form a sort of curtain for the light to bounce back on. Will you all step out of the room, please?' he asked.

We all stepped into the hall and were followed by Shiv, who then shut the door. Akhil switched off the lights in the hall. There was still some light escaping from the cracks in the door which Shiv masked with the gum tape. After a couple of minutes, we heard the familiar gurgling sound of the water boiling in the steamer, followed by a steady hiss as the steam was let out. It seemed much more faint here than earlier. After a couple of seconds, Shiv opened the door with as much force and low behold, we saw the exact same effect in the room.

'If you guys had stayed a couple of moments more back there in the building or decided to enter the room,' Shiv explained, 'maybe the effect wouldn't have been that dramatic. You would have managed to see through the whole thing. The timing was important and so was shutting the door from inside.'

'Brilliant,' I said, clapping, 'you are truly amazing, Shiv.'

Shiv took a bow and looked at Mohan, hoping to hear a compliment.

'This is all fine,' Mohan said, shaking his head, 'but there still is something beyond science.'

Ship slapped his forehead with his palm and looked around at us helpless.

'What more do I do to convince you that there is no such thing as a ghost?' he asked, despondent. 'We visited the house in question, we went room by room, and we did everything possible—'

'It still doesn't answer what happened to Stella,' Mohan said, his voice barely a whisper.

The mention of Stella brought down a heavy curtain of gloom into the room.

'But we called the same damn number remember,' Shiv said, now starting to lose his cool.

'We tried just once,' Mohan said. 'Stella tried many times over.'

'Okay,' Shiv said, trying to calm himself, 'if we call the number over and over again, we should get connected as per your hypothesis, right?'

'Maybe,' Mohan said, noncommittal.

'Akhil, does your landline have caller ID?' Shiv barked.

Akhil nodded. He was clearly uncomfortable that this was leading nowhere.

'Let us call from your landline so that we do exactly the same things that Stella did,' Shiv ordered.

We walked up to the landline. Shiv turned on the speakerphone and started to dial the number 81366630.

We heard the familiar faint blips of the number being dialed. We waited for a couple of seconds and heard the message 'Please check the number you are dialing.'

44

'Look,' Shiv said, 'you will hear the same message over and over again, no matter how many times you dial.'

To prove his point, he disconnected and dialed again. 'Please check the number you are dialing' was the message.

That is when the thought hit me. I had finally managed to work out the nagging feeling I had been having.

'That's it!' I exclaimed. 'I know why we are not getting through.'

'Oh, so you decided to join the bandwagon too?' Shiv questioned.

'No, listen to this,' I said. 'The message we are getting, "Please check the number," is because we are not dialing the area code preceding the phone number.'

'What do you mean?' Christie asked.

'We should be hearing the message that this number does not exist. Instead, we are hearing "Please check the number."'

'How so?' Akhil asked.

'In a landline, if you are calling from one service provider to the same service provider's connection, you don't need to add the area code. Dialing the number directly should do. Am I right?' Shiv asked to help me out.

'Correct. However, if you are dialing a number which is provided by a different service provider, you have to add the area code. For example, Shiv's home number starts with a 3 and the service provider is different. If we were calling from a service provider whose number started with 8, then there is no need to dial the area code,' I chipped in.

Shiv dipped into his pocket and brought out his purse. He fetched the receipt Christie had given him a few days back.

'He is right,' Shiv said. 'Stella called from a number starting with 8 and so she did not dial the area code.'

45

'Then let us try calling the number with the area code,' Akhil suggested.

Clearly, Mohan was not excited. 'I am not for it.' He sounded uncomfortable.

'I think we should go for it,' Shiv said and looked around. No one said anything. Part of me was regretting having given the probable solution.

Shiv reached for the phone and started to input the area code followed by the phone number.

Again the familiar sounds of the phone connecting.

We waited anxiously for something to happen. After what seemed like eternity, the phone rang. Mohan jumped and, in a moment of panic, disconnected the call.

'Why the bloody hell did you do that?' Shiv screamed.

'Are you nuts? Don't bloody finger the unseen,' Mohan screamed back.

'Unseen? What makes you feel there is something if it can't be seen?' The slugfest continued.

'Doesn't it prove a point that the phone rang?' Mohan did not let go. 'What more proof do you need?'

'The phone ringing does not mean a thing,' Shiv said.

'*Guys,*' I said, fear gripping me as I pointed to the display of the landline, which had lit up. Everyone turned to look at the phone.

In the eerie silence of the night, the only sound I could hear was the shrill sound of the phone ringing.

I could feel the adrenaline pumping through my veins as I stepped closer to look at the display to see who was calling.

The number 8163330 flashed.

Nobody except Shiv had the courage to move. Even he was hesitant when he moved forward and pressed the answer button and meekly said, 'Hello.'

I felt my throat go dry when I heard an old woman's voice on the speakerphone.

'Shiv?'

'Yes,' Shiv said, his voice shaky and barely audible. Only the fear was palpable in his voice.

The same old woman's voice boomed through the phone.

'I have nothing to say to you. Give the phone to Christie. I have a message for him from Stella.'

And then I heard the laughter on the speaker. The cackle of an old woman ended in the deep-throated chuckle of a man.

# THE TEMPTRESS

S trange things happened to him ever since he met her.
Rajeev Chauhan enrolled in his MBA program at IIM (Bangalore). Not that it was his first choice. Given half a chance, he would have opted for the one at Ahmadabad. However, his scores were not as supportive as his father was, and so he had to settle for the second best, not something that he liked at all. The only son of Giridharilal Chauhan, a self-made millionaire, Rajeev Chauhan prided himself on being aggressive and an achiever. Like his father, the son was at his best when pushed to a corner, a trait that especially came to the fore when he took the podium at debating circles. In all fairness, Rajeev Chauhan was a very good speaker who modeled himself on his idol Barack Obama. He watched hours of the speeches made by Barack Obama and spent many more hours standing in front of the mirror rehearsing every subtle action of the American president.

He never missed an opportunity to showcase his skills in front of other envious students, because he attended each and every debating competition held in the campus or outside. Every time, he came back with the first prize and added the trophy to his overflowing showcase of trophies.

He considered himself as the numero uno when it came to debating and was confident that no competition could stand up to him. All that changed on that fateful day he set foot in the VXL college of medicine.

On the face of it, there were no looming threats in the form of strong contenders and the format called rapid-fire was something he was quite familiar with. Each participant would have to speak on a topic previously announced. The topic for the round was 'Are the politicians the world over failing their nations?' The topic as simple as this could only have been chosen to separate the novice from the old hands. No sweat.

A pool of the best ten speakers would then move on to the next round where they would be directly pitted against another competitor. The final two contestants would then move to the last round, which was to be an extempore round.

Rajeev scanned the room, looking at his competition. There were twenty to twenty-five nervous youngsters rehearsing for the event. Rajeev was familiar with Anand from Bangalore University (a good speaker but now considered a spent force), Sid the flash in the pan from AIMS, and screechy voice Maya from Deccan—no one who could give him trouble. This was once again going to be a piece of cake, Rajeev figured.

When his name was called out as the fourteenth speaker, Rajeev adjusted his blazer and dusted off a speck of invisible dust from his lapel. He then closed his eyes for a couple of moments as he recalled the last speech of his idol before walking to the podium at a pace which was neither casual not hurried. He stood in front of the crowd, looking directly at them with his feet slightly apart, and smiled. He waited until the whole auditorium fell into a calm of anticipation.

Somewhere there in his mind was an invisible camera focused on his every micro expression and gesture.

'Everything is changing,' he started and paused for effect before continuing. 'People are taking their comedians seriously and the politicians as a joke.' He heard laughter from the audience. 'Ladies and gentlemen,' he continued, 'these are the words of American social commentator Will Rogers and they have never been as apt as in today's society.'

The next three minutes, Rajeev ensured that the audience was eating out of his hand as he launched an acidic attack on the political class, making sure his speech was peppered with humorous anecdotes and hard-hitting quotes.

When the names of the qualifying ten speakers were announced, it was no surprise that his name received the maximum cheers and a few catcalls. Sid had dropped off, Anand had clung on, and Maya would continue to torment her audience for one more round.

The topic for the second round was on death penalty. Rajeev spoke passionately about how the world needed death penalty as a deterrent for the rarest of the rare cases. He quoted from the speeches by Margaret Thatcher, Al Gore, and Ronald Reagan. He reminded the audience that over half the world population lived in just four countries where death penalty was still applicable to a capital offense. In conclusion, he reminded an audience listening in with rapt attention that the government saved over 50 crore rupees a month by opting to hang Ajmal Kasab, the lone terrorist who had been captured during the 26/11 attacks in Mumbai, than by opting to put him in a high-security prison.

After delivering his address to the usual thunderous applause, Rajeev quickly walked out of the auditorium because he was aware that the next speaker was Maya and he couldn't bear to hear her squeal.

He felt hungry and asked for the directions to the canteen from one of the organizers. He walked to the canteen and found it bustling with activity. Students from various colleges were crowding the counter, trying to catch the attention of the couple of service staff who seemed totally lost in the entire din. Reaching the counter seemed like half a battle won for Rajeev, who then waited patiently until he caught the eye of one of the service boys. He had originally planned to order a sandwich but there was nothing to eat. Instead, he ordered a cup of coffee. Picking up the hot cup of coffee, which he any day preferred to a bottle of soda that he found other customers ordering, he turned around to fight his way back only to be rudely shoved. He lost his balance for a split second and saw his cup turn over and the contents spill on a girl standing behind him.

'Sorry, I am so sorry,' he offered apologetically. The girl just raised her hand and said, 'It's okay, accidents happen,' and looked up to lock eyes with him.

When he re-entered the auditorium almost an hour later, the last of the speakers had already done their job to the best of their abilities. Only the names of the finalists remained to be announced.

Rajeev found it strangely amusing when he heard the names of the finalists. He wasn't the least bit surprised to hear his own name. He was, however, surprised to hear the name of his challenger, a name he had never heard of in the debating circles before.

As per the format, both the finalists were invited on stage. The topic would be announced, and the winner of a toss of the coin could choose to be the first one to speak on the subject or let his challenger take the first shot. The second speaker would then have to take the opposing side of the argument. Ninety-nine out of one hundred times, the winner would choose to speak second and thereby make effective use of the time to prepare a rebuttal.

Rajeev walked up on stage, resolved that he would choose to speak second. That way, he figured he could mercilessly tear into his hapless competitor's arguments, ensuring the judges did not even remotely remember the name of his ill-fated rival. He anxiously waited for his challenger to come on stage. He liked to see whom he was going to launch an assault on that day.

He was actually caught unawares when she stood opposite him. He was expecting someone who would have been very nervous on stage. The girl who stood in front of him radiated calm confidence as she intently listened to one of the judges explaining the rules of the format. The first time she looked at his face, he felt extremely uneasy. There was something in the way her eyes pierced him, almost as if she could read his thoughts. He felt compelled to look away, though she held her stare. It took him a few moments to compose himself before he decided to risk a second look at her. The result was no different. She seemed to be enjoying his discomfiture.

'I am going to toss the coin,' the judge called out, 'and the lady gets the first choice of call.'

'Heads,' she called and waited for the coin to fall on the floor.

'Tails it is,' the judge announced, picking up the coin. 'What will it be, Rajeev? Would you like to go first or follow on?'

Rajeev stood transfixed, looking blankly at the judge.

'Rajeev, what will it be?' the judge repeated and, seeing no response from him, gently shook him by the shoulder.

'What?' Rajeev asked, suddenly realizing that he was expected to say something.

'Exactly my question, Rajeev. What will it be? Will you go first or would you like to be the second speaker?'

'I will go first,' Rajeev blurted out. A pall of silence descended the auditorium. Rajeev was himself perplexed as to why he had opted to go first.

'Good,' said a rather surprised judge. 'Before I announce the topic, I need to ask you one question. You understand that you have 60 seconds to prepare your speech and an additional 210 seconds to make your point?'

'Yes,' Rajeev replied, still very confused, 'I understand.'

'The topic for the last round is', the judge announced on the public address system, 'the aftermath of the American invasion of Iraq.'

Putting behind his curious choice, Rajeev took a couple of moments to compose himself. He quickly jotted down a few points on a sheet of paper until an alarm sounded out to let the contestants know that the one minute of preparation time was up. Trying to put on his usual arrogant swagger, Rajeev walked up to the podium to a deafening round of applause from the four hundred-odd students who had gathered there just to see him speak. He did not disappoint the audience and ended his discourse in the allotted three minutes thirty seconds, closing on the dot. At the end of the discourse, most people were convinced that Iraq, and more importantly, the world, was much better off without Saddam Hussein or his two infamous sons.

Rajeev never heard her name being announced nor did he notice her walk to the podium as he was busy soaking in the adulations of a cheering audience. He stood there waving to the crowd much like Barack Obama would do after rendering a successful speech to the US senate.

She however waited for the cheers to die down and the audience to reclaim their seats before she started.

'That was very impressive, Rajeev, I doubt even George Bush or his secretary of defense Donald Rumsfeld could have put it any better,' she said amid chuckles. 'Let us, however, not forget that there is one important point we are missing and that is what use is freedom if it is to be enjoyed only in the confines of one's home?'

The next three and half minutes she rubbished everything about the American foreign policy and interspersed it with enough quotes from Donald Rumsfeld to enforce her point that he had no idea what was happening in the US, forget about Iraq. She ensured that she did not at any point of time directly attack Rajeev or any of his statements. She closed her talk with a final quote from Donald Rumsfeld when he was testifying before the US congress on the number of Iraqi insurgents by saying, 'I am not going to give you a number for it because it's not my business to do intelligent work.'

The audience burst out in laughter and the guffaws could be heard for quite some time before the audience realized that she had in fact finished her speech. The fact that she had overstepped her time by an extra seventeen seconds was something the judges were happy to overlook as they heard the audience applaud for more than the time her speech actually took to deliver.

The next few minutes before the judge's final decision was announced were the longest ones Rajeev spent. He looked around anxiously for her and found her calmly staring at him from a distance without interacting with anyone. He still felt there was something about her stare that made him uncomfortable. Was she able to read his thoughts? Was she able to sense his anxiety at finally having met his match?

Every once in a while, someone would walk up to Rajeev and shake his hand and say, 'Good job, mate', but Rajeev knew otherwise that it was basic courtesy they were administering. There was no sincerity in their voice. He found it strange that no one was extending the same courtesy to her. No one approached her to congratulate her.

Rajeev busied himself looking intently at the huge digital clock mounted on the wall in the auditorium almost as if it would sound out a loud alarm and the world would come to an end. Secretly he wished it would. He was aware of her eyes boring into him, but refused to look at her.

He, however, could not avoid her when she came walking right up to him and offered her hand.

'Good job, Rajeev. You were fantastic. Every bit the amazing speaker I was expecting you to be,' she said. There was a certain sincerity in her appreciation that he couldn't overlook.

He avoided looking at her straight in the eye and left her hand suspended in the air for a long time. He was, however, aware of a strange but divine perfume emanating from her. She stood in front of him, persistently holding up her hand. Almost as if in a trance, he extended his hand, much to his own dislike, and shook her hand. And for the first time he took a good close look at her. What he saw unnerved him. It would take a blind fool to say she was not pretty. But it was not her beauty that disturbed him. It was something in those eyes. He quickly looked away.

'Thank you. You did pretty well yourself,' he heard himself say.

'Well?' she asked. 'I managed to toast you, boy,' she admonished, much like a high school teacher would if she caught a kindergarten boy wetting his shorts. Even before he could recover from the smarting, she laughed as if she had cracked one of her best one-liners. Rajeev ensured he kept away from her after the exchange.

It didn't surprise anyone, Rajeev included, when the judges announced the results and declared Rajeev second best. He went on stage and picked up his trophy and certificate, not bothering to shake hands with the chief guest or any of the dignitaries on stage. He did not even stop for the customary photograph of him accepting the award. Even before the announcers had called her name to invite her on stage to claim the first prize, he was out of the venue.

He returned home and parked his bike. His neighbor's dog, which usually came around for a petting, stayed behind the stairs growling at him.

'Here, Rufus,' he called out, only to see the animal now start revealing a pair of lethal-looking canine teeth. This had never happened to him before, not good old Rufus.

'Crazy!' he exclaimed and walked inside his home.

He hadn't shared the happenings at the VXL College with anyone except his best friend and roommate Abid. Abid was more amused that Rajeev found it disturbing to look at a girl's face and speak to her than that he had ended up as runner-up in the debating competition for the first time since Abid had got to know Rajeev.

'Was she pretty?' Abid teased him.

'I don't know,' Rajeev said, smiling for the first time that day.

'What crap,' Abid exclaimed, 'you stand on the stage speaking to a hundred people over and over again, looking them in the eye, and you couldn't speak to one little girl?'

'I guess I was perturbed,' he said, taking a sip from a bottle of soda he was drinking.

'Disturbed by her beauty?' Abid exclaimed. 'How can that be?'

'I said I don't know,' Rajeev retorted. 'Something's strange about her. Anyway, I just met her once. Chances are, I will never meet her again.'

'What is her name?' Abid asked inquisitively.

'Strange,' Rajeev replied, 'I don't even remember her name.'

'Even more strange', Abid quipped, 'is you drinking soda. You always prefer to drink coffee.'

The next morning when he stepped out, he discovered that poor old Rufus had not recovered and continued snarling at him. No amount of coaxing would get the dog to come and get petted. The rest of the week remained uneventful except for Rufus now managing to even nip at him for getting too close.

'*Seriously!*' he thought to himself, '*The dog must be sick. Can't the neighbor take him to a vet and care for his pet?*'

The following week, Rajeev attended another debating competition held by the Rotary club. He did not expect a lot of the regulars at the competition. He sat reviewing his notes for the upcoming debate on government's involvement in the daily life of citizens.

'Working hard to bag the first prize?' he heard a girl's voice.

He looked up for a moment to see who it was and saw her. She stood a couple of feet away from him, waiting for him to respond. Rajeev was not too sure about whether he was happy or uncomfortable seeing her again. She looked prettier than the first time he had seen her, and her hypnotic gaze made it difficult for him to look away this time. With a lot of effort he managed to return his gaze back to his notes.

'I need to beat someone. This time I will take the winners' cup,' he said without looking at her.

'Still smarting from the last defeat?' she laughed. 'Don't worry, I assure you, you will win this round.'

'Looks like someone is not well prepared,' he said again, not looking at her.

'Winning is not an obsession for me like it is for others,' she remarked. A hint of curtness was not lost on Rajeev. 'It is good to lose smaller battles for bigger rewards,' she continued.

He ignored her remark and continued to show great interest in his notes. She waited for his repartee and, when she saw none coming for some time, decided to leave him alone and walked away.

At the end of the day, though he won the trophy, he was strangely disturbed. Something didn't feel quite right. She had not been half as good as she had been the other day and did not figure in the top three. He wondered if she too was a one-time wonder like Sid.

That evening while he waited at the prize distribution ceremony, she again approached him and extended her hand.

'Friends?' she asked, raising an eyebrow.

He smiled and extended his hand. He wanted to give her a firm handshake but was surprised that her grip seemed much too strong for a lady. What surprised him even more was her next question.

'What are you doing tomorrow evening?'

'Why? Are you asking me out?' he asked.

'No, silly. There is a debate competition at the YMCA. Wondered if you were participating.'

'I had no clue,' he said.

'Would you be going?' she asked.

'I would love to,' he remarked.

'Good, I will meet you there at 7 p.m.,' she said and walked away even before he could respond. He didn't see her for the rest of the evening, though he did look around, trying to spot her. After all, she had looked quite pretty that evening and he wouldn't have minded spending some more time with her.

He reached the YMCA at 6.45 the next evening and found her waiting. He was surprised to not find any crowd at the venue and remarked as much to her.

'Oh, the competition has been called off,' she said. 'I did not have your mobile number to inform you. Thought I might as well meet up with you here,' she added.

For a change, she was not looking him in the eye when she said that. He found that strange but remained silent.

'Now that we are here, shall we do something together?' she asked, excited.

'Like what?' He asked. She did look pretty. He realized that he liked to look at her when she was not looking at him.

'Movie?' she asked.

'Not sure' he remarked.

'What is the matter?' she asked. 'Afraid to go out for a movie with a girl?'

She found him squirming and added, 'I promise I won't try and sneak my arm around you or try to steal a kiss.'

'Which movie will it be?' he asked, mostly to assert himself.

He couldn't help notice a mischievous grin on her face, like she had achieved what she had set out to do. He somehow felt he had played into her hands.

The movie she chose was a horror movie. He felt uneasy that the theater was almost empty. He moved reluctantly when she chose two seats that seemed to be far away from anyone. During the first half, as one of the characters in the movie walked into a dark basement all alone, she slowly reached for his hand and held it. He was again confused by the mixed signals his brain sent out. Every time a zombie appeared, she squeezed his hands, but this time it was more feminine than the handshake he had experienced the previous day. Her hands did feel smooth like satin.

He was happy when the lights came on in the intermission and excused himself to get some popcorn. The popcorn vendor's behavior in the theater also struck him as weird, as he was handed a bucket of corn, with a sinister smile, even before he had placed the order. It was only on his way back to the seat that he realized that he had ordered a bottle of Coke rather than the customary coffee. He quickly dismissed it as forming a new habit, a habit he would soon kick anytime he felt he wanted to.

After the intermission, the screaming and bloodshed increased and so did her proximity to him. A couple of times she hid her face in his arms to look away from the screen and he felt himself freeze, not knowing how to react. He did enjoy the smell of her perfume though.

Once the movie was over, much to his discomfiture, she continued to hold his hand.

'Dinner?' she asked.

'Not after all those gut spilling scenes. I lost my appetite,' he said, excusing himself. The disappointment on her face was visible for a moment.

'Maybe some other time,' he offered as an afterthought.

Abid rolled on the bed with laughter much to the chagrin of Rajeev when he narrated the incidents of the evening.

'You screwed up a fantastic opportunity, brother,' he howled. 'Did you at least exchange phone numbers?'

'Yes. We did,' Rajeev answered, opening a can of soda.

'Good. So you finally got her name?' Abid asked.

Rajeev just smiled. He didn't want to tell Abid that he still didn't have her name and had stored her number under 'Mystery woman' in his cell phone. How do you ask a girl her name after you have met her twice and been to a movie with her?

Strangely, he just couldn't stop thinking of her the next day. He kept thinking of the way her hand felt in his and the way she hid her face in his arms. Her perfume remained fresh in his mind and her smile replayed in his mind a hundred times.

Sometime towards evening as he came out of his class, he got an SMS from her with a ☺.

What shocked him was the message trail displayed on his phone. He saw a message which originated from his phone in the morning, which said, 'Been thinking of you the whole night.' He could have sworn that he had never sent the message.

'Bloody idiot Abid. Must be playing cupid,' he cursed.

Next afternoon he got a call from her.

'Yes,' he said, trying to sound as uninterested as possible.

'KFC near your college', she said, 'and make it fast.' She disconnected even before he could say anything. He tried calling her back, but the call just wouldn't go through. He decided to send a message but was again shocked to see three messages sent from his phone. All of them the same message, 'Can V meet 4 lunch 2day?'

This time he checked the timing the messages were sent. The first message had been sent at 10.14 a.m., the second at 12.18 p.m., and the third immediately after at 12.22 p.m. He checked the time on his watch: 12.35 p.m. All the time, the phone had been in his pocket. Did the keys get punched in by mistake when it was in his pocket? He wondered. He scrolled his phone for other messages. Just a day back, Abid had sent him the exact same message. He swore and decided to make it to KFC anyway.

He thought it would be better to explain to her that he had never sent the messages to her. 'It got sent by mistake.' Yeah, tell me more! No matter how he put it, it didn't sound convincing. He decided to let it go.

She smiled and waved to him as soon as she saw him. Her smile was not too different from the one Colonel Sanders was flashing in a poster right behind her. God, she looked stunning.

Like two academicians, they conversed over the next half hour on various topics, from rising petrol prices to the turmoil in Syria and Iraq. He caught people looking in his direction. He still found it difficult to maintain eye contact for a prolonged period of time. He had definitely improved from his first meeting though.

'Drop me home,' she said after the meal.

'Why?' he intended to ask, but ended up asking, 'Where do you stay?'

Any onlooker would have found it amusing to see him on his Honda CBR 250R. He was almost perched on the petrol tank, his body lunged forward. For he felt her clinging on to him nearly as if she was holding on for her life.

They hardly talked until they reached the suburbs, except for a few times she had to give him directions. From there, she directed him onto interior roads, and at some point, the roads ended and there was just a dusty cycling track leading to nowhere.

'Keep going,' she urged him even as he wondered where she was leading him to. He was left quite restless because there was not a house in sight anywhere in the vicinity. As they finally reached her home, he discovered that it was an independent house which almost seemed like a remote island in the middle of an ocean. The building did seem like it was new and it came with a compound wall that was seven feet high and ran all around the house.

'Did Osama Bin Laden stay here sometime?' he asked only half jokingly.

'Why?' she asked not lost on his caustic humor.

'Why would someone have a seven-foot-high compound wall?'

Her answer shocked him even more. 'Because I need all the security I can get,' she said, 'and I happen to live here alone.'

'What? You stay alone in this godforsaken place?' he asked, shocked.

She shot him a look which told him that she didn't appreciate the comment about her home.

'Where do your parents stay then?' he asked.

'Away,' she said and quickly changed the topic. 'Aren't you coming inside for a drink?'

His first instinct was to run away. He saw that she had already opened the front gate and was opening the front door. He looked around waiting for a couple of moments, unsure of what to do. He felt uneasy standing outside all by himself without a life form anywhere in sight. He decided it was probably safer inside the house.

The first thing that he noticed as soon as he entered the house was a life-size portrait of an elderly couple on the opposite wall to the entrance. In the picture, an old lady sat on a cushioned chair and beside her an elderly man stood holding his wooden walking stick. The lady, dressed in a silk sari, was perhaps wearing all her finest jewelry. She must have ensured that the artist who painted the portrait captured each one of them in its finest grandeur. The man wore what looked like a silk suit with a turban tied to his head that had some pearls hanging from it. The wooden walking stick that the old man held had an ivory handle and the exquisite engravings were well captured in the painting. The artist had managed to render the painting in a very lifelike manner, with both the subjects appearing to lock their gaze with anyone viewing the picture. The effect was so lifelike that anyone who saw the picture would think the aged couple was actually alive and standing in front of the house to greet visitors. Rajeev stepped forward to take a closer look of the portrait.

'That's a picture of my great-grandparents,' she said, entering into the room.

'Where are they now?' he asked, still admiring the painting.

'Mister, that painting is almost seven decades old and was made when they were in their sixties. Where do you think they would be now?' she asked. 'They have been dead for years.'

She walked into the kitchen as he surveyed the room. There were no other photographs or paintings adorning the walls. In the corner of the room was placed a settee that could seat two, with a small center table. No books were on the table. Nothing. Not even a lampshade. Strange. Yet for some strange reason, the room did not look barren.

'Soda?' she said, returning within a couple of minutes. She had changed her dress and was holding up two bottles.

'That was pretty quick,' he said, a tone of suspicion apparent in his voice.

'I have a spirit imprisoned in my house that helps me change my clothes,' she said with a poker face.

The problem was that he couldn't be too sure if she was joking or was dead serious. It wasn't making him any more comfortable. He reached for the bottle and drank a couple of huge gulps.

'So? How come you were so desperate to meet me today?' she asked, taking a sip from her bottle.

'I wasn't,' he retorted.

'Three messages in a span of one hour sound pretty desperate to me,' she said, looking at him, 'unless you are going to say that you didn't send those messages and your phone did it by itself.'

He fidgeted. He noted a hint of sarcasm in her tone. Was it intended? In case it was, he couldn't make out for sure. He was lost for words anyway.

'Who are you?' he asked suddenly.

'What?' she asked, her expression suggesting she was not sure what the question meant.

'Who are you?' he asked a little more firmly this time.

'I am a witch,' she said, laughing. 'I am here to kill you and drink your blood,' she said, moving her hands around like a cat scratching around.

'That's not amusing at all,' he said. 'Tell me, who are you?'

'I told you I am a witch,' she said. 'I ensnare young, handsome men like you and kill them. All right, I first take them to bed, if that sounds more interesting.' She laughed hysterically this time.

'I need to leave,' he said, getting up.

'Leave after you have finished your drink,' she ordered and he sat down meekly to comply. 'I will tell you more about me when I need to tell you.'

Later that evening as he sat with Abid, he said he had no idea why he meekly sat down to gulp his drink like an obedient school kid who had been asked to complete his homework.

'I need to meet this lady,' Abid laughed. 'You make her sound like a real witch.'

Rajeev did not mention the messages sent out by his phone. He decided even Abid wouldn't believe him.

'I don't know,' Rajeev confided. 'She looks even more beautiful every time I meet her, but sometimes she really makes me uncomfortable.'

'Then why don't you stop seeing her?' Abid asked curiously.

'This is strange. When I do not meet her . . . I feel like I need to meet her.'

'Look it up in the dictionary, boy. It is called *love*,' Abid said, smiling. 'Tell you what, let us invite her and a friend of hers for dinner this weekend,' Abid suggested. 'Make it sound like a kind of double date.'

'Are you suggesting that because you want to meet her or are you desperate for a date yourself?' Rajeev joked.

Later in the week when they met again, Rajeev suggested a double date. Her reply suggested that she was not very interested.

'I don't like the idea,' she said, 'gets complicated when we involve others. Anyway, if you want to go out with me, you just need to ask. No need for excuses,' she laughed.

'She didn't seem very interested.' Rajeev sounded apologetic to Abid. 'I got a sneaky feeling that she does not have many friends. Come to think of it, I have never seen her speak to anyone . . . Shucks, that's really strange . . . I don't remember seeing the poor thing speak to anyone,' he said, sounding bewildered and sympathetic at the same time, making Abid smile.

'Relax, man. Chill. Enjoy the courtship,' Abid said. 'Are you meeting her anytime this week?'

'Yes. We are going to a movie at the Inox,' he said. 'Why?'

'Don't tell her, I will drop by to meet you both. Also remember if her feet are on the ground, she is not a ghost,' Abid laughed.

'I never said that she was a ghost,' Rajeev said, protesting and punching Abid in the arm.

The following Saturday, Rajeev did not have to wait long at the theater for her. He saw her walking into the theater and the first thing he did was to check her feet. He felt reassured that they were very much on the ground, though he had no idea why he had checked them out. Within a few minutes, they headed for the screen, only stopping to pick up a bottle of soda each. As usual, it was a horror movie much to Rajeev's discomfort.

'Why do you always pick horror movies?' he asked her and just received a smile for an answer. Rajeev was thankful that this time around, the movie house was almost full. During the intermission, he again excused himself to get some refreshments. Abid stood beside the counter, holding a pack of wafers.

'Soda again,' Abid remarked, looking at the cans he was holding and followed up. 'Where is she?'

'She is sitting inside. Come, let me introduce her to you,' Rajeev said. They walked in and found the seat empty. 'She was here a few moments ago,' Rajeev said.

Soon the trailers started rolling.

'No problem. I am a few rows behind you. I will try and meet you after the movie,' Abid said. 'Also, I can see you from back there.'

A few minutes after the movie resumed, she returned.

'Where were you?' he asked.

'Washroom,' she replied.

After the movie ended, she turned to him and said, 'Got to go. Have a test on Monday.'

'Wait for a few minutes,' he said, his eyes searching for Abid amongst the crowd that was rushing to leave the theater.

'Sorry, some other time,' she said and left.

A few minutes later, Abid turned up.

'Where is she?' he asked.

'Was here a few minutes back. Had to leave because she had a test on Monday,' he said, disappointed.

'You mean she was with you for the second half of the movie? I thought the seat beside you was empty!' Abid said.

'The one to my right was empty. She was sitting to my left.'

'But . . .' Abid started to say and left it at that. Abid was certain that he had seen both the seats beside Rajeev empty.

Strange things continued to happen, and now surprisingly, he had started to accept it as part of his life. Rufus attacked him when he tried to reach out and pat the dog. Thankfully, he had moved his hand away before the canine managed to bite him. More disturbing, Rajeev discovered that his cell phone had a mind of its own. It had started sending out text messages at will, all to the one person he was trying to figure out all about. Every time he tried to call her, the call wouldn't go through. However, she would call him back within a few minutes.

'Why do you keep giving me missed calls?' she asked one day when they met just outside his college. 'Too cheap to pay your phone bills?'

'The call never goes through when I dial your number,' he protested. 'Let me show you,' he said, pulling out his phone and dialing her number. Her phone rang.

'Cheapskate,' she laughed, pulling out her phone and disconnecting the call.

'But I swear, it never goes through' he insisted.

'It's all right,' she said, 'I believe you.' He wondered if she truly did.

'Do you have an email ID?' he asked her one time when she had called him. He figured he would get her name through her mail ID.

'No,' she laughed, 'on our planet, we communicate through smoke signals. Of course I have an email ID.'

'Need to send you some forwards,' he said.

'Only send them to me if they are jokes or pornography,' she laughed. 'My mail ID is UR4ME@yahoo.com.'

He was not too sure whether she was serious. 'What kind of a person has a strange ID like that?' he asked.

'For starters, a witch who likes to ensnare young, handsome men,' she said, laughing.

'That joke has run out of steam,' he replied and noted down the email ID anyway.

He sent a joke to her mail the same day. He received a smiley within a couple of seconds. He assumed she would be accessing her mail on her phone. For the next few days, he followed it up with a lot of interesting trail mail and jokes and received a smiley for each one of them within a few seconds, almost as if it was an automated reply. All he wanted to check out was if his laptop acted as weird as his cell phone when he communicated with her. He was reasonably reassured that the problem lay in his phone.

Through the next week, he kept meeting her at various places like restaurants and movie theaters. He was getting a little bolder with her and slipping his hand around her waist when they walked. She never objected and seemed to enjoy the attention he showered on her.

And then one day something happened.

'We met exactly a month back for the first time,' she said on the phone.

'What do you have in mind?' he asked.

'Come over to my house, around four in the evening for some coffee and a quiet dinner. We can cook together, and since it's a weekend, maybe we can . . .' She left the sentence hanging.

'Maybe we can what?' he asked, but the line had gone dead. He thought of a hundred things she could have meant. He smiled at the thought of quite a few probabilities.

At home, over a bowl of noodles, Rajeev talked about how he felt to Abid.

'Maybe you are right, Abid,' he said. 'I think it is love.'

'But you have hardly known her for a month,' Abid said, not sounding amused. 'You haven't met any of her friends or her family. Nobody, Rajeev, not a single one. You hardly know anything about her, Rajeev.'

'I have been to her house,' Rajeev defended himself, 'and I think I know fairly a lot about her.' He felt strange saying that because he did not even know her name.

Over the next few minutes of the conversation, Rajeev felt it strange that Abid was almost talking him out of the relationship.

'Moreover,' Abid said, 'most of the time you have been telling me that this girl is weird. Now you are telling me that you are in love with this girl?'

'Don't forget, you are the one who insinuated that,' Rajeev muttered. 'I anyway intend to find out more about her when I meet her this evening.'

'You are meeting her today?' Abid asked, aghast. 'Rajeev, you have been bunking off classes to meet her. You are way back on most of your project assignments and you are meeting her again today?'

'Yes,' Rajeev said doggedly.

'Your call, mate,' Abid said with an exaggerated expression of resignation. 'I am leaving for Calcutta in the afternoon. I will be back on Monday by the early morning flight. I want you to be careful, buddy,' he said.

For the second time, Rajeev felt something strange about Abid's behavior. He had gone out of town on numerous occasions but had never displayed any concern for Rajeev's safety.

'Why did you say that?' Rajeev asked inquisitively.

'Just like that,' Abid said, forcing a smile of reassurance.

After Abid left, Rajeev started readying himself for his evening date like never before. He changed his shirt thrice before he was convinced he looked really good. He kept admiring himself in the mirror, patting his hair down several times and spraying his most expensive perfume over and over again. He felt a nervous energy building up inside him. As he stepped out of the house, he found his neighbor standing right outside his gate.

'Rufus died this morning,' his neighbor informed Rajeev. 'Thought I would tell you because you always cared.'

Rajeev felt genuinely sorry, hearing the news. He had known the dog ever since it was a pup and came to live with his neighbor. That was roughly two years back. It was too young an age for a dog to die. He wondered if the dog had contracted rabies. At least it would explain the strange behavior of the dog in the last couple of weeks.

'How did he die?' Rajeev asked.

'Absolutely no idea' his neighbor said sadly. 'He was fine and healthy a couple of weeks back. He started to act strange lately. He stopped eating and kept wailing through the night. We took him to a vet. Hard luck, I must say.'

Rajeev nodded his head sympathetically, but his mind was on being near her as soon as he could.

He reached her home at four and parked his bike in front of her gate. He popped in a mouth freshener and checked himself in the rearview mirror. He wiped his face with a wet tissue and combed his hair. A passerby gave him a strange look before walking away.

He walked to the front door and rang the bell. She opened the door and the first glance floored him. He had never realized that she could be as stunning. She was wearing a sari, something he had never seen her wear before. Her tresses were left untied.

He said a silent 'Wow.'

'Are you ever going to come in?' she asked, smiling.

For the next few minutes, he hardly said a thing and kept admiring her. When he got a chance, he held her hand and drew her close to him.

'Shouldn't we be making dinner?'

'Can I have you for dinner?' he asked, sounding romantic.

'Actually, I planned to have you for dinner. I am the witch, remember,' she said matter-of-factly. The statement had the desired effect and he let her go, some of the old fear resurfacing. She just smiled and said, 'I am sorry. I know it's a stale joke.'

He just smiled and let the comment go, but somewhere the nagging fear had started. Over the next couple of hours, nothing else happened to alarm Rajeev and he slowly got over his apprehensions.

'You said something about tomorrow being a weekend and maybe we could do what?' he asked her. 'The line went dead and I couldn't hear you.' He smiled mischievously, anxious to know what she had in mind.

He saw her blushing, but she recovered soon enough to say, 'What about tomorrow being a weekend? I don't remember saying anything.'

'You did,' he insisted.

'Maybe you could help me with the dinner,' she said, trying to sound serious.

'And what after that?' he asked.

'Help me with the dishes,' she said.

'And what after that?' he asked.

'Depends on how you behave,' she said, smiling coyly, which was enough to make him imagine a thousand things; each one made him smile.

When he came to, she had already entered the kitchen and had started making dinner. He stood in the kitchen, helping her cut the tomatoes and peel the potatoes, all the while talking about his father and the family business.

'What happened when your father went to Bhopal last year?' she asked out of the blue.

'Oh, he had a tough time getting out of the mess . . . How do you know my father went to Bhopal last year?' he asked, surprised.

She just smiled.

'Tell me, I don't remember having told you anything about my father's visit to Bhopal last year. How do you know about that one?' he asked in a tone mixed with surprise and shock.

She just continued to stand there smiling.

And the phone rang. He kept looking at her as he fetched his phone from his trouser pocket and looked at the display. It was Abid.

Still looking at her as she stood there smiling at him, he answered the phone.

'Hello?' Rajeev said into the phone.

'Where are you?' he heard Abid's voice sounding worried.

'With her,' Rajeev answered.

'Is she in front of you? I need to talk to you in private. Can we talk?' Abid said.

'Can we talk later?' he asked Abid. He was still perplexed that she knew something about him that only he or his father knew. Not even Abid was aware of that dreadful visit to Bhopal.

'Now!' Abid insisted. 'I need to talk to you now. It's urgent. Do you understand?'

Rajeev realized that Abid would not be insisting if it was not really serious.

'Yeah,' he said and turned around and walked to the living room. 'I am alone now. What is it?'

'Listen to me carefully,' Abid said, 'she does not exist.'

'Who does not exist?' Rajeev barked into the phone.

'That girl you are with,' Abid said as calmly as he could.

'What are you talking about?' Rajeev asked, irritated. 'Are you okay? Are you on substance?'

'I am perfectly fine, and no, I did not take any substance. I want you to listen to me carefully and keep your voice down. Your girlfriend does not exist. She never did,' Abid repeated.

'You idiot,' Rajeev said, almost whispering into the phone. 'I am with her. She is cooking dinner in the kitchen. We just shared a bottle of soda some time back. You must be out of your mind—'

'Where did you meet her?' Abid asked.

'I told you. At the debating competition at VXL. She won the first—'

'Was Anand there?' Abid asked to cut him short.

'Yes. He was.'

'I talked to Anand. A guy called Shivshankar Dubey won the first prize there. You did not even turn up after the second round. Everyone was surprised that you walked out after the second round. Because you did not turn up, Shivshankar, who came third in the semifinal, was offered a place in the finals. You just disappeared after that. Do you get me? In fact Anand won the second prize. Anand sent me a picture of his winning certificate on Whatsapp. I can forward it to you if you want.'

'I don't understand,' Rajeev said.

'Let me ask you a question. All of the time that you met her, it was at a public place. Movie houses, restaurants, colleges, and other places, right?' Abid asked.

'Yeah, most of the times. Except at her home,' Rajeev agreed.

'Do you recall a single instance of seeing her interact with another person?' Abid asked.

'I don't understand. What are you getting at?' Rajeev asked.

'Do you remember her talking to someone at the cash counter or ordering food or buying the movie tickets? In short, do you recall her interacting with anyone?' Abid did not wait for an answer. 'Try as you may, you will not. Because she couldn't have.'

Rajeev kept listening, trying to understand what Abid was telling him.

'One last thing,' Abid continued. 'Remember, I met you at Inox? You had gone to a movie with her. I came to your seat to meet her. She wasn't there. She couldn't be there because she doesn't exist and I am absolutely certain that both the seat on your left and to your right were empty. I did not know how to put it across to you then. That is when I decided to track down Anand. I got the confirmation only a few minutes back and—'

'So what you are telling me is that she doesn't exist?' Rajeev said. 'Well then, tell me, if she does not exist, who is the girl who is cooking dinner inside the kitchen right now?' Rajeev asked.

'I don't know,' Abid confessed, 'either she is a figment of your imagination or '

'Or what?' Rajeev asked. The answer sent a shiver down his spine.

'Or she is something purely evil. Just get out of that place, man. Go someplace safe. Not home. Someplace else. Just make sure—' The line went dead.

Rajeev looked at his phone. The battery was dead. He placed his phone in his trouser pocket and turned around and walked into the kitchen.

He was stunned at what he saw. Nothing in his life had prepared him for the sight in front of him. There was no one in the kitchen. The potatoes he had been peeling had disappeared. The stove was missing. In fact the whole kitchen looked different now. No utensils. The fridge was nowhere. Spiderwebs were all over the place and the place was covered in dust as if no one had lived in the house for ages.

He staggered back in horror and went back to the living room. The scene was no different. The settee was there, but it was torn, with rodent droppings all over it. The center table was badly broken and the glass was lying around in shards. He felt a strange presence in the room almost as if someone was watching him. He turned to look at the life-size painting on the wall. It was still there, but now it looked different. He stared at the picture in pure horror. Just beside the old couple was a third person. Rajeev recognized her just as he had seen her a few minutes back, the same sari and her tresses left untied.

He staggered towards the door and wanted nothing but to get out of the house. He suddenly felt as if someone was choking him inside the house and fell with a thud raising a plume of dust all around him. As he fought to breathe in fresh air, he felt the dust entering his nostrils. He started to crawl out of the home, but it was difficult as he felt as if someone imaginary was pulling him back into the house. A power that was difficult to fight off.

He conjured up all his energy in one pull and kicked in the air and, for a moment, felt the imaginary grip released from his legs, which was enough for him to crawl out of the house. He did not stop until he was out of the front gate. He gasped for air as soon as he reached outside. He turned around to look at the house. There was enough light for him to see a very dilapidated structure with weeds and moss growing all around the place. Some of the walls had cracked and given way and the windowpanes were broken. He stood outside, still gasping for air, looking at the building.

He reached in his pocket to search for his bike key. He did not find it there. He remembered having put it on the center table. He decided that he was not going back there. He turned around and started running to where he remembered the main road was. He seemed to have lost all sense of time and direction. It was getting dark.

He kept running and sweating profusely. Finally, at a distance he saw the lights of passing vehicles. He ran to the road and stood waving to catch the attention of passing vehicles. Not a single one stopped until he saw a bus coming his way. He waved frantically, almost standing in the middle of the road until the bus pulled over. He entered the bus and was relieved to see quite a few passengers in the bus. He sat down at an empty seat to catch his breath suddenly aware of his whole body aching.

The ticket collector approached him. 'Where to?' he asked.

'Last stop,' Rajeev replied, still gasping for air. The ticket collector gave him a strange look as he handed over the ticket.

Almost an hour later, he got off at the main bus terminal. He tried to recall what Abid had told him. 'Don't go home. Go someplace safe.'

He wondered where he could go. 'Back to Ahmedabad. No place is as safe as home with Dad around,' he thought. But he had to head back home first to pack. His credit cards were at home. He did some quick thinking on how he could solve that.

He searched for a public phone and found one at the bus terminal. He made a quick call to a taxi service and asked for a cab to pick him up from the terminal. He found a place teeming with people at the terminal and waited for half an hour before a cab arrived to pick him up.

It was already dark and he wanted to reach the airport as soon as possible to catch the last flight out.

He gave his address to the cab driver and sat at the back trying to make sense of what had happened.

'*Do you remember a single instance of seeing her interact with another person?*' Abid's voice kept echoing through his mind. He punched his head with a fist. At KFC? At the theater? He drew a blank every time. Then it hit him. At KFC and other restaurants when he had caught people looking at him, he had misunderstood them as appreciative glances. They must have been wondering whom he was talking to.

'*At the theater, I came to your seat to meet her. She wasn't there. She couldn't be there. She does not exist.*

'*Either she is a figment of your imagination* or . . .' Rajeev shuddered when he recalled what he had heard next.

'*Or she is something purely evil.*'

'Sir, we have reached your home,' the taxi driver said, bringing Rajeev back to the present.

'I need to go to the airport. Can you take me there?' Rajiv asked the cab driver before he got out.

The taxi driver replied in the affirmative.

But Rajeev realized that his problems were far from over. What if she was waiting for him in his home? Rajeev reached into his pocket and pulled out his wallet. 'A 500 to come up to my room and help me carry my luggage down here.'

The taxi driver's eyes lit up. Rajeev got out of the cab and waited for the taxi driver to step out. He walked up to his front door and unlocked it.

'The light switch is to the left of the door. I forgot something back in the car,' Rajeev lied, stepping away from the door as the taxi driver entered the house and switched on the light. Rajeev entered the house only when he felt it was safe.

'My bedroom is to the left,' he told the cab driver. 'There must be a black suitcase. It will be heavy. Can you bring it out please?' Rajeev was now working overtime to find excuses not to enter any place which could be a potential risk to his life. 'You will find the light switch to the right as soon as you enter,' Rajeev added.

'There is no suitcase here,' the cab driver called out from inside.

Rajeev entered the room and looked around as if searching for a suitcase. 'My maid must have forgotten to pack it' he lied.

He quickly grabbed a few clothes and put it into a suitcase even as the cab driver waited in the room. Once done, he grabbed his laptop bag, checked for his credit cards, and rushed out of the house, not even waiting for the cab driver to come out of the house.

The cab driver stepped out and said, 'The lights are on.'

'Don't bother. I will be back by tomorrow,' he said, quickly locking the front door. 'Just rush me to the airport and you get an extra five hundred as a tip,' he added.

They reached the airport in fifteen minutes. The driver had kept pushing the pedal and had overshot two red signals. Rajeev got out of the cab at the airport and paid the driver as promised. He ran to the ticketing counter of the only airline he found open. Spicejet.

'Next flight to Ahmedabad?' he inquired.

'Tomorrow morning,' the booking clerk replied without even looking up from the computer monitor.

'Are there any flights out of Bangalore now?' Rajeev asked.

'To where?' the clerk asked.

'Anywhere,' Rajeev hurried.

That got the booking clerk's attention all right. He looked at Rajeev curiously. Rajeev didn't mind. He was getting a quite a few of those looks ever since he had met her.

'Hyderabad,' the booking clerk replied, 'but you need to hurry up. Boarding is just about to commence.'

'I will take it,' Rajeev said, thrusting his credit card onto the counter. The counter clerk was astonished that the guest did not even ask for the fare.

Rajeev felt much more reassured once he had boarded the flight. He did check out the other passengers sitting next to him just to be doubly sure she was not on the flight. The flight landed at Hyderabad International airport fifty minutes later.

The first thing Rajeev did on arrival was to walk up to the information desk and ask for the details of the first available flight to Ahmedabad. The first flight was at 8 a.m. but it was overbooked and the clerk at the booking counter offered a seat in the 2 p.m. flight instead. Rajeev took it. He then stepped outside the airport to hire a cab to the city and on the long drive to the city opened his hand baggage and fetched his laptop.

He switched the laptop on and opened Outlook Express. He started scrolling for mail from her. He found none. Mysteriously, they had disappeared, but he was not surprised anymore. He checked once again. None. He checked the recycle bin. He didn't find any.

He shut the laptop, feeling exhausted. He felt himself sweating profusely.

'Increase the AC,' he barked at the cab driver.

'It's running on maximum,' the driver replied.

There were still some answers he was looking for. He recalled Abid's words: '*I talked to Anand. A guy called Shivshankar Dubey won the first prize there. You did not turn up after the second round.*' Where the hell did I go then? Rajeev wondered.

He tried to recall what happened in the intervening period between the second and the third round. He remembered he had visited the canteen. He had spilt the coffee on a girl's dress. The girl was standing behind him. Something strange had happened. What was it?

'*Oh yes,*' he recalled. *Nobody seemed to notice when he spilt the coffee on the girl. Nobody turned to look in his direction. Wait a minute. Something even more bizarre—the coffee was steaming hot and yet the girl did not flinch when it fell on her.*

He closed his eyes, trying to recollect the face of the girl he had spilt the coffee on. He ran the scene in his mind over and over again and opened his eyes in a state of shock when the realization hit him. '*It was her!*'

How the hell did he miss it? he wondered.

He reached the five-star property on the Banjara hill road, paid the cab driver, and walked to the front desk.

'Good evening. How may I help you?' the front desk executive greeted him.

'Need a room just for a night,' Rajeev informed him. He was starting to feel relaxed that he had gotten out of the godforsaken city. 'I also need a cab to take me to the airport at twelve noon tomorrow.'

After the front desk staff had booked him into a room on the seventh floor, he walked to the lift. One of the lift doors opened. It was empty. He did not get into the lift. He waited for it to leave and waited for the next one, which also turned up empty. He didn't feel safe enough as yet to get into an empty lift. He realized that he would have to spend the night alone in a room. Not a comforting thought. On second thoughts, he should have remained in the airport.

A bellboy appeared by his side with his luggage. He decided to take the next ride in the lift.

As soon as he entered the room, he turned on the television while he made the bellboy wait.

'Turn on the news. CNN,' he said, not because he wanted to catch the latest edition. He was sure that the news channel was the only channel which wouldn't show any late-night horror show. While the bellboy got busy with the television, he turned on the lights even in the washroom.

After the bellboy left, he locked the door and sat down to watch the news. He did not unpack because he didn't feel the need to do it right away. He sat on the bed watching the news and fell asleep watching a rerun of the Piers Morgan show. When he got up with a start after a couple of hours, Anderson

Cooper had taken over. The clock on the wall showed the time as two minutes to three. He got up and walked to the washroom. He just splashed some water on his face and avoided looking in the mirror . . . just in case.

He wiped his face with a hand towel lying on a shelf nearby and walked back into his room. He stopped dead in his tracks when he saw his laptop out of his bag and open. He walked slowly towards the bed and looked at the monitor.

It was on and running. He saw the cursor move all by itself to the Skype icon and double-click it. He was too scared to move. The Skype program was initiated and the system waited for something to happen. It didn't take long before he heard the ringtone of a Skype call. The cursor moved to 'Accept Call'.

At ten the next morning, Ajoy wondered what the commotion was all about. He looked out of his office window to see a stream of police cars drive in and out of the five-star property across the road. He wondered if any VIP was about to attend a gathering at the venue and worried about the impending traffic jam.

He decided it was time to take his first coffee break and walked to the coffee shop across the road. He saw an ambulance drive out of the five-star hotel without the sirens blaring. He sighed as he entered the coffee shop and paused to look at any faces he could recognize in the café. There was an ensemble of his colleagues settled at different tables, no one he was particularly interested in chatting up that morning. And then his eyes fell on the lone girl sitting at the corner table all by herself. She was probably waiting for someone because he noticed that she had not placed her order yet.

He walked to the counter and waved to the attendant serving behind the counter. He didn't have to place an order as within a couple of minutes the attendant placed a cup of hot machine-made coffee on the counter for him. In exchange, he left a couple of notes and coins on the counter, which the attendant quickly pocketed with a smile.

He picked up the hot cup of coffee and turned around. He was taken by surprise to find someone standing right behind him and there was no time to halt the turn. His hand crashed into the person and he saw his cup turn over and the contents spill out. It was the same girl whom he had noticed sitting alone earlier.

'Sorry, I am so sorry,' he offered apologetically. The girl just raised her hand and said, 'It's okay, accidents happen,' and looked up to lock eyes with him.

If he had been observant enough, he would have noticed that the girl did not draw back when the hot coffee fell on her.

# THE GHOST WRITER

I would be lying if I said that I was not scared. Driving in the dead of the night on a deserted road, with no sign of any civilization anywhere around, was indeed unnerving.

The truth was that I had been caught off guard. Even though the plans to visit the forest resort were made some time back, I had never expected that it would happen so soon. I should say nature played its part and so did my own desperation at not wanting to lose an important client. Truthfully speaking—my only client. The confirmation of the visit came only at five that evening and I was hardly prepared for the long drive.

The first thing I did was to give my wife a call and inform her. I was hoping that she would throw a few clothes into my overnighter.

'How many days will you be away?' she had asked, coldness evident in her voice.

You see, it hasn't gone well at home for quite some time now. My recent financial instability had added extra pressure on our already fragile relationship. This was not what I had bargained for when I quit my job as assistant vice president at Icon Advertising six months back, much against my wife's wish. My wife had always been against the idea of me giving up a lucrative job, especially since we had just purchased a new apartment. When I decided to quit, I had assurances from two or three major clients of Icon that they would be willing to move their accounts to my new agency. On that assurance, I had also poached a few employees from Icon, promising them higher salaries and a share in profits.

However, the couple of clients who had promised business backed out. Now they were not even returning my calls. Apart from a small number of miniature tender advertisements, there was nothing much to show as revenue for the new agency. I was under tremendous pressure to pay mounting bills. Added to that, I had also rented out an office space in the center of the city which was eating into my savings.

Thankfully, my wife worked as an SAP consultant in a software company that did keep the food served on my dining table. However, pressures at my office had started to show at home as I had got increasingly anxious. I had stopped talking to her about any developments, or rather the lack of them, because every conversation in the recent past had ended in acrimonious exchanges. I had started to dread the I-told-you-so look I had been getting at the start of every conversation.

And then a glimmer of hope appeared like the proverbial light at the end of the tunnel. A couple of weeks ago, an ex-colleague at Icon called, asking if I was willing to take up a new account of an NRI investor, Jagan, who had invested in a local resort. Was I willing? At the desperation levels I was in, I would have taken up the contract of the Taliban if they were looking for an advertising agency!

I first met Jagan at the Indian Gymkhana Club. I had worn my dark-blue blazer more because I considered it lucky than to improve my appearance. Though it had been a weekend, the club was sparsely occupied as most of the members had still not sauntered in to hone their swimming skills or try their luck at the bridge room.

We chose to occupy a corner table in the lounge by the side of the library. At the other end of the lounge, an old rerun of a Wimbledon match played on the huge plasma TV without gathering much attention. Jagan ordered for some grilled sandwiches and was quick to get down to brass tacks.

'I bought this place near Bandipur reserve forest,' Jagan said during the first meeting. 'We are looking at revamping the whole place. The work started six months ago and is nearing completion, though work has been slow. But that is what I am told to expect in India,' he laughed.

Jagan, as I got to know, had moved to Atlanta thirty years back. He was a businessman running a chain of twelve Indian stores all across the east and southeast of the US. His stores were located all across Louisiana, Georgia, Pennsylvania, and Florida. He now wanted to invest in the tourism industry in India.

'India is the growing market,' he said.

'Though things move at a very slow pace,' I reminded him, laughing.

'We are looking at an advertising agency which is not too big,' he said. 'Big agencies don't give the time or respect to a small client like me. Moreover, I am not too charmed by these big names. I am looking for someone for whom my resort, the Spotted Leopard, will be the most important client.'

And so my agency fit the bill. We were not too big. In fact, we were so small that we faced the danger of being invisible any time soon if we didn't get a client. And surely Jagan was going to be our most important client since we didn't have any at the moment.

The client brief said that the resort would be planning advertisements in the print and social media to start with.

'We will surely venture into television,' he promised, 'but that will be at a later date.'

I tried hard not to drool and make a mess.

'Your team', he said, 'will start with designing and maintaining a website and as we get closer to the inauguration, we will also look at releasing a half-page advertisement at least in the major English news dailies.'

I couldn't control my excitement when I broke the news to my team at the office. I did not feel it appropriate to discuss the same at home until I had my client sign on the dotted line.

Over the week, I and my team made a few presentations to the client. Some corrections were suggested and we went back to the drawing boards a couple of times. It was almost a fortnight later that Jagan finally approved our concepts but reminded us that he expected the pace to be much faster. I did give him a guesstimate on the financials and was happy that I did not see him flinch at the figures.

And then on Thursday morning, Jagan called me on my mobile and requested me to visit the resort in the weekend to experience the resort personally.

'Get your wife along,' he said. 'She will enjoy the place. I will ask them to set up a bonfire, especially for you this weekend.'

Though the original plan had been to leave for the resort on Friday afternoon, the meteorologists' predictions of heavy to very heavy thundershowers for the weekend forced me to change my plans. I decided to leave in the evening and spend the next three to four days at the resort. That way, I figured, I would not be forced to spend the weekend with my wife. I immediately called Jagan on his mobile to inform him of my plans.

'What time will you reach?' he asked.

'Maybe 8 p.m.,' I said.

'I am not too sure that is a good idea,' he said. 'You see, it is difficult to find your way to the resort in the dark. You have to drive a good two or three miles from the nearest road and I am not sure you will be able to find the way.'

'I have a very good sense of direction,' I assured him. 'However, I am not able to find the place on Google Maps though, can you give me the directions?'

'I will have Raghav give you a call,' Jagan said. 'Raghav works at the resort and stays in a village close by. He knows the place well.'

'Will you be there at the resort or make a visit in the next couple of days?' I asked.

'No,' he replied, 'I have a morning flight to Singapore. I am sorry I will not be able to join you.'

The call from Raghav came a good two hours later and we both struggled to understand each other. He only knew four words in English which I could understand: yes, no, left, and right. The generous sprinkling of Kannada in between these four words ensured our conversation led nowhere and I very soon felt there was clear and present danger of me forgetting English altogether. After struggling for ten minutes, I finally decided to take the help of my office boy, and thankfully managed to get some clarity on the location. On the face of it, it looked quite simple. I was to drive on the Coimbatore–Ooty highway for thirty-two kilometers after which I was to look out for a now-defunct Reliance fuel station. Pass the fuel station and drive on for approximately one kilometer and just before the next milestone to the left, I was to find a tar road with a billboard of the resort, the Spotted Leopard.

'You can't miss it,' Raghav assured my man Friday Lingappa as I kept noting down the instructions as rapidly as it was being translated to me. 'Drive thirty-five kilometers interior and to the right you will find a milestone number 3. To the right of the milestone you will find a dirt road. Do not take any turns anywhere before that. It is a straight road until you find the milestone. Follow the dirt road for around three kilometers and you will find a newly erected cement arch. Enter the arch and follow the direction from there. It is around two kilometers from the arch.'

After some time, the translation stopped and Lingappa continued to converse in Kannada. I thought the call ended abruptly as Lingappa continued to parrot 'Helloo, helloo' into the phone while moving around the room to catch signals.

'What is it?' I asked, looking at the strange expression on Lingappa's face after he had given up hope of establishing contact with the lost connection.

Lingappa looked worried and with some amount of hesitation blurted out, 'He tell you be careful.'

'Careful of what?' I asked, still wondering about the perplexed look on his face.

'I no hear clear.' Lingappa continued searching for words from his limited English vocabulary. 'Lot of phone disturbance. Signal very poor. That man just says ask your boss to carry holy water,' Lingappa said.

'Holy water?' I asked. 'What does he mean by holy water?'

'No idea,' Lingappa said slowly, still trying to make sense of the broken messages he had heard. 'That man say something about losing head or headless person.'

I tried to make sense of the whole thing and then it struck me and I started laughing out loud.

'What is funny, sir? I said joke?' Lingappa asked, trying to figure out the reason for my laughter.

I shared with him the conversation I had with Jagan in the morning wherein he had told me, 'You will not get any liquor at the hotel. Carry your own brand of spirit and holy water,' he had laughed. 'Don't blame me if you lose your head over it.'

Lingappa laughed nervously, but I saw that he still nurtured some doubts about the conversation.

'Don't worry. I will be fine,' I said, reassuring him.

I had Lingappa pack a few things for me for the trip from the office which included my Canon Eos 600D SLR camera to take pictures of the resort, after which I called my wife.

'I will be gone for a day or two,' I told my wife. I wanted to add that things would look up and that we were on the verge of signing up a new client, but the disinterested tone in her voice stopped me. I was desperately hoping that as the situation improved in office, so also it would start looking up at home.

That evening, I finally managed to leave office shortly after five and reached home almost an hour later. My wife was already home as expected as she worked from eight to four. As I opened the front door to my apartment, I saw her sitting on the beanbag, with a cup of coffee, watching television. She just looked away from the television only to check who was entering and, promptly deciding I was not worth the attention, turned her focus back to the program. I walked into the bedroom and had hoped to find my luggage packed as was customary every time I went out of town on official work.

Obviously, these were different and difficult times. I went about looking for a suitcase which was neither too big nor too small for a two-day sojourn which I finally found under the cot. I opened it to find it empty and proceeded to fill it with a pair of almost everything I could think of. As was always, by the time I finished packing, I couldn't help the nagging feeling that I had forgotten to pack something important.

I walked back into the living room with my briefcase and found my wife still sitting in exactly the same position as I had left her a few minutes back. She continued to ignore me and did not make any attempts to even make eye contact. She sat watching a rerun of *The Big Bang Theory* and was not even smiling at the antics of Sheldon Cooper, whom she usually found extremely cute.

I did not wait to say goodbye and left. I left the door wide open on my way out. I wanted her to take the trouble of closing it.

The city traffic was unusually busy and it took me almost another hour to reach the suburbs, by which time I was very hungry. I noticed a McDonald's on the way, but resisted the temptation. I figured that if I stopped for a bite, it would only delay me further.

I had hoped for the traffic to be lighter on the highway, but there was no respite. Two traffic jams on the highway further delayed my progress. I noticed one of them had been because a truck had rammed into a tree. What was the idiot doing? I wondered. It was around 9 p.m. when the traffic finally thinned out and I managed to spot the redundant petrol station. There was a small restaurant attached to it which was still operational.

A light drizzle started as I pulled up at the restaurant. There was hardly anything to eat in the restaurant that caught my fancy. I just filled my flask with hot coffee and picked up a few packets of biscuits from a store attached to the restaurant. I figured that I would make it to the resort within an hour anyway. The biscuits were insurance just in case I did not find anything to eat there. I also picked up a few paper cups from the store for the coffee.

By the time I left the restaurant, the light drizzle had developed into a heavy shower. I drove on the highway for a kilometer and found the turning to the right. As I had been informed, there was a billboard advertising the resort on the road. Some signage should have been put much earlier on the road too, I felt. I made a mental note of it.

The rain was pouring very heavily now and I could hardly see a few feet ahead of me. Thankfully, I did not encounter any traffic coming towards me on the narrow single road. I kept looking at the sheet in which I had written down the direction, every once in a while to reconfirm if I was in headed in the directions. On hindsight, I should have checked the odometer when I took the last turn. Somehow that detail had slipped my mind.

After having driven for about half an hour, I still had not spotted the milestone number 3. I had no idea if it would appear to my right or left. After driving around for another half an hour at a snail's pace, I still couldn't locate the milestone and came to the conclusion that I had somehow missed it. There was not a soul in sight and what seemed earlier like a blessing, now didn't seem as much.

I stopped by the roadside and poured myself a cup of the coffee. The hot cup of coffee somehow seemed to be reassuring for me. Placing the cup in the cupholder, I took out my phone, hoping to make a call to Jagan. I dialed Jagan's number only to see the message 'No network available' flashing on the display. Very soon the low battery warning signal too flashed on the display. I searched for the car charger and cursed out loud. I had not replaced the car charger back in the car after my last car service.

The rain continued to pour heavily and I could hardly see a couple of feet ahead of me. I wondered if it would be any better with the windowpane down and lowered it a tiny bit only to feel my sleeve drenched in a couple of seconds. I quickly closed the window and sat down to plan my next move as I reached for my coffee and slowly sipped it. I decided it was better to return to the highway and start my search for the milestone once again from there. Going back home was not an option I was ready for.

What if the milestone is just a few meters ahead? I thought. Probably persistence was the key. After all, I had been planning to shut down my agency a couple of weeks before Jagan appeared as my knight in shining armor. The indecision was killing me.

I decided not to turn around and planned to continue a little further to search for the damn milestone. I must have driven for a few minutes when I suddenly recalled the conversation with Lingappa. Could he have really heard the words 'headless ghost' and 'spirits'?

Knowing that I seemed to be hopelessly lost added to the fear of encountering a headless ghost, and I started to get truly scared. With the rain continuing to lash down without any respite, I decided the best way was to head back to the highway. I stopped the car and tried to maneuver it to turn around on that narrow single road. I was worried about getting the tires getting stuck in the mud. Moving cautiously, I had just about managed to complete a total turn when a knock on the window startled me.

I looked out of the closed window to see the figure of a man standing by the car. I was not sure whether I was pleased or terrified to see a person at this point of time. The fear of the headless ghost still worried me. The man soon put me out of my misery by bending down and attempting to look inside the car through the glass. I brought the glass down an inch even as he knocked on it again.

'Excuse me, sir,' he said. 'You seem lost. Is there any way I can help you?'

I was taken by surprise, hearing someone speak to me in English at such a godforsaken place. I guess the predicament I was in, only added to the surprise.

'What makes you feel I am lost?' I asked a little rudely. I was just making sure that the man would have second thoughts about mugging me, just in case he was indeed a mugger.

'Why would someone turn a car around on such a road if he wasn't lost?' the man reasoned with me. 'I was just wondering if I could help you and you could return my favor.'

The man seemed reasonable and surely didn't sound like a mugger. Not that I knew how a mugger sounded. I had not encountered a single one all my life. I doubted a mugger would speak in quite as much a polished way as this stranger did.

'I am looking for a resort called Spotted Leopard,' I said. I then remembered that being a new resort, its name would not be familiar to many.

'I am looking for a milestone number 3,' I rephrased.

'Milestone number 3?' he asked. 'But you have come way too far ahead. It is quite some distance back. I know where it is. In fact, I am headed there. If you so want, I can show you the way,' he said.

'Come in,' I said, opening the central lock of the car.

'Thank you,' he said and opened the back door of the car. As an afterthought, he shut the back door and decided to sit in the front passenger seat. His movements were slow and deliberate, and I understood that he did not want to involve any sudden movements that would alarm me. I still looked at his feet. Someone had told me a long time back that you could spot a ghost by looking at their feet: 'Either they are not on the ground or they are turned away from the face.'

He caught me looking at my feet and laughed. I looked at him quizzically.

'If you need to spot a ghost, you need to touch them. They feel cold as ice,' he said, continuing to laugh. 'In fact, don't touch me now, I have been standing in the rain for a very long time, I am bound to be cold.' I sensed that he was trying to put me at ease. I just shook my head, smiling.

By now the windshield had totally misted up and I couldn't see a thing. I wiped the windshield with a tissue. I had already put the car in gear when I realized that the man could be feeling really cold.

'Do you want a cup of hot coffee?' I asked. It felt so nice to be talking to someone besides myself again.

'That would be most welcome,' he said. I put the car back in neutral and fetched the flask from the back seat. I poured him a cup and offered it to him. Rather than readily drink it, he accepted it and placed it in the cupholder on the passenger side.

I put the car in motion and moved ahead.

'What are you doing here at this hour?' I asked, wanting to make small talk.

'My car broke down,' he said. 'I have been walking miles since. I was walking towards the highway when I saw you. What about you?' he asked.

'Oh, I was searching for this new resort and got lost,' I replied.

'What is the name of the resort again?' he asked.

'Well, you wouldn't know it. Not even started operations,' I said.

'Try me,' he said.

'It's a resort called Spotted Leopard,' I replied. 'It is a little distance from the milestone 3.'

'Hmm,' he said. 'So now it is called Spotted Leopard, is it?' he asked.

'So, you know the place, eh?' I inquired.

'Yes,' he said, 'very strange place.'

I did not say anything, expecting him to continue. But he remained silent, maybe wanting me to ask. Curiosity got the better of me.

'Strange?' I asked.

'Why are you looking for the place?' he questioned me back.

I told him the bit about how I had been approached by Jagan to be their advertising agency.

'Did you say Jagan?' he asked.

'Yes. Do you know him?' I asked, looking at him.

He pursed his lips and nodded thoughtfully. That is when it struck me that I didn't even know my fellow traveler's name. It would have been rude to ask him so I introduced myself and told him my name.

'I am sorry, I should have given my name earlier,' he said apologetically. 'My name is Vikram Rao.'

'So, Vikram,' I said, 'you didn't answer my question. Do you know Jagan?'

'Yes. I do,' he said. 'I could tell you how, but it is a long story,' Vikram offered.

'I thought we had a long way to drive?' I asked.

'Yes, we do,' he laughed. 'However, I need to ask you one question before that. Did Jagan ever tell you anything strange about this resort?'

'No,' I said, trying to recall our conversation. 'Definitely *no*.'

'But, as I recall, he did tell you that he bought the place six months back and work has been slow. Any reasons he quoted?' Vikram asked.

'No. Only that he felt it was the work culture,' I replied, recalling our conversation as if it happened yesterday.

'That means he hasn't found out yet,' Vikram said to himself, shaking his head. I was about to ask him what he was referring to, when Vikram followed it up immediately with his next question: 'Did Jagan say he was married?' I was curious that Vikram had so many questions to ask me.

'No,' I replied, 'actually I never asked him if he was married and neither did he tell.' I said, 'Strange, you asked me so many questions. I am sensing a very interesting story behind all these questions.'

'Strange is not the word, my friend,' he said. I sensed a chuckle hidden behind his remark.

'So tell me,' I almost pleaded.

'Well? Where do I start?' he asked and, without waiting for my answer, started narrating his story. 'Five years back, I took over my father's garment business after his death. Since my mother had also expired long time back, it was just me and my sister Diya. The business was in a mess when I took it over and it took me a long time to set things right. We were doing well in terms of turnover, but everything else was a mess. There were no processes, the union had started creating problems, and government regulations and taxes were not in order. I started setting things right one by one and it took me almost four years to bring some semblance of normalcy into the whole thing.'

'Four years is a long time. Why did it take so long?' I asked.

'Before I took over my father's business, I used to stay in London studying music. Dad's death changed all plans that I had set for myself. Diya was in the US doing her MS. I did not know anything about the business, nor about the local rules and regulations,' he answered.

'Okay. Continue,' I prodded.

'In the interim period, I did not have either the time or the inclination to get married,' he continued. 'Around a year back, after Diya had returned from the US, I happened to meet this chap called Nathan at a friend's party. The three of us hit it off well and seemed to share a common wavelength. Nathan was also from the US and had good taste in Western classical music and so we three had some common topics to share and life went on. Six months back, we decided to come to Bangalore on a holiday.'

'Wait a minute,' I interrupted. 'I thought you were from Bangalore.'

'No,' Vikram replied, 'Delhi.'

'And the name of your company was?' I inquired.

'DiVi Garments,' he replied.

'The name sounds so familiar,' I said, 'can't recall where I heard it.'

'Maybe you will remember soon enough,' Vikram said. 'Where was I?'

'You decided to come to Bangalore on a holiday,' I helped out.

'Did I say we decided? Well, actually, it was Nathan and Diya who picked Bangalore. I wanted to go to a beach resort, but Diya insisted on a forest reserve. The plan was made hurriedly and we hardly had any time to plan out our schedule. However, when we landed here in Bangalore, we couldn't get any accommodation in any of the popular resorts around. Nathan said he knew a few people in Bangalore and kept calling just about anybody he had in his phone book to get us rooms. He seemed pretty nervous, but I was all chilled out as I was in a holiday mood. It was the first break I was taking since I took over the businesses.'

I turned to look at Vikram. He could have been in his mid thirties. Prominent cheekbones added character to his round face. He had a long forehead and I couldn't make out the color of his eyes. Quite a handsome man, I thought.

'Finally, Nathan returned with some good news. He said that he had managed to find a resort in the forest reserve. It was not much, he said, but we would be comfortable. The resort was called the Brooke or something like that. We drove down all the way from Bangalore to here.'

'Here?' I asked, curious at the sudden revelation.

'Yeah, here,' Vikram said, amused at my surprise. 'This is only going to get even more interesting,' he warned, smiling.

'I am all ears,' I offered.

'Surprise!' he said. 'We were to find milestone number 3 and take a turn there. Sounds familiar?' he asked.

'Small world,' I laughed, 'and then what happened?'

'Strange things, my friend . . . strange things.' It almost sounded like a premonition of things to come.

'We reached the resort around 3 p.m. The first thing I noticed was that unlike the usual resorts, which have many cottages, this one was a single building. A heritage structure, if I may call it. I found it strange because it didn't look like a resort had been planned and built there. It was like an old building was taken over and converted into a resort.'

'Jagan never told me anything about that,' I mentioned. 'I always thought it was a modern resort like any other resort.' Could have been the reason he picked on a small agency like mine, I reckoned.

'That was not all. I also noticed that we were the only guests booked to stay in the resort,' Vikram said.

'What is so strange about that?' I asked.

'How come all the other resorts were full?' Vikram reasoned.

'Oh. Okay,' I replied, 'that is strange.'

'We took three rooms on the second floor because the view was good. Forest reserve resorts are funny places, if you have ever stayed in any one of them,' Vikram said.

'Never did,' I replied.

'All the lights except in your rooms are out by 10 p.m. No loud music is allowed and they scare the hell out of you, warning you not to venture out after ten in the night, and that they are not responsible if you get attacked by a wild animal and end up in its stomach, blah-blah. I think they say all that to give you the experience of staying in a forest reserve. I have never heard of anyone who had gone to a forest reserve and got attacked by a wild animal. Have you?' Vikram asked.

'Me neither,' I agreed.

'I was not someone you could tie down with such dumb rules,' Vikram said, 'and so I ventured out at around eleven on the very first night.'

'You did?' I asked. 'Don't tell me.'

'I did,' he said, 'and that is when I discovered something even more strange.'

'And what is that?' I asked.

'I told you that all the lights get switched off in the corridors and at the front desk. And added to that, I found that not a single hotel staff was to be found anywhere in the hotel. No front desk, no housekeeping, and no room service, and brace yourself, not even a security guard!'

'Don't tell me,' I exclaimed. 'Not even a security guard?'

'I am telling you,' Vikram said. 'Isn't that strange?'

'Very,' I concurred.

'Though I was quite surprised then, the reason only became clear to me later. You too will understand in a short while from now.'

I was all eager to hear the whole story.

'After my first night out, I went to bed trying to sleep. I was disturbed that there was no security guard and even a wild dog could find its way inside the resort. As I was telling you, I was trying to sleep when I first heard the footsteps in the corridor, and soon I heard someone knock on my door. I didn't bother the first time, but then I heard the knock again. I was worried that it could be my sister and opened the door. There was nobody outside.'

I started to feel a bit uneasy. I do love to listen to a good thriller, but surely not on a night like this one was.

'I went back to bed and the same thing happened again,' he said. 'I walked to Diya's door and knocked softly. No answer. I thought she must have been asleep and did not want to disturb her. As I turned towards my door, I heard the sound of someone running down the stairway. I could hear the sound of bangles and I wondered if it was Diya. I walked to the stairway and looked down. I could find no one. Only the sound of the footsteps and the bangles just speeded up as if someone was running away from the stairway on the ground floor. Though I felt very uncomfortable, I returned to bed. I heard the knocking again a couple of times more.'

'What was it?' I asked, concerned.

'Patience, my friend,' Vikram replied. 'Don't worry, I will complete the story before we part. The next day, I did not want to mention the incident to either of them. However, when we were having breakfast, Diya mentioned that she had heard someone walking in the corridor just outside her door in the night. Nathan also mentioned that he had heard someone knocking on his door. I did not contribute to the conversation.'

'Why did you not say anything?' I asked.

'It was a casual conversation. Neither of them seemed alarmed or scared. I didn't want to say anything I was not sure about. I wanted to investigate if any of the hotel staff had come near our rooms. I approached the front desk and demanded to know why all the staff had disappeared the night before. The staff swore that they had been around. But I knew they were lying. I asked them about who was walking around the hotel corridors in the night and from the nervous looks they gave, I was sure something was not right.'

I glanced at Vikram nervously. I did not want to ask any questions at that point of time. I was partly preoccupied trying to figure out where I had heard the name DiVi Garments.

'That night, I was resolved to get to the bottom of the issue,' Vikram continued. 'I went on my customary round around eleven and as usual found the place deserted. I called out for the security guard, but no one was around to respond to my call. I waited at the front desk for quite a long time, hoping to see who was playing the fool. Nothing happened till 1 a.m., after which time I decided to go back to sleep. Around 3 a.m., I woke up feeling thirsty. I drank some water but couldn't go back to sleep. I sat up on my bed with a feeling that something was about to happen, and in a few moments, it happened.'

'What happened?' I asked.

'One side of my bed . . . it felt as if someone had just sat down on the bed,' Vikram said.

I felt my hair stand up on end as I heard it.

'Someone was in the room. Trust me, till that day, I never believed in ghosts. But that day, I started to wonder. There was first a distinct creak of the bed, followed by the feeling that someone actually sat on the bed. I distinctly heard the sound of bangles and I just held my breath and waited. Whoever or whatever it was that sat on the bed waited for a long time and finally decided to get up and go. An uneasy calm enveloped the room. I waited for something else to happen, but nothing else happened that night. The next day, I again did not mention it to the other two. As an afterthought, I thought I might have imagined the whole thing.'

I tried hard to focus on the road.

'We went on a safari that day and when we got back it was around six,' Vikram continued. 'After dinner, I walked to the front desk and requested for a change of room, stating that the room was very warm. I had decided that if anything strange happened that night, I would convince my sister and Nathan to leave the resort.'

'And did it?'

'Something strange did happen. But it had nothing to do with anything supernatural,' Vikram replied.

'What happened?' I asked.

'That night as I went out on my walk a little early, around 9.30 p.m., I saw Diya and Nathan talking near a small garden behind the resort. I found it strange because it was cold out there and though the lights had not yet been put out, it was still dark and they could have been in the room talking, or anywhere else for that matter. Behind the resort, in the dark shadows . . . somehow it didn't seem just right. At first, I thought they were romantically involved. But the body language, the hushed tones didn't seem romantic at all. Without making my presence known, I closed in on them. I was just a few feet away from them and I heard them talking. It was really shocking and to this day, I feel sad about that moment of my life.'

'What were they saying?' I asked impatiently.

'Nathan was telling my sister how he had planned on killing me that night, and my sister, my very own sister, was asking him if he had it all covered.'

I looked at Vikram, shocked. 'What are you saying?' I asked.

'It is indeed shocking, my friend, when you face such a situation. Nothing in life prepares you for such a situation. You can go to the best business schools, travel the world, and speak to the finest minds. You will still be lost when you face such a situation.'

'And then?' I asked.

'The plan was well thought out. Choosing the resort, the modus operandi, disposing the body, saying that I disappeared in the forest one fine day . . . all that was discussed,' Vikram said, sounding depressed.

'But why?' I asked.

'Money, inheritance. What else?' Vikram said. 'You see, that day I came to know another truth that I never knew. Diya called Nathan by his real name.'

'Which is?' I asked.

'Jagan' Vikram said.

I slammed the brakes as a reflex action. I was not sure I had heard it right and turned to look at Vikram.

'Shocked?' he asked. I most definitely was. 'His full name is Jaganath and his pet name Nathan. Keep driving, we are almost there,' he said.

I reluctantly put the car in first gear and drove on. I had a thousand questions running in my mind. Most importantly, I was disappointed that it was a criminal I had been dealing with all along. A fleeting thought was also about the lost business opportunity. But then, I wondered, what if all this is not true? What if Vikram was lying? I decided to wait for the story to end before I drew any conclusions.

'Do you want to hear the rest of it?' he asked. 'Or have I really shocked you too much?'

'Tell me' I said, sounding distraught.

'Remember, I had not told them that I had shifted the room. I wanted to see if they would really carry out their devious plan. With the door slightly open in my new room, I watched the corridor to check their movements. Around twelve midnight, they both walked to my room. They had flashlights with them, and a duplicate key, with which they opened the door without making a sound. I saw them enter the room. After a few minutes, I saw them come out. And Diya spoke to Nathan or rather Jagan. I could sense the panic in her voice as she said, "I think he has found out about our plan and escaped. We have to find him." I saw them run towards the stairs. I broke down and cried in my room. It was obviously a shock for me. Seeing my sister talk like that sort of broke me. I mean, your own flesh and blood plotting to kill you! I must have sat there sobbing silently for about fifteen minutes after which I decided that I needed to do something. I needed to get away from that place. Run someplace safe and think this over.'

'In the middle of the night?' I asked.

'Would you have stayed back, knowing someone was coming to kill you?' he asked.

All of a sudden, my question sounded stupid to me. 'And then?' I asked.

'Remember at the beginning I asked you a few questions? One of them was—' Vikram started.

'Did he say anything about being married?' I chipped in. 'I figured it was to find out if he married your sister.'

'It is the second one I want you to recall,' Vikram interjected, '"Did Jagan ever tell you anything strange about the resort?" to which you replied in the negative. I concluded that he did not know the place was haunted.'

'Haunted?' I asked. 'But you yourself admitted that you could have imagined someone sitting on your bed'.

'Yes. But what happened afterwards definitely was not my imagination,' he said.

'What was it?' I asked. Personally, I do not believe in ghosts. I always believed that science has an explanation for every paranormal or supernatural experience. I believe that when we get scared, we do not see a rational explanation to the situation. Now, here I was with a perfectly sane man who was saying something to the contrary.

'When I decided to make a run for it, I was all the time planning as to how I could get away from the place at twelve in the night,' Vikram said. 'During one of my interactions with the front office staff, I distinctly remembered one of the drivers coming to the desk and handing over the keys of the resort van to the front office clerk. He in turn had dropped it into the second drawer of one of the tills in his desk. I knew that there were two vehicles that belonged to the resort, and if I managed to find the keys, I could make a quick getaway.'

'But it must have been pretty dark for you to find your way around?' I asked.

'Yes,' Vikram replied, 'I did plan to use my mobile phone to find my way around but it could have attracted attention. Thankfully, there was a huge window running along the stairway and there was enough moonlight streaming in for me to find my way down the stairway. And so, without waiting to gather any of my belongings except for my mobile phone, I started to make my way down the stairs and that is when it happened.'

I wondered what new twist this story had in store for me. I braced myself.

'As I walked down the stairway with the help of the little moonlight that filtered from the stairway window, I heard the sounds of the footsteps and the bangles again. Somebody was approaching the stairway from the ground floor. I stopped dead in my tracks. At first I thought it was Diya coming back to check the hotel once again. But then I figured that if it was indeed Diya, she would surely have used a flashlight. I couldn't see any. It had to be somebody else.'

'Who was it?' I hurried Vikram.

'Nobody' Vikram said.

'What?' I spat out. 'How can it be nobody? Don't tell me it was—' I didn't complete my sentence.

Vikram just turned to look at me. I could see the terror of that night play out on his face.

'I just waited on the stairway,' Vikram said, clearly reflecting on the incidents of that night, 'listening to the sounds of approaching footsteps. I heard the sound of the bangles get closer and closer to me, but there was nobody on the stairway except me. I was scared out of my wits until I felt someone touch my hand gently.'

The tension was building up inside me. I felt my heartbeat race. The story could have been a figment of his imagination, but I didn't care. The way he said it had got me all tensed up. I realized I was breaking out into a cold sweat. I increased the air conditioning by one level and directed the vents directly at my face.

'It was the touch of a woman,' Vikram said. 'I couldn't see her, but I could sense her, smell her, and touch her. She held my hand and gently guided me towards the front desk. On one hand, I was paralyzed by fear of this unseen entity, on the other, the will to survive was prodding me on. I got down the remaining stairs with someone still holding on to my hand. The woman let go of me as I reached the front desk. I wondered if someone was really there, or was it me just imagining everything? I tried to banish the ghost from my thoughts and focus on the task at hand. I used the light from my mobile to find my way around.'

'I reached for the till and tried to open it. It was locked. I panicked even more. I started to wrestle with the till handle, trying to force it open. It wouldn't budge. I don't know how many seconds went by with me standing there, not knowing what to do. I tried the till handle again and again, but it wouldn't move. I could feel the desperation building inside me and I finally said aloud, "Please, please help me."'

I felt the need to stop the car and hear the whole story. I resisted the urge.

'And then all of a sudden I heard the familiar sound of bangles again and saw another till open by itself. In it was the key of the till I was trying to open. I grabbed the key, saying 'Thank you,' and opened the till I had been struggling with. I found a key that looked like the one I was searching for. I took it out and ran out. I heard the sounds of the footsteps and bangles following me. There was only one van parked outside and I tried opening the door with the key I had. It opened and I got into the van. The passenger door opened and I felt the presence move into the passenger seat. I just started the car and I made a dash for it.'

'Wow,' I said, 'that is quite a story.'

'Not over yet, my friend,' Vikram said.

Obviously there were loose ends. What happened to Jagan and Diya? Did Vikram finally go to the police? If he did, then how the hell was Jagan not in prison? And most importantly, what was that thing that helped him find the key?

Somewhere at the back of my mind, another answer came alive. I suddenly recalled where I had heard the name DiVi Garments. DiVi Garments was supposed to be signed up by my ex-company Icon Advertising. For some reason, the sign-up had been called off. I just couldn't recall the reason.

'Well, we had barely managed to reach the milestone number 3 when we got caught in a heavy rain,' Vikram continued. The reference to the word 'we' was not lost on me.

'Something similar to today's rain, I must say,' Vikram said, bending low to look out of the front windshield. 'I figured that Nathan and Diya would be searching for me on the route to the highway. I decided to turn in the opposite direction. I drove for a few minutes, but the damn vehicle stopped.'

'Oh damn,' I said.

'I tried starting the van many times over. No luck,' Vikram added. 'I decided that staying in the van was not a good idea. I had to get out. I figured that without the vehicle, proceeding on foot and heading towards the highway gave me better chances of survival even though there was a risk of running into Nathan and Diya. On the other hand, if I continued in the same direction, I could be going into the forest and might never find my way out. So I got out of the car and started walking back towards the highway. I had walked quite a distance in the downpour and I finally reached the milestone number 3 again. I saw a car approaching and I hid behind the bushes till I could see who was in the car. The car stopped near the milestone and out stepped Nathan.'

'Oh my God,' I groaned.

'I saw my sister step out too. I hid behind the bushes waiting for them to leave,' Vikram said. 'I did not even dare peep from between the branches as they had a flashlight. While I waited there hardly breathing, a hand grabbed me.'

'Was it the same ghost which helped you in the resort?' I asked with anticipation.

'I wish,' Vikram said wistfully. 'I heard a voice saying, "Excuse me, sir, you seem lost. Is there any way I can help you?"'

I had a feeling of déjà vu.

'It was Nathan,' Vikram said. 'He was holding a revolver in his hand.'

'And?' I asked. I could feel my heart thumping in my chest.

'You have to stop here,' Vikram said, pointing to the road ahead. 'We have reached milestone number 3. You have to go left to reach the resort and I will get off here.'

I stopped the car just beside the milestone with the number 3 marked on it. I wondered how I could have missed it the first time.

I turned to Vikram. 'You didn't tell me what happened next,' I said, almost pleading for him to finish the story.

'Remember when I got in I asked you for a favor?' Vikram asked, smiling.

'*I was wondering if I could help you and you could return my favor.*' I remembered the words distinctly.

'I do,' I replied. 'I assumed that you wanted a lift.'

'Not really,' Vikram said, looking in the distance. 'I am going to ask you that favor now.'

He turned to look at me. He had an expression I couldn't read.

'I have asked this favor of so many people. No one has helped me till now,' he said. 'Approximately four feet behind the milestone number 3 . . .'

I waited with a sense of fear engulfing me. I knew what he was going to say next.

'Please go to the nearest police station and tell them that they will find the body of Vikram Rao of DiVi Garments buried there.'

And then he was gone. I sat in the car suddenly all alone. I felt a sense of horror grip me and I pushed myself against the car seat. A feeling of numb pain in my chest hit me and then I heard the sound of the bangles in the seat behind me.

The pain came and went with increasing frequency. Above all, while the pain tore through my chest and paralyzed me, I keep continuing to anguish over the need to carry out his request. If only one of you can do me a favor? Please go to the nearest police station and report to them that approximately four feet behind milestone number 3, they will find buried the body of Vikram Rao of DiVi Garments.

As for me, I wonder if my wife will come to see me after she hears that I died of a heart attack near milestone number 3 . . .

# THE NEW ORLEANS GHOST TOUR

'Did you ever visit the New Orleans ghost tour when you visited Louisiana this summer?' the voice boomed on my cell phone.

The voice seemed very familiar to me though I couldn't readily place it. Not many people have that baritone voice which commands instant respect. I thought I knew who was on the other end but wondered why he would call me all of a sudden after so many years. I decided to play it safe.

'No,' I replied. 'Who is this?'

'How many people you know have a voice like mine?' the caller bragged and, after a couple of moments of silence, said, 'Rudrasen Verma.'

'What are you doing this evening?' he asked, and even before I could reply, he ordered, 'Dinner, my home. Be there at 8 p.m. sharp. I have a surprise waiting for you. I will send you the directions by SMS.'

The line went dead and I had hardly placed the phone back on the desk when I heard the familiar beep of an incoming message. I flipped open my phone and saw an address from the same number I had received a call from.

I saved the number under new contacts. Interesting, I thought, saving the number under a listing called 'new contacts!!!' I had known Rudrasen even before cell phones came to India. I pressed the save button and was flooded with memories of our association.

I first met Rudrasen in my first year of graduation. I had been studying commerce for two years after school at Xavier's. I decided to move over to the Indian Institute of Business Studies because I found the faculty at Xavier's too highbrow for my liking. Rudrasen, similarly, had been studying math and had decided it was something he couldn't quite agree with. It was a new college for both of us and so an opportunity to interact with a new group of students.

I had found his temperament very endearing the very first time we met. I had walked into the college quite anxious, having arrived late on the very first day to college. The professor, who had already started the class, stopped midway through on seeing me enter, which was embarrassing to start with. Added to that, I found the classroom with just about every seat taken. I scrambled to the last row and was desperately trying to spot a place and disappear in the crowd when my eyes fell on him. I noticed him because he was the only one smiling at me, while the rest of the class waited impatiently for me to find a place and settle down so that the professor could continue explaining the law of diminishing marginal utility. He promptly pushed aside on the already crowded bench he was sitting on to make space for me to sit. After the class, he sat down to explain the theory to me in detail.

As I got to know more about him, I realized that he had a genuine interest in people. He would be the person who would inquire about your well-being and ensure you were comfortable talking to him. He was always there to help you with the assignments and, during the month end, happily pay your canteen bills. There was also something about the way he spoke to people, maintaining just about the right amount of eye contact to make you feel at ease. Though he had a deep voice, he knew how to modulate it well to never give anyone a feeling of being aggressive.

And then I realized there was another side to him. During the college election, one of the candidates standing for the general secretary's post came to canvass during our statistics class. After having given a discourse on how nice a chap he was and having advertised his academic brilliance, the candidate suggested the class vote for him.

A hand shot up in the row right ahead of me.

'You still haven't told us why we should vote for you.' It was Rudrasen.

'I am the best candidate for the post,' the candidate defended himself.

'Says you,' Rudrasen shot back. 'Tell us what you will do for the student community and how it will impact us for the next two years.'

There was a shocked silence in the room. It was not common for us freshers to question a senior, especially one standing for elections.

Clearly nervous and taken aback by the turn of events, the candidate mumbled some gibberish before beating a hasty retreat amidst catcalls. The prospective secretary did more to create an icon out of Rudrasen than he had served his own cause.

That interaction had confused me initially. I wondered who the real Rudrasen was. Was he someone who was soft-spoken and ever ready to charm you one day or the guy who could be arrogant and in your face the next day? However, his ability to stand up and question authority was something that clearly impressed me. During the short bursts of interactions over the year, mostly at the college canteen, I found even more different shades to the youngster, which I found intriguing.

Rudrasen in many respects was totally the opposite of me. To start with, Rudrasen was the best in anything he did. He was an amazing sportsman, representing our college in cricket, football, table tennis, and chess, a gifted orator and dramatist, and always scored A's in all the subjects.

Added to this was the abundance of charm he displayed with women. Without an exception, the specimen of the opposite sex found him hard to resist. In turn they tried their very best to seek his approval in whatever they did.

'Rudra, do you think this shade of lipstick goes well? Rudra, do you think I should opt for combined studies or study alone? Rudra, do you think modern wear suits me more than traditional?' They would go on and on. His opinion was indeed most sought after by women. And as for me? Even my mom never asked me what I wanted for dinner.

I really thought it was the pits when our English professor, an attractive lady in her early thirties, once met us near the staff room. Ignoring my presence altogether, she turned to ask Rudrasen, 'Do you think it is a good idea to schedule a surprise assessment in the coming week?' Rudrasen thought for a moment and replied, 'I don't think that is a good idea, madam. Maybe the week following that should be better.'

I realized that the trick was that Rudrasen was a fantastic listener. He would listen attentively, without any interruptions, and gave his counsel without being judgmental. And the women loved him for that.

I wouldn't be doing complete justice to him if I didn't mention his aristocratic good looks. The truth is, it helped him get away with murder. I say this because Rudrasen was two-faced when it came to dealing with women. In front of them, he behaved like a thorough gentleman, full of chivalry. And in private, his conversations reflected scant respect for women. I had personally witnessed an incident where he had made some very impolite remarks about a girl in college. The girl, who had stormed into the classroom to question Rudra about his uncharitable remarks, had made a turnabout and was sweetness personified during her interaction with him.

I decided that him being a hypocrite was no concern of mine as long as it did not affect me. To me, it was an allowable weakness. After all, though we continued to share the same bench in college, Rudra was not my best friend. Hence, I did not think it necessary to influence any change in his behavior.

It was during our last year in college that we found ourselves together in the inaugural conference of the Club 13, a club started to dispel superstitious beliefs. Rudrasen was the only other person I knew amongst the thirty-odd prospective members who had gathered on Friday the 13th at 13.13 at the state public library's meeting room. The venue had been deliberately chosen since it was rumored to be haunted. I sat beside Rudrasen for most of the two-hour ceremony when each one of us was spiritually inducted to the club with a solemn oath that our mission would be to spread the light of science and destroy superstition in any form until our dying day.

We shared many experiences during that day, and for the first time, on my way back home, I realized that Rudrasen and I shared something in common: our dislike for superstition.

We met regularly at the college with a newfound shared vision of the Club 13. The club regularly doled out tasks to the group like conducting seminars on dispelling superstition, or visiting haunted houses and spending the night there to prove that ghosts were nothing more than imaginary beings that dwelled in our minds. Over the next eight years, we continued to be active members of the club, with Rudrasen even going on to become the chairperson of the now 200-plus-strong club. During this period, we had spent over thirty days investigating various haunted settlements.

Rudrasen, though still never got to be counted as one of my best friends, was always counted in the circle of close friends, nevertheless. After graduating from college, he continued his pursuit of scholastic achievements in management while domestic pressures forced me to find a job. Our interactions came down from daily to fortnightly, since we only interacted either during our club meetings or at dinners hosted by common friends. I did visit his home, a palatial bungalow, a few times with other friends. Rudrasen was the only son to his parents, who were of royal lineage and had inherited a fortune in the form of ancestral properties. It was only a matter of time that Rudrasen started to be actively involved in his father's real estate business.

During our rare visits to his home, Rudrasen made it a point to introduce us to all the people residing at his home including the family man Friday, Janardhanan. The group got very fond of Janu, as we called him, because the man was extremely resourceful. He could cook a delicious meal of a minimum four dishes for six people in fifteen minutes flat.

The phone rang to shake me out of my memories of those blissful days of bachelorhood.

'Are you at the office?' my wife asked tersely.

I thought that was a strange question because she had called me on the landline.

'Yes,' I replied. 'Why?'

'I was not able to reach you on your cell phone,' she said. I waited for the next set of instructions to be delivered to me. She had left for Mumbai to attend an official conference only that morning. This had been the fourth phone call of the day from her.

I waited for her to complete all she had to say before I informed her that I was going to be out for dinner.

'Oh, okay,' she said, apparently preoccupied with her conference, 'will it be the boys from the office again?' she asked. The way she had used the word 'again' was obvious to remind me that this was my third outing with the same group within a span of a week. For every ten words my wife speaks, there are a hundred unspoken meanings.

'No,' I said and, after a moment of hesitation, added, 'Remember Rudrasen? I think he is having a party at his home. He called to invite me.'

What followed was a long moment of pregnant silence. My wife was one of the very few rare women who detested Rudrasen. It probably had to do with his marriage. Two, in fact. And both had ended sadly though they had been love marriages.

I recalled that my wife and I had bumped into a very bitter Rima, Rudrasen's first wife, at a shopping mall, shortly after she had filed for divorce. Rima had recounted her shocking tales of having to put up with her ex-husband's idiosyncrasies to my wife, even as my wife kept giving me disapproving looks as if I had inflicted all that torture on the poor lady.

'That man is so two-faced', Rima had recounted, 'that he proclaims his undying love for me in front of the whole world and does not even bother to remember my birthday.'

I wanted to butt in and say, '*Tell me more. You choose to fall in love with him and marry him after seeing him for over two years.*' I however kept my mouth shut, because only recently I had been guilty of forgetting my wife's birthday, and I didn't want my wife to think that I was justifying my own shortcomings.

'He is arrogant and a slave driver. He can drive you insane,' Rima continued her tirade against her estranged husband. It turned out to be quite an accurate prediction when, a few years later, we found out that Rudrasen's second wife Anita ended up in a mental asylum.

'All right,' my wife said, sounding clearly displeased on the phone, 'make sure Amog has his dinner. Order a pizza, he likes that.'

The call ended quite abruptly.

That evening after the pizza had been delivered and devoured, I reviewed my son's homework and later tucked him into bed before leaving for Rudrasen's place. As I drove through the dense traffic, I wondered how much Rudrasen would have changed over the years. I had last talked to him seven years back when he was still living with his second wife Anita. I couldn't even recall who had called whom last or what we had discussed on the last call. On and off, I did get to hear from common friends on how Rudrasen and his wife Anita went off on frequent trips abroad to exotic places like Maggiore in Italy, Big Island in Hawaii, and Santorini in Greece, places I had only seen on *National Geographic*. The last piece of news I had heard was about how Anita had slit her wrists twice in an attempt to commit suicide before being admitted to a mental asylum.

I deliberated on why he was having a get-together that day and who else could have been invited. Was he getting married again or was this a dinner to announce the inauguration of yet another real estate venture? Nothing would surprise me about Rudrasen. Talking of surprises, I recalled his last words on the phone: '*I have a surprise waiting for you.*' I wondered about what he meant by having a surprise waiting for me? An old friend? Or did he have a gift for me?

I reached his home a few minutes after eight and was surprised to find the compound walls had been raised by another couple of feet more than I last remembered. I honked at the gates and waited for the watchman to open it; however, very soon the massive gate opened all by itself. I recalled Rudrasen's penchant for electronic gizmos. The remote-controlled gate had not been installed during my last visit, but then that had been many years back.

I wondered if Rudrasen was suffering from anthropophobia or any other anxieties that I was not aware of.

As I drove towards the porch of the palatial bungalow, another intriguing sight was that no other cars were parked in the driveway. I had imagined that Rudrasen was having a large gathering. Absence of any other guests would mean having to put up with a few embarrassing moments, a consideration that left me a wee bit uncomfortable.

I parked my car under the huge porch and saw the short flight of stairs to my right leading to the front door. I did not bother to lock the car; obviously no one was coming in to steal it.

The double door was made of teak with a beautiful piece of oval-shaped etched glass set on it. The doors were over seven feet tall, and each of the doors must have been three feet wide, with a polished brass handle that had intricate designs carved on it.

I searched for the doorbell and was about to reach for it when I heard a faint click and the door opened all the way through automatically. I noticed the closed-circuit camera installed a couple of feet above the imposing doors. 'Impressive gadget,' I reflected as I entered the house.

I walked into the huge hallway, which had a carpeted stairway leading to the rooms on the first floor. The house was exactly as I remembered it, but for a few minor changes. The walls had been freshly painted and decorated with tasteful paintings, the wooden floors spotlessly clean and artifacts from across the world placed strategically with accent lighting. The settee in the room had been exchanged with a more modern set of recliners. The old grandfather clock still stood proudly making its presence felt in the room. It was still working.

'In here,' Rudrasen's unmistakable baritone voice called out from inside the living room.

I walked to the living room and was taken aback by the figure who greeted me. Rudrasen looked lighter by almost fifteen kilos from when I had met him last. His cheeks were sunken and traces of gray hair were very visible on his now not-so-thick tuft of hair. He wore spectacles which were a size too big for his long narrow face, now even more accentuated by his thin frame and a long gray beard. He looked like a pale shadow of the old Rudrasen who had women swooning all over him. He looked ten years too old for his age.

'You old rascal,' he called out, looking at me. 'Surprising nobody killed you yet.'

'I survived,' I said, laughing. 'Word is out that many people want to kill me just because I was your friend.'

Rudrasen walked across the room slowly and embraced me warmly. I was happy that he seemed genuinely affectionate and appeared to have forgotten a lot of bitterness that had in the past crept into our relationship.

'Long time, friend,' I said, looking at his face. 'Very long time.'

'Yes,' he replied, gesturing me to sit on the comfortable-looking red-and-beige-colored chaise lounge. I eased myself, taking a few moments to study my friend.

'But I did keep track of you. Always,' Rudrasen smiled.

'Really?' I asked, surprised.

'I know which college your son goes to, which company your wife works for, and which places you visited recently . . . everything,' he said grinning.

'Working for the FBI or the CIA?' I asked, laughing.

'I wish,' he replied, studying me deeply. 'You haven't changed much though.'

'I seem to have found all the weight that you seem to have lost,' I laughed.

'Don't be too harsh on yourself,' Rudrasen said. I found his stare a bit unnerving.

'The house is as I remember it,' I said, looking around and eager to find some topics to chat about. 'Even the furniture hasn't changed much. Having a tough time maintaining it, eh?' I asked.

'Come, let's have a drink,' he offered. 'What will it be? Scotch?'

'I prefer beer,' I said as I got up and walked with him to the dining area. I noticed that the old wooden dining table which could accommodate over fifty guests had been replaced with a much smaller glass table surrounded by eight chairs.

I remarked about the change to Rudrasen.

'Don't get as many guests now,' he said. 'I started feeling lonely sitting at the damn table. Donated it to charity.'

He opened a huge refrigerator, another new addition, which seemed more like a cabinet and I noticed that it was stacked with bottles of beer and champagne.

He pulled out a bottle and held out for me to check if it was cold enough for me. After I had approved, he proceeded to open the bottle.

'Still drink from a mug?' he asked.

'Prefer to,' I said as he reached for a beer mug placed on a shelf nearby. I was happy to note that the glass mug did not have any smudges of dried water droplets.

'You must be spending a fortune to keep this place clean,' I remarked.

'No. It gets done free,' he said, laughing.

'Then you must be married . . . again,' I remarked, regretting the remark.

'Not with my reputation,' he replied, not taking offense at my comment. 'No living female will take the risk.' He then waved a hand to dismiss the topic.

He filled the glass to the brim and handed it over to me. He selected another glass from the hundreds placed on the shelf and adequately satisfied that it was the right pick, opened another cabinet which presumably was the bar. I saw the cabinet had almost a hundred bottles of liquor in it. Each one seemed to be exquisite and rare. He proceeded to pull out a bottle of whisky. He opened the cap and smelt the contents and proudly said, 'Glenfiddich twenty-one-year-old single-malt Scotch. Cost me 133 dollars at New York duty-free.'

He poured the contents into a glass and added two cubes of ice from an ice bucket placed nearby.

'I thought you were having other guests over,' I said, looking around. A plate with some starters had been placed near where I had been sitting a few moments ago. I had not noticed it before.

'How many days did you spend in the US this time?' he asked as I staked my place back at the chaise lounge.

'Forty days in all,' I replied.

'Which places?' he asked.

'California, Atlanta, and New Orleans,' I replied.

'Business or pleasure?'

'Neither,' I replied, picking up a slice of cucumber from the snack tray. 'Visiting relatives.'

'I remember your sister-in-law stays there,' he replied.

'Both,' I replied. 'The elder one in New Orleans and the younger one in Atlanta.'

'And California?' Rudrasen asked.

'Friends,' I replied as I picked a piece of diced chicken from the plate. The chicken pieces were all cut into perfect cubes. I placed the chicken in my mouth and felt it melt, cooked to perfection. The tangy taste of lemon lingered on my taste buds and I was sure it was one of the best dishes I had ever eaten in my life. Old man Janu had not lost his touch.

'So what did you see in New Orleans?' Rudrasen asked, forcing me to take my mind off the succulent chicken.

'Lots,' I replied. 'The swamp tour, insectarium, Lake Pontchartrain, the aquarium and there was a jazz festival,' I said, trying to recall the whole list of activities I had indulged in.

'An apology for an aquarium,' he corrected me.

'True,' I agreed. 'It was pathetic compared to the one in Atlanta, but much better than the ones we get to see in India,' I rebutted.

'I couldn't agree with you more,' Rudrasen replied. 'I just wondered how you missed one of the most popular attractions in New Orleans. The ghost tour!'

'You seem to be pretty fascinated by the tour,' I remarked. 'That is the second time you have mentioned it today.'

'It was fascinating for me all right,' he said, reflecting, 'but you may not find my experiences interesting after all that we have been through over the years.'

The way he said it made me arch up my brow. I was not sure what to make of the remark. Regret? Anger? Resentment?

'Why don't you tell me about it?' I asked.

He smiled. 'Care for a smoke?' he asked and, without waiting for an answer, walked to the cabinet by the wall. He searched for something in the drawers of the cabinet for some time and seemed to have miraculously found it lying right there on the top of the cabinet.

'Ah,' he said, picking up a pack of cigarettes, 'Parliament. The best cigarette money can buy. Rarely advertised.'

He signaled me to follow him to the open veranda a few feet away from where I was sitting. I followed him out and once we reached there, he studied the pack almost as if he was checking for an expiry date on the pack. I noticed that it was a fresh pack as he tore open the plastic seal and offered me a cigarette. I placed it gingerly on my lips and waited for him to light it. He proceeded to light his own cigarette and I watched as the flames danced from the spout of the lighter. He paused to look at the lit end of the cigarette before pocketing the lighter.

'The New Orleans ghost tour departs at a voodoo shop on St Joseph's Street, between Bienville and Canal streets, across from Pat O'Brien's bar,' he started before pausing to inhale the cigarette smoke. He spoke even as he exhaled a column of dense smoke. 'The tour starts at 11 p.m. and costs twenty-five dollars per head. I understand that an average group which gathers for the tour is usually anywhere between thirty-five to forty people.'

He paused to check if he had managed to get me interested. I looked at him intently.

'That night, there were much fewer tourists gathered for the tour, probably because it was unusually warm,' he continued. 'There is a tour guide who usually accompanies you on the tour, and ours was an old fellow called Mike, which I seriously doubt was his real name.'

Rudrasen paused to inhale at the cigarette again and did not continue until he had blown out another column of thick smoke. I noticed that his cigarette had already burnt halfway with him having had just two drags at it.

'The tour started with a trip to the cemetery and visits to some of the oldest heritage sites, where Mike told us an awful lot of boring stories of how the movie actor Nicolas Cage got to purchase a property which was haunted and all that.'

At this point, Rudrasen understood my interest level dipping a bit as I turned to look at the vast garden beyond the verandah.

'Anyway to cut a long story short,' he said, hurrying it up a bit, 'I turned to Mike the guide and told him, "Mickey, this is a whole lot of nonsense, why don't you show us the real thing?"'

I think my eyebrows arched involuntarily for Rudrasen understood he had managed to get me interested again.

'Refill?' he asked, looking at my mug. I still had more than half a mug of beer left.

'You go ahead,' I said. I watched him walk back to the bar cabinet and refill his glass. He added a few cubes of ice and walked back to me. As I watched him return, I was beginning to think of the reasons for convening the club.

'Where was I?' he asked, looking at me.

'You asked Mike, or whoever your guide was, for the real thing,' I said contemptuously. Rudrasen didn't read it, and even if he did note the sarcasm in my voice, he let it go. I was mocking him because I had started to realize where this conversation was heading.

'Yes, I asked Mike to show me the real thing, and good old Mike, with a twinkle in his eye, asked the group if we indeed wanted to see the *real* thing. The whole group got into a huddle and discussed seeing the *real* thing. Except for one young lady, who was not comfortable with the idea, just about all of us agreed that we wanted to see the *real* thing,' Rudrasen said emphasizing the word *real* over and over again.

'I approached Mike and informed him of the group's decision,' Rudrasen continued. 'I also offered Mike a twenty-dollar tip, which he gratefully pocketed, and he asked us if we were ready for an extra hour of fun and we agreed. Mike guided us back to the tour van and took over the wheel himself. He drove for about twenty minutes, a route which took us along the Mississippi River, and finally we reached a building which resembled the old French Quarter.'

I took a huge gulp of the beer, masking any display of emotion and stubbed out my cigarette.

'By the time we reached the building, it was dark outside and there were no lights near the building. Obviously it was a deserted structure; Mike promised to return in a few minutes and entered the building alone. I surveyed the brick structure and figured it was almost three hundred years old. The building was three floors high with long French windows facing the road.'

Rudrasen threw away his cigarette and lit a new one. He offered me one, which I refused.

'Ten minutes later, Mike returned and grouped us into a close circle. He then went on to give a brief history of the building and its occupants. He said that there had been many sightings of ghosts and other paranormal activities in the place. Before we entered, he wanted to get some rules in place. No running, no screaming. Mobile phones were to be kept on silent. "If you see something, do not panic," he said, and most importantly, he reminded us that we were there of our own accord and that he was not responsible for anything that could happen there. I just thought he wanted it to sound dramatic.'

'I know,' I laughed. 'That is what our guide did during the swamp tour.' I recalled my own swamp tour when the tour guide had asked us what we would do if the boat overturned in the middle of the swamp. 'After you have finished screaming, just stand up and walk because the swamp at its deepest is not more than four feet,' he had advised.

'Exactly, but it did have some effect on an old couple. They decided that they had had enough excitement for the day and decided to stay back in the van. However, thanks to the buildup, there was enough excitement within the rest of the group as we prepared to get into the building. But Mike had more to say.'

I gulped the last drops of the beer from my glass.

'Refill?' Rudrasen asked, his glass only half empty.

'I can wait,' I said, more eager to end this charade so that I could head back home. I had started to wonder if Rudrasen was turning senile.

'Mike told us that there were reported sightings of various ghosts or apparitions in the building,' Rudrasen continued. 'There was a sultan who was rumored to have been buried alive in the building, the black slave who was tortured and killed in the dungeons, the little mischievous boy who drowned in the bathtub, and so on and so forth. We could run into any one of them, he warned, and we heard the stories in rapt attention until Mike finally announced that it was time to go in.'

At this point, Rudrasen stopped to empty the contents of his glass. He pulled out one more cigarette to light, changed his mind, and asked, 'Shall we eat dinner or do you want to have another beer?'

I was more than happy to opt for dinner, since I was already looking forward to returning home.

'Dinner,' I opted.

Rudrasen led me back to the dining table, which now had a generous spread of food placed on it.

'Is Janu still working his magic around here?' I asked.

'Janu?' Rudrasen asked. 'Janu who?'

'Janardhanan. Your man Friday,' I reminded him.

'Oh, Janardhanan,' Rudrasen said. 'You still remember him?'

'How could I forget him?' I asked. 'Such a resourceful chap. I have eaten quite a few delicious meals cooked by him.'

'Good. Good,' Rudrasen remarked pensively. 'No. This is not the handiwork of Janardhanan. He died three years back. Actually, he quit my services five years back because he had to go back to his hometown. He did keep in touch on and off.

The last I heard from him was three years back when he called me, asking for monetary assistance for his granddaughter's surgery. I was in Hamburg I think. I told him that I would send him the money after I returned. It was too late, I guess. The kid didn't survive. And then shortly afterwards, I heard Janardhanan died of a heart attack.'

I was truly sorry to hear the news. I wondered if the whole story was true. Was Rudrasen really meaning to send the money? Was he truly in Hamburg at the time?

'Help yourself,' Rudrasen said as I sat down at the dining table. I grabbed a plate and looked at the spread. There was a bowl of soup for starters, fried fish, chicken gravy, naan for bread, rice, and for dessert, a bowl of trifle pudding.

The food smelt divine and I helped myself to a large helping of chicken and naan, not bothering to start with the soup. I dipped the bread into the chicken and stuffed it into my mouth. It tasted even better than it smelt.

'Let me complete my story,' Rudrasen insisted. 'Like I said, Mike decided to take us into the house. We entered the huge compound, and though it was pitch-dark, Mike had a flashlight which helped us to navigate our way through the compound into the building. We went through a series of rooms. All through, we ensured that we talked only when necessary, ensuring we kept as silent as possible. Some of us had our cameras and Mike allowed us to take a few pictures in the rooms.

'Finally, Mike led us to one of the interior rooms and told us in a hushed tone to wait and watch. Since we were not aware as to what was expected, we waited in edgy anticipation. A few minutes passed without incident, after which we heard footsteps just outside the room. All of a sudden, the room grew icy cold and then we heard a loud *bang*.'

Rudrasen made a loud sound, obviously trying to startle me. I had anticipated this coming and so deprived Rudrasen of the pleasure of scaring me. By now I was pretty clear where this conversation was headed.

'With a loud sound, the door of the room banged shut,' Rudrasen continued without showing his disappointment at not being able to startle me as intended. 'Mike focused the flashlight onto the door and we heard the door latch being secured from the outside.'

I found the fried fish sumptuous and helped myself to a couple more pieces.

'There were loud gasps from the group in the room,' Rudrasen continued without respite. 'One young girl started to cry hysterically. Suddenly there was pandemonium as the group started getting agitated. Mike calmed us down, saying that this had happened numerous times before and that there was nothing to worry about. He informed the group that this was the ghost of the mischievous child who had drowned in the bathtub.'

I would have helped myself to some more chicken and rice, but I noticed a tray with trifle pudding lying at arm's length. I reached for it.

'The child would lock up the visitors and open the door after some time,' Rudrasen persisted. 'This sort of calmed the group a bit, and within a few minutes, we heard the door latch being opened. Mike went to the door and pushed it open. There were gasps of relief all round the room and the group was more than happy when we stepped back into the compound and entered the van.'

I looked at Rudrasen, waiting for him to pause. 'Interesting', I said, 'but very naïve.'

Rudrasen did not offer an opinion. I helped myself to another serving of the pudding. 'This is amazing food,' I said, almost as if providing an excuse for my binge eating. Rudrasen smiled and waited for me to continue speaking.

'Let me tell you what happened and put it in the right perspective. Mike entered the building a few moments before you all did. He had his people inside to whom he briefed on what to do. Once done, he walked out and told you some lame ghost stories which served two purposes,' I said, setting the dessert spoon on the bowl.

'And what were they?' Rudrasen asked, amused.

'First to set up the mood, and second, more importantly, to buy some time for his flunkies to set up the whole show,' I replied, 'not having more than a flashlight added to the eerie atmosphere. He took you to the exact same room where the action was expected to happen. It was also a signal for his team to start the act. The footsteps were heard and the door closed by some mechanism or even by hand.'

'And how could that have been possible?' Rudrasen asked, still amused.

'Simple, my friend,' I said. 'If the incident was routine as claimed by Mike, he would have informed you of it. However, he didn't want to keep you prepared about the planned act.'

Rudrasen continued to watch me silently as I absent-mindedly rolled the spoon on my plate.

'What followed was unanticipated by the group,' I continued. 'The group was not prepared for the door to bang shut and so none of you noticed the person walk up to the door and bang it shut. If you knew what was expected, you would have been directing the flashlight at the door and seen the whole setup. I am sure Mike was paid a handsome tip by everybody from the group.'

'Not everybody paid a tip,' Rudrasen offered as if it was a piece of crucial information.

'Fair enough,' I replied. 'Even by a conservative estimate, I would say he pocketed a neat two hundred dollars for pulling the scam on you all.'

'What about the chilliness that enveloped the room?' Rudrasen asked, not wanting to be dragged into a financial debate.

I suspected there was more to this coming. Even Rudrasen could have seen through all of this, and he was asking me the most basic questions.

'A fan with any fabrication that sprays mist would have done the trick,' I said. 'Come on, even you can figure that out. We have investigated this kind of stuff day in and day out.'

Rudrasen shook his head and replied, 'I am not done yet. But I wonder if you will be ready to buy my story after the Blue Mountain episode.'

The Blue Mountain episode. Finally the cat was out of the bag. I had suspected all along that all this had to do with the incident that happened more than a decade back. It was no mere coincidence that Rudrasen was calling me after my visit to New Orleans. The fact that he kept tabs on me all these years had to be premeditated. It had to be that incident at Hotel Blue Mountain. The incident which led to much acrimony between Rudrasen and me was still fresh, almost in its entirety in my mind. No wonder it was traumatizing Rudrasen so much. After all it was he who had to face all that humiliation.

For a moment, my mind raced to that fateful incident.

Rudrasen had been president of Club 13 for two years in a row. As per the rules of the club, he could contest for one more term. Rudrasen had hoped to win uncontested but was unaware of the ground realities. I was aware that he had inadvertently rubbed quite a few of the members the wrong way, which made his position untenable. Many people approached me to advise him to withdraw from the race rather than face the ignominy of losing an election. There was a lot of talk about how the presidency had made him arrogant and a hypocrite. Since I always knew him to be hypocritical, I was sure the presidency had nothing to do with it. Arrogance was subjective. After all, one man's pride could easily have been perceived as arrogance by somebody else. Further, Rudrasen, unlike whatmany believed, was not my best friend. I did not feel the need to pass on any advice that was unsolicited. Rudrasen contested the election and, as predicted, faced a humiliating defeat, which unfortunately he did not take too gracefully.

The same year, some more interesting developments transpired. Club 13 was approached by a four-star hotel called Blue Mountain to carry out an independent survey. The hotel, a 140-room property, faced a peculiar predicament.

Two years prior to the management approaching Club 13, a twenty-four-year-old lady of Swedish nationality, Elsa, died in a mysterious yet horrific fire in room number 409 on the fourth floor of the hotel. The death was mysterious because some eyewitnesses reported seeing Elsa leave with another Caucasian male, late in the night, while some others swore that she was seen entering her room alone, too drunk even to open her door. Police investigations conducted later were inconclusive on the reason for the fire. The police eventually closed the case, stating that Elsa had fallen asleep smoking a cigarette in bed. She must have realized too late that the room was on fire.

However, the eyewitnesses had a dreadful tale to narrate. I had met one of the front desk staff who had been on duty that night. He revealed that by the time he reached the fourth floor after he had received a call from one of the guests, he saw Elsa running in the corridor screaming for help. Her clothes were still on fire and the smell of burning flesh was evident in the air. The employee had confided to me that he was still unable to come to terms with the incident and still had nightmares about it. The incident had occurred early in the morning, around 3 a.m. Elsa never even managed to make it to the hospital alive, with many claiming that she had died on the fourth floor.

The hotel had shut down the entire floor for a year for renovation. Soon after it was reopened to guests, the rumors started spreading. Some guests had complained that around 3 a.m., they could hear a young woman scream for help in the corridor outside. A man and his wife, who had returned to their room on the fourth floor after a late-night party, claimed to have seen an apparition of a woman running in the corridor, her clothes in flames. The hotel finally decided to shut down the fourth floor after a guest jumped out of the window of room 409 and suffered multiple fractures after he saw a woman in flames inside the room. His own clothes had caught fire, the guest claimed, showing off the burnt shirt he was wearing.

The hotel was considering a sellout and feared that it was interested parties that were busy spreading a rumor of the haunting to get the price reduced. One of the parties interested in the purchase of the property was a group well known to Rudrasen's family. They planned to construct a mall in the property. After the hotel promoters approached Club 13 for an independent survey, the club members met up to discuss the proposal and scope of activity involved. A long deliberation followed, and some members were vehemently opposed to getting involved in the survey, stating that the findings could be influenced by Rudrasen and his group. The majority opinion was to go ahead with the survey as they felt that the club motto was to dispel superstition and hence would not be directly influenced by any group.

The real shocker was when Rudrasen's name was included in the list of investigators. Despite stiff opposition, he had managed to get himself included in the final list. My name too figured in the final list of nine investigators, and I later discovered that Rudrasen had insisted on me making the final cut.

The investigators held two meetings to finalize the finer details of the investigation prior to making a field visit. Rudrasen did not contribute anything significant in the first meeting. In the second meeting though, he did propose the name of Sachi, a well-respected member, as the team leader for the investigation. The group was only happy to endorse the motion without any opposition. During the second meeting, the scope of activity was once again discussed and members were allotted specific roles and responsibilities. The group resolved to undertake the field activity on 7 November, which was exactly two years since the fire accident.

The group assembled in the hotel lobby at 11 p.m. on 7 November to carry out the field study. Sachi debriefed the group for the first thirty minutes and each one of us was asked to reiterate our role. Rudrasen's role was to secure the fourth floor and ensure no staff or outsiders entered the floor. I was to be stationed in room 409, the room where the incident happened, along with Sachi and two other members. The other two members carried tape recorders to record any audible activity. I handled the Panasonic video camera which I set up on a tripod to record any unusual activity.

Before we took up our positions, Sachi informed the group that we were expected to assemble in the lobby at 5 a.m. for coffee should no untoward incident occur. I had found the last bit of instruction a bit strange because never before in all our investigation did an untoward incident happen. I however did not draw anybody's attention to the statement. Clear instructions were that no one apart from the four of us would be in room 409.

A couple of incidents made that night different from the innumerable stakeouts we had successfully conducted in the past. To start with, a room service staff entered the fourth floor and reached us to deliver coffee. This was strange not only because it was a direct dereliction of duty on Rudrasen's part, but also because we never took any refreshments once our watch had commenced, a rule enforced to ensure that investigators were not influenced with any substance that could possibly impede their judgment.

The second incident happened shortly before 3 a.m. when we heard a knock on the door. I opened the door to find Rudrasen waiting outside the room. He was sweating profusely and requested he be allowed to enter the room. He said that he was feverish and so felt uncomfortable in the corridor and preferred to spend the rest of the time in the room with us. I touched his forehead and did not detect any increase in temperature on his forehead. However, Rudrasen insisted on being in the room with us. One of the members handling the audio equipment took up Rudrasen's position securing the fourth floor. I had, however, found the whole episode very out of the ordinary. I was sure that Rudrasen was faking illness to be in the room.

The last and final incident happened at 3 a.m. when we saw Sachi jump up from the couch she was sitting on. She was startled and disturbed. It took her a few minutes to compose herself, after which she said that she had felt someone pulling at her arm. No other untoward activity was reported till 5 a.m., post which we decided to reconvene in the lobby. Every member reported nil activity and so Sachi felt it best not to mention anything to the other members of the group. The audiotapes and videotapes were handed over to our member-archives, a woman named Richa, for safekeeping. I considered the chapter closed and was waiting for the final report to be submitted, signaling the official closure of the episode. This was not to be.

That weekend, I got a call to mark my attendance at an emergency meeting convened by Sachi to discuss the Blue Mountain file. I knew something was amiss when I saw the club in full attendance. I was only expecting the nine investigators or, at best, the core committee to turn up at the meeting.

After the meeting was officially underway, Sachi informed the group that certain specific incidents had been brought to her notice which were required to be addressed on an urgent basis. Sachi went on to explain that as a regular practice it was customary for the member in charge of archives to review the audiotapes and videotapes before considering the case officially closed. Richa had followed the usual protocol, but some strange developments had transpired during the review of the tapes which required the group's intervention and guidance before the final report was submitted.

Sachi then invited Richa to take over the proceedings. Richa hardly spoke a word and proceeded to connect the tape recorder to the speakers and pressed the playback button. We all heard the long static interspersed with early conversation that had taken place in room 409. There were some murmurs in the room as the tape continued to play in the background. I was unsure what to expect, like most others in the room. Richa quickly pressed the pause button and silenced us, saying that she needed us to focus on the tape. We all waited in silent anticipation as she pressed the play button once again.

I waited for something to be heard and was greeted by just static. I remembered that prior to Rudrasen's entry into the room that fateful night, nobody had talked in the room. Not much talking had happened even after Rudrasen had convinced us of his need to be in the room.

'There,' Richa screamed, excited.

I hadn't heard a damn thing and looked around to check if anyone else had. Interestingly, most of us hadn't. A couple of the club members who had been sitting close to the speakers were wide-eyed in excitement.

'Did you all hear that?' Richa asked, looking around the room.

I heard a couple of people say 'Yes.' The others all looked at each other bewildered as if they had missed Halley's comet.

'Let us hear it again,' Sachi requested.

The tape was rewound and played back. I continued to hear the static as Richa stood with her right arm raised. She suddenly brought it down as we heard some of the members bark out in excitement. I noticed that this time around, many more people had claimed to have heard it. I still drew a blank. A small commotion started with some people urging others to listen in more closely.

'What was it?' I heard someone ask.

'How could you miss it?' someone else replied.

'Does anyone know what I am supposed to hear?' I asked, confused.

'You can hear a faint feminine voice crying out, "Help me",' Richa proclaimed over the din.

'Really?' I asked more sarcastically than with disbelief.

'Let me increase the volume to the maximum,' Richa said and played the tape again. The room fell silent again.

Richa took her now-familiar stance with her right hand raised. I closed my eyes and covered my face with my hands, focusing on the sounds coming from the speakers. I did not want to be influenced by her actions. This time around, I did hear something just before the members went 'Ahh.' The group went into a tizzy once again.

But for me, there was no way to say that I heard the words 'Help me.' Hell, I was not even sure the sound was human. For all I cared, it could have been a crow cawing outside the hotel.

'I still didn't hear anybody say anything,' I said, raising my voice above the din.

'You would if you heard it again,' some idiot responded.

'If you made me listen to the tape over and over again, I eventually might,' I replied. 'Not because I will hear it, more because I am bored to death and can't stand this torture anymore,' I shot back.

The room fell silent for only a few seconds. As soon as what I had said sunk in, somebody shouted out in my defense, 'He is right.'

'If only you guys heard more and talked less,' someone else commented.

A heated debate had started to ensue. People were talking across the table, some directing their views at the chair. A small group stood watching helplessly. I saw Sachi trying to listen to the views of an agitated member with a sympathetic look on her face. I bet she couldn't hear a word of what was being said in the room. I turned to look at Rudrasen. He was telling another member that he could hear the words. I heard someone bang on the table. It was Richa. The group fell silent.

'I have clinching evidence,' Richa informed the group. Everyone fell silent to check out the new evidence. 'We all know that there were two sound recorders used that night. The second one too has captured the voice at exactly the same time.'

Another commotion erupted. 'How can that be new evidence?' someone asked. 'Of course it is new evidence,' a rebuttal came. 'How can we believe it is not the same tape?' was another unnecessary remark. Now people were questioning integrity.

Richa did not offer any comment, but proceeded to present the second tape. The tape was fast-forwarded and played with maximum volume. I continued to draw a blank. This was getting nowhere. We went through the whole cycle of people swearing they had heard or not heard anything. Interestingly, I noticed that the believers were increasing in numbers. Rudrasen became even more vocal with his arguments claiming the hotel required another closer look.

Even as the floor debated the issue, the tape continued to run in the background and then we heard a startled cry.

'What happened?' I heard my own voice on the speakers as everybody turned to look at me. It was the conversation we had after Sachi had felt someone pull her hand in the hotel room. There was a moment of silence before we heard Sachi's voice.

'I felt someone pull my hand,' we heard Sachi's voice on the speaker.

'Your sleeve must have got caught in the armrest,' I heard myself reassure Sachi.

'No. It definitely was someone pulling my hand,' Sachi reiterated.

I heard myself groan and say, 'Come on, Sachi. Don't be ridiculous. It was nothing.'

'You are right,' Sachi said, sounding doubtful. 'It may have been the armrest.'

The members took turns to look at me and Sachi. I noticed her turning red as the silence got louder.

'I didn't think much of it,' she said anxiously. 'I thought I imagined it.'

Nobody said anything to me though I got a feeling that people had started to view me as an extremist. The voices grew in the room and I saw Rudrasen trying his best to convince as many people as he could. For a moment, his eyes met mine. We looked at each other for what seemed like an eternity. I figured out that I knew what he was doing. I felt disgusted and got up.

'Enough,' I shouted at the top of my lungs. 'I think you people are forgetting the very reason we are here.'

'And what is that?' Richa asked defiantly.

'We are a club that does not support superstition,' I reminded the whole group.

'But that can't be at the cost of clear evidence,' Richa shot back. 'I say we go with the truth.'

I was not angry. I was not even upset. Disillusioned was more like it.

'Truth is subjective,' I replied. 'Whose truth? Yours or mine?'

I did not get a response. Nobody wanted to say anything. I wanted to end this controversy as soon as possible.

'Fair enough. I need to ask a few questions before we discuss this any further,' I said. The group fell totally silent and waited for me to speak.

'Firstly, my question is directed to the group leader Sachi,' I said. 'Are you truly convinced that you heard a feminine voice in the tape?'

Sachi looked undecided for a moment. She looked around for help and her eye fell on Rudrasen, who was also staring at her. 'Yes,' she said slowly.

I just raised my brow in surprise. The expression was not lost out on the other group members. I had expected more from Sachi than a meek capitulation.

'My second question is to Richa,' I said and watched Richa look at me in anticipation. 'When did you discover these new findings?'

'Yesterday evening,' she replied almost as if she had rehearsed the answer.

'And?' I asked. She didn't seem to understand what she was expected to say. 'And what did you do?' I repeated.

'I immediately brought it to the notice of the group leader,' she replied.

'And?' I asked again.

'And nothing. We are here,' she said, shrugging her shoulders.

'By "And?" I meant, did you inform anyone else apart from the group leader Sachi?' I asked, almost like I was speaking to a toddler.

Richa seemed hesitant to answer the question. She didn't like to be put on the dock like a criminal and questioned. She looked around for help and, seeing none coming, decided to reply.

'I informed Rudrasen Verma,' she said slowly.

Some murmurs started in the room.

'Why did you think it necessary to inform him?' I asked. From the corner of my eye, I could see Rudrasen glaring at me and Richa alternately.

'Because I thought he would be interested,' she said.

'That is nice of you. One last question,' I said, looking at an uncomfortable Richa. I felt Richa knew my next question already. I still decided to ask her. 'Tell me were the tapes in your custody from the time of our investigation till now?'

'No,' Richa pronounced. The group gave out a collective gasp.

'They have also been with Rudrasen,' she concluded. Rudrasen got up to say something in his defense, but it was too late, for the room broke out into a frenzy. Arguments broke out and voices were raised. I stood there and looked at Rudrasen, who stood there baffled like a defeated man. I walked out of the room.

---------***---------

I had thought that the Blue Mountain incident was dead and buried. These many years are a long time for people to change, for priorities to change, and in some cases, for even values to change. Given a chance, I would have handled the same situation very differently.

I looked at Rudrasen, who was still waiting for my response.

'Tell me the rest of the story,' I said.

Rudrasen grinned and continued, 'Two days later, I went back to the voodoo shop on St Joseph's Street.'

'The same place from where the tour originated?' I clarified.

Rudrasen nodded in the affirmative. 'My objective was to interview Mike. Mike was surprised to see me there. I told Mike that I had figured out his scam and explained it to Mike in exactly the same way you had summarized a little while ago. Mike heard me out and started to tell me that there was no scam. I asked him to prove it by taking me back to the same spot. Mike contemplated for a moment and asked me for my real motive in being there. He asked me what I actually wanted. I repeated what I had asked him the other day. I said, "Mike, I want to experience the real thing."'

I mulled over what Rudrasen was telling me. I was not yet completely sure where this story was heading.

'I offered Mike a thousand dollars,' Rudrasen said proudly.

'Why in the three worlds?' I asked.

'Because Blue Mountain did something to me that I could never recover from,' he answered, looking despondent. 'It broke me. People doubted me. They wondered what had gotten into me. They said I was untrustworthy, all that just because some family friends of mine were interested in the property. Everyone doubted my integrity. I couldn't live with that. I survived a divorce and I was partly responsible for Anita going mad,' he confessed.

'What do you mean?' I asked.

'I had become obsessed,' he continued, on the verge of a breakdown. 'I traveled around the world to encounter a ghost, to see one face to face, so that I could get some evidence. Anita couldn't take it. She went insane.'

'Why was it so important to you?' I asked. I was not aware that it had become an obsession for Rudrasen.

'It was important for me because after the Blue Mountain incident, I was left friendless. I felt alone. I knew that people smirked when they met me. I could feel it. All because I did not speak up.'

'Did not speak up about what?' I asked, intrigued.

'I did not speak up about two things. Firstly, I got hold of the tapes only after Richa claimed she heard something in the tapes. I swear, I never got my hands on the tape anytime before. But the way she put it, looked like I had the tapes before the hearing and that I had doctored the tape.'

'Oh my God,' I exclaimed. 'I always thought you had the tapes before she heard them.'

'Yes,' he said, crestfallen, 'that is what everyone assumed. I never held a grudge against you for that night.'

I suddenly felt sorry for Rudrasen. Even I had judged him. 'And what was the second thing you never spoke about?' I asked.

'That night when we went to investigate at Blue Mountain,' he said tentatively, not sure how I would react, 'remember I came into the room stating I was not well?'

'I remember,' I said. 'Always wondered what got into you. You were not sick. You pretended to be sick.'

'Yes,' he replied, 'I got scared.'

'Scared?' I blurted out. 'Scared of what?'

'I saw the girl Elsa in the corridor,' he said. From the expression on his face, I knew he was not lying.

'I saw her running in the corridor. She was on fire and screaming for help. She collapsed in my arms and I felt my flesh burn. I still have the mark,' he said, rolling his sleeve to

149

expose a huge discolored part of his forearm. I looked at the mark in disbelief.

'Really?' I asked, still trying to overcome the shock of this new revelation. 'Why didn't you say something then?'

'Would you have believed me, if I had told you?' he questioned.

I reflected on his question for a brief moment and replied, 'In all fairness, *no*.'

'For a long time, I cursed myself for insisting on being on the panel,' he reflected. 'I never should have been on the cursed panel. But after the hearing, with all that I experienced, with people looking at me like a liar, I figured the only way to redemption was to get proof. Have another encounter, a photograph, something. I was clutching at straws. And so I offered Mike a thousand dollars.'

'And?' I asked, urging him to continue.

'Mike took me back to the same place. All the time, he kept swearing that it was not a scam. We reached the place after noon. Must have been 2 p.m., I guess. We went back to the same building, the exact same room, and waited. It was much brighter and this time I was prepared.'

'Continue,' I said.

'After a few minutes, we heard the footsteps and the door banged shut. This time, like I said, I had been prepared and was watching the door all the time and so I am certain, I didn't see anybody close the door. And just like the other night, after a few minutes, the door was unlocked.'

'Oh, come on now,' I said. 'How can you be sure there was no hanky-panky involved?'

'I checked the doors myself. They were made of solid oak wood. No wires running. No metal protrusions. Nothing. I made myself absolutely certain.'

I offered no suggestions. I had started to have mixed feelings now. On one hand, I felt sorry for Rudrasen, and on the other, his insistence to convince me of the existence of ghosts was disturbing. One thing was for sure, this man was clutching at straws. He so much wanted me to say that I believed him.

'I then asked Mike to wait outside,' Rudrasen continued. 'I wanted evidence, you see. Mike thought I was crazy. Just like hundreds of other people.'

The thought had not crossed my mind until Rudrasen mentioned it. I started to look at him in a new light. With his flowing beard and large-framed reading glasses, he now seemed queer to me. What if he started to tear his clothes apart and started a jig? What if he attacked me? I tried to block the unnecessary thoughts.

'After Mike left, I waited for a long time alone. Like a hunter waiting patiently for his kill.'

Now Rudrasen was also starting to sound like a lunatic.

'Mike was wrong,' Rudrasen said.

'About what?' I asked.

'It was not the mischievous boy who had drowned in the bathtub. It was a young woman, Clara, who died waiting for her lover to return. Her lover died in the Civil War.'

'What are you saying?' I asked. 'How do you know that?'

'I talked to Clara. Clara, she told me everything. I know you will not believe me when I tell you this. I talked to Clara just like I am talking to you now.'

I was clearly not prepared for this loony talk. My sympathy for Rudrasen was now slowly turning into alarm. I felt uncomfortable with the conversation and wanted to close it and get back home as soon as I could. Rudrasen was a raving lunatic to me now.

'I need to leave,' I said, getting up from my chair. 'My son is alone at home and it is quite late.'

'I know you don't want to hear me out,' he said, dejected. 'Nobody wants to believe me.'

I turned to look at Rudrasen sitting dejected. Maybe he would become normal if someone heard him out. Maybe all he wanted was for someone to tell him it was okay. Maybe, I was that someone. I reached out to him and placed my hand gently on his shoulder.

'It's okay. I believe you,' I said, not sounding convincing at all. 'I believe you because you want me to believe you.' That sounded much better.

Rudrasen looked up to give me a wry smile. I stood there and offered him a hand to stand up. He took my hand and got up slowly.

'I really need to leave,' I said. 'My wife is not in town and my son is alone at home.'

'I have something for you,' he said, walking towards the cabinet. He opened it and brought out three packets of varying sizes. 'This one is for you,' he said, pointing to one of them.

The surprise, I figured. I opened it slowly and smiled when I saw a beautiful gray T-shirt with a picture of the fictional comic character Tintin on it. The words 'I was at Brussels' were neatly printed in red on it. Rudrasen had forgotten to remove the price tag. I took a closer look at the tag—twenty euros. I thought it was worth every penny. It indeed was a pleasant surprise.

'There are some Belgian chocolates for your son,' Rudrasen said, still sounding sad.

'Thank you,' I said, embracing him. 'If you had given me this before the Blue Mountain episode, I would have believed every word you said,' I joked.

The remark made Rudrasen smile. 'And the last packet is for your wife. It is a bottle of perfume.'

I thanked him for the gifts as he walked me to the main door, which as usual opened automatically. 'You are a gadget freak,' I said, punching him in the arm.

I climbed down the stairs and walked towards my waiting car. For one last time, I turned to wave to Rudrasen, who had an amused look on his face. I wondered what he was smiling at as I turned around and froze in my tracks.

My car door was opening all by itself.

I heard Rudrasen say in his baritone voice behind me, 'Don't scare the poor man, Clara. Let him go home now.'

Then I heard the soft laughter of a woman.

# THE SOOTHSAYER

Nobody was prepared for the plethora of strange and intriguing incidents that took place that evening at the third anniversary party—least of all Raghuram Bhat.

He had been extremely anxious right from the morning. In fact, it was an extension of how he had felt for a full week now. If only he knew what was in store for him that evening, he wouldn't have pushed for the program as hard as he did. As the head of the Talent Engagement Division (TED), a name he had coined himself only because he felt it sounded much better than plain HRD, he believed he had quite a task to pull off that evening. There was no way the evening program was going to be anything but spectacular.

'The best show that the employees have ever experienced' was how he had put it to his team. 'The previous anniversary parties should look like an apology for a party.' His team had just nodded in acquiescence. None of them would have dared to say what they personally felt anyway, lest they found themselves searching for a job at the slightest hint of dissent.

He picked up the intercom and dialed Rithu, the senior manager of TED. He waited for what seemed to him like hours for her to answer the call.

'Pick up the phone, pick up the damn phone,' he muttered to himself before finally giving up and disconnecting the call after the sixth ring. He dialed once again, hoping that she had miraculously appeared at her desk within the intervening seconds. Again, no response.

Where the hell were these people when you needed them? He wrung his fingers anxiously as he decided to amuse himself with some other distraction. He turned his attention onto his laptop lying open on his desk. He pressed the send/receive button on his mailbox. As the mail started to download, he was pleased to see that the only messages which were unread were the ones downloading. He loathed seeing a number beside the unread mail icon.

'It just shows how pathetic you are with managing your time,' he had lectured to a hapless employee justifying why a promotion was denied.

A cluster of mail landed in his inbox. He sorted the mail by the senders' names and selected the one sent by his boss Sandesh Mehra first. It was a message addressed to all employees of the organization, congratulating them for having completed the third year of operations. It went on to state that as the organization entered its fourth year, there were greater challenges up ahead. The CEO talked of the need to focus on cutting costs, increasing revenue and customer satisfaction.

Raghuram looked at the mail for some time and smiled. He clicked on the 'reply to all' button and drafted a message.

'Thank you for all the motivation you have given us . . .' he started, and paused. It looked too patronizing. He pressed the backspace button and started afresh. He continued typing at a feverish pace and stopped only after a couple of minutes to admire his work of art. He congratulated himself as he read his reply.

'Our organization has always been good. Now is the time to move from good to great. We are blessed to have with us the level 5 leadership . . .' And it went on. He had ensured that he had used terms like synergizing the basics, singular modular operability, evolved competency mapping; the meanings of most of these even he didn't understand. But then he was sure nobody would ask.

'Perception management,' he sighed, 'so important these days.'

He looked at the other mail. He opened the one sent by his counterpart Badhrudin, the vice president in the marketing department. The mail was marked to the leadership team, updating everyone on the progress achieved with a new client based out of Sydney, Australia. It also intimated the TED team that approximately 150 new agents needed to be recruited on a war footing and went on to give a detailed description of the skills and competencies required by the agents, as specified by the client.

'Bloody idiots,' Raghuram groaned, 'where do they expect me to find so many flunkies with these competencies at such short notice?'

He clicked on 'forward to' and marked his team the mail with a terse FYNA.

'Delegation', he smiled, 'is the art of survival. If they manage, take the credit. If they don't, blame them.'

The third mail he opened was from a training company in Sweden marketing their competency development workshop to be held in Mumbai. He deleted it. If it was to be held in Sweden, it would have been worth considering for him to personally attend.

The remaining mail was either forwarded or archived. The ones he was marked a cc to were opened and closed without reading. He did this until the number of unread mail disappeared. He smiled in blissful satisfaction.

The mail was handled and done. He drummed on the table with his fingers, wondering what to do next. Of course it had to be the program in the evening. He picked up the intercom and dialed Rithu once again. After a couple of rings, Rithu picked up the phone.

'Where are you?' Raghuram barked.

'In my cabin obviously,' Rithu replied.

Raghuram realized the stupidity of his question.

'I mean, where were you?' He didn't wait for her to respond and asked, 'Can you come here?'

'Is it urgent?' Rithu asked.

Raghuram controlled an urge to say, *'No. You can come by next year.'*

'Yes, it is urgent,' he said, not bothering to sound polite. I am the boss!

'Give me a couple of minutes,' Rithu replied.

'Make it fast,' Raghuram said curtly and slammed the intercom down. *I am the boss.*

A few minutes before the call, just a few feet away from Raghuram's cabin, Rithu had been pondering over the evening's agenda. She had just returned after a coffee break and was not happy that she had to spend a major chunk of her time on this assignment. She would have preferred to spend more time working on the new compensation structure she felt the company so needed, to prepare for the new office being set up in Chicago. She had always requested for the event to be outsourced to an event management company. Her boss disagreed because the event management companies charged too much. Moreover, Raghuram had argued that an event management company never understood the culture of an organization.

She looked at the three HR managers sitting in front of her. Zia, thirty-something and committed to his job, handled recruitments for the company. What he lacked in the form of a postgraduate degree from a fancy management college, he made up with his passion and commitment. Shriya, in her early forties, was not very smart in handling payroll but made up for it with her infectious enthusiasm. She was ever ready to take on any assignment. Sheon, the weakest link, handled general administration. He was manipulative and a bootlicker. He considered himself an ardent fan and devotee of Raghuram. Thankfully the dumbest of the lot, Rithu thought.

'Do you have the venue and the food all covered?' Rithu turned to Zia first.

'All done,' Zia said without the least bit of excitement showing in his face.

'The lists?' Rithu asked, turning to Shriya.

'The list is prepared, checked, and rechecked. I have the list in separate envelopes marked for the CEO. I shall hand it over to him just before he gets on the dais,' Shriya said, pointing to a bunch of Manila envelopes she had in front of her.

'Good,' Rithu said, 'make sure it is handed over to him just before he gets on the dais. He has a habit of misplacing things, and just to be sure, do make a duplicate copy and keep it with you.'

Rithu next turned to Sheon. He had a few sheets of papers haphazardly placed in a folder. Rithu gave out a deep sigh before she started talking to Sheon.

'You have changed the program a dozen times now,' Rithu started. 'Do you have the final flow of events marked out now?'

'It is almost done,' Sheon started.

'Almost done?' Rithu asked, irritated.

'Well,' Sheon replied, 'Raghuram sir wanted a couple of changes incorporated and—'

The phone rang and Rithu picked it up.

'Is it urgent?' Rithu asked to the person on the other end and let out a soft groan as she added, 'Give me a couple of minutes.'

She put down the receiver, trying hard not to show her irritation.

'It is Raghu,' she informed her team sitting in front of her. 'He wants to meet me, no doubt, to check our preparations for this evening's event.'

'That is the fourth time he is checking,' Zia complained. 'We have better things to do.'

Rithu ignored the comment. There was no point in displaying personal differences in front of the team.

'I want you to come with me,' Rithu said to Sheon. Sheon seemed happy that he would get one more chance to interact with his idol.

A few minutes later, Rithu opened Raghuram's cabin. She was closely followed by Sheon, who was holding the folder close to his chest almost as if it contained the secret files of the FBI. Raghuram continued to work on his computer and did not acknowledge either of them. It took him a full three minutes to complete whatever he was doing before he turned to look at them.

'Yes?' he asked.

'You asked to see me,' Rithu said, not making a move towards seating herself in the vacant chair opposite Raghuram. She did not want to sit because she wanted to leave at the first opportune moment.

'*Is everything for today's program in order?*' she mimicked Raghuram in her mind.

'I hope everything is ready for today's engagement?' Raghuram asked and didn't wait for an answer before continuing, 'Who are the caterers?'

'We have the college of catering to take care of the food,' Rithu said. This was probably the sixth or seventh time she was going through the drill in the last three days.

'Do you have the menu worked out?' Raghuram asked.

Rithu silently held out a sheet that was already lying on Raghuram's desk. She hated every minute of this.

'I left this on your desk two days back when you asked for it,' Rithu replied.

'I don't remember having seen it,' Raghuram lied as he took the sheet from her hand and ran through the list. 'Vanilla ice cream?'

Rithu was aware that he would object to something. It was in his nature to change plans just for the sake of changing it.

'You asked for it to be put on the menu,' Rithu said.

'I don't remember any such thing,' Raghuram confronted her and looked at Sheon almost as if for support.

'I don't remember either,' Sheon agreed.

Rithu rolled her eyes in subdued frustration.

'*Of course you wouldn't remember, you idiot,*' Rithu almost blurted out to Sheon.

'Please have this changed to fruit custard,' Raghuram said.

'Excellent choice, sir,' Sheon chipped in.

'I am not sure it can be done now,' Rithu said, frustrated. 'It is too late in the day and—'

'I am not asking you to change the whole menu,' Raghuram insisted, 'just one dish. Tell them Raghuram sir asked for the change.' The emphasis on the words 'Raghuram sir' was not lost on anybody.

Rithu started to object, but held back and decided that she did not want to get into a pointless debate. She had decided that she wouldn't change the menu. 'After all,' she thought, 'this idiot wouldn't even remember what he ate tomorrow morning.'

'I will see what I can do,' Rithu informed him.

'What about the entertainment?' Raghuram asked.

'Sheon here will explain it himself,' Rithu said. This was going to be fun. Who doesn't enjoy a conversation between a despicable dogmatic despot and a fumbling first-rate idiot?

Sheon stepped forward most respectfully and pulled out a sheet of paper from his million-dollar folder and handed it over to Raghuram.

'What is this?' Raghuram asked, perplexed, looking at the sheet. Even from a distance, Rithu noticed that the sheet would have confused anyone who would have cared to look at it. What was originally a computer printout had red lines striking out some of the line items. There was a lot of matter scribbled in blue, black, and green ink at various places on the sheet.

'The agenda for today's entertainment, sir,' Sheon said with a flourish.

'All right, I understand that, but what is this?' Raghuram said, losing his patience.

'The list of programs for today's entertainment, sir,' Sheon repeated, unable to understand which word in his sentence was confusing Raghuram.

Rithu stood silently by the side, holding back a smile that threatened to escape her lips.

'Do you understand English?' Raghuram asked, visibly irritated.

'I was at 88 per cent in my tenth class, sir,' Sheon said proudly.

'Looks like the 12 per cent was the most important part you missed,' Raghuram said, distressed. 'I am going to repeat this question once again, look at my lips closely.'

Sheon, as always, took his skip-level boss seriously, took a step forward, and focused his eyes on Raghuram's lips.

'Can you please tell me what the programs are that are listed on this sheet?' Raghuram asked, stressing each and every word.

'It is all there on the sheet, sir,' Sheon said, almost mimicking Raghuram.

Raghuram lost his cool and crumpled the sheet into a ball and flung it on the floor. He looked at Rithu for help, aware that she was quietly enjoying the show.

Rithu was indeed enjoying the show. At the same time, she wanted to be out of the cabin as soon as possible. She thought it best to intervene.

'He says he can't read what is written on the sheet because it is illegible,' Rithu said, stepping in. 'He wants you to tell him all the programs you have listed on the sheet.'

'Oh,' Sheon replied with a 'You should have told me so' look. He walked to the sheet which had been thrown and picked it up. He proceeded to spread out the sheet on Raghuram's desk and eased his palms over it to clear the creases.

'To start with—' Sheon started.

'Wait a minute,' Raghuram said, holding up his hand to stop Sheon. 'Do you have any other sheets with the agenda written down or is this the only sheet?'

'This is the only sheet, sir,' Sheon confirmed with a broad grin. 'Didn't want anyone else to know the programs. Wanted it to be a sort of suspense.'

Raghuram covered his face with his palms, hiding his irritation, and said, 'Do you know the flow of events?' Rithu wondered if he would break down and cry any moment now.

Raghuram was greeted by a long silence. He uncovered his face to glare at Sheon.

'I want you to go and get me a printout of the flow of events clearly marked with the amount of time each event will take. Is that understood?' Raghuram asked.

'Yes, sir,' Sheon said, for the first time feeling a bit nervous.

'How much time will you take to get me that?' Raghuram inquired.

Sheon looked over to Rithu, half expecting her to give the answer. He found her looking at the ceiling and realized he would have to come up with the answer himself.

'Two hours?' Sheon asked.

'Are you asking me or telling me?' Raghuram clarified.

'Telling you, sir,' Sheon replied.

'And why would it take two hours?' Raghuram asked in a patronizing manner.

'One hour?' Sheon asked and waited to determine the response on Raghuram's face. Seeing no change in expression, he pushed himself further to say, 'Half hour.'

'Good,' Raghuram remarked. 'Now get the hell out of here.'

Sheon left with much less enthusiasm than he had come in.

'Anything else we haven't covered?' Raghuram asked Rithu.

'Nothing I can think of,' Rithu lied, wanting to leave the cabin as soon as possible.

'Is the R & R list ready?' Raghuram demanded.

'Shriya has the list,' Rithu said.

'Shriya who?' Raghuram asked, frowning.

'Shriya handles payrolls,' Rithu replied, not surprised that Raghuram did not remember names of staff in his own department.

Raghuram hardly interacted with members of his own team. He was not one known to greet you in the hallway and inquire about any personal well-being of the employees of the organization. He never dwelt on the personal lives of any team members primarily because he did not want anyone to know about his own personal life. Raghuram was presently involved in a messy divorce case with his second wife whom he married three years back—an improvement, considering his first wife left him within the first year of marriage.

If anyone had bothered to talk to his ex-wives, they would come away believing Raghuram was close to an American version of Saddam Hussein. The list of allegations that Raghuram's present wife had filed in her divorce complaint included a compulsive drinking problem, domestic violence, mental harassment, and a host of other issues. Rithu and more than half of the employees of Oak Tree Talent Engagement Resource (OTTER for short), where Raghuram worked, would have gladly testified that Raghuram was an icon of all these traits and more. Rithu suspected that quite a handful of the employees would have been happy to include sexual harassment and sexual discrimination too as some of the charges against Raghuram.

'Might not be too good-looking else I would remember her,' Raghuram said aloud, referring to Shriya.

Rithu was hardly surprised with these comments from her boss. Unfortunately, he was much too powerful in the organization and no one was ready to speak against him.

'Ensure there are no screwups,' Raghuram said. 'I am already quite concerned about that joker Sheon.'

Rithu continued to maintain a stoic silence. Anything you say might be and will be used against you.

'Anything else?' she asked, more with the need to run out of the cabin.

'Yes,' Raghuram said, 'I hope you remember that tomorrow I am catching an early morning flight to Bangalore to meet up with our client Spark Technologies.'

*'Finally, something to do with actual work,'* Rithu thought.

'I had asked you to put together that presentation,' Raghuram continued.

'I sent you one yesterday,' Rithu intervened.

'I am coming to that,' Raghuram cut her short and ordered, 'Redo the whole thing.'

'What is wrong with the one I sent you?' Rithu asked.

'Everything,' Raghuram said, sounding displeased and lost. 'It lacks any spice. The colors are not vibrant in the slides, it looks tacky, and please use some high-tech jargon like reverse brainstorming. Don't say challenge, say conundrum.'

'By when do you need the corrections made?' Rithu asked to show no hints to express her displeasure about what she thought was a good presentation.

'My meeting is at five in the evening,' Raghuram said. 'You can mail me the PPT by tomorrow morning.'

'I will do that,' Rithu said, moving towards the cabin door and opening it.

'I want you at the venue by five to personally supervise the preparations,' Raghuram said as a parting shot.

Rithu closed the door behind her and was silently mouthing obscenities directed at Raghuram. She walked to her desk and sat on her chair. She closed her eyes and prayed that the evening program would be uneventful. With a Sheon in her team, she greatly doubted that.

She tried to dismiss any scary premonitions she fostered about the evening's program and tried to focus on the presentation she had to get ready for the next morning. It was 5.30 p.m. by the time she finally mailed a presentation that was high on nonsense quotient and low on quality.

It was 6 p.m. by the time Rithu started for the venue.

The venue, Apex Convention Centre, was one of the most modern convention centers in the city. The massive air-conditioned hall could easily accommodate over a thousand people. A gigantic stage was set up at the far end of the auditorium with two huge screens on each side to project the events live for anyone who had not managed to get a seat close enough to the stage. The company logo presently adorned the screens. The stage by itself was brightly lit with fresnel lanterns, LED stage lights, and parabolic aluminized reflector lights. A couple of followspot lights kept roaming the stage as lighting experts tested every bit of the equipment they had brought in.

Food stalls had been lined up on one side of the auditorium and the opposite side housed a huge bar counter. The bartenders had started to stock up different types of liquor and soda for the evening. A dozen people ran around, ensuring they attended to last-minute orders barked out by just about anybody who felt like contributing to the confusion. A few employees had already started filling up their glasses, probably worried that the bar would run out of booze before the night was over.

Rithu found Sheon, Shriya, and Zia managing the proceedings from the stage and walked up to them.

'Everything under control, I assume?' she asked them.

'Everything except the audio system,' Shriya announced. 'The collar mikes we got for the master of ceremonies wasn't working. Should get corrected anytime now.'

Rithu turned to Sheon.

'All the performers will be here anytime now and I have a list of the schedule here with me,' Sheon answered. 'I did leave a copy on Raghuram sir's desk.'

'Can I have a copy?' Rithu asked.

Rithu ran a cursory look across the sheet. The program was expected to start at 7 p.m. and end at midnight. There was a live band, a magic show, a standup comic act, a couple of dance shows, a Russian gymnast, and other programs listed on the sheet, including the rewards and recognition program. She folded the sheet and placed it in her handbag.

'What time does the bar open?' Rithu asked Zia. She felt she needed a drink badly.

'Supposed to be at seven sharp,' Zia said, 'and as you can see, some of them haven't waited for a formal announcement. We plan to keep it open till well past midnight. All required permissions have been taken and filed. The food service will start at seven with starters. We have four vegetarian and four non-vegetarian . . .'

Rithu listened to Zia with interest as he clearly explained the food arrangements made for the evening, and the efforts were clearly impressive. He had left nothing to chance. It was not Zia who worried her anyway; it was Sheon. She felt there was hardly anything she could do about it now. She would just have to pray and hope for each performer to arrive and start entertaining the crowd.

The crowd slowly started to trickle in. Rithu stood by the entrance and greeted a few of the senior management staff and personally saw to it that they were seated comfortably close to the dais.

'Quite a show you have put up for the staff,' Alegeshan, the CFO of the organization, remarked, half complaining to Rithu.

'Everything is within the budget,' Rithu reassured Alegeshan, who was seated next to Badhrudin, VP Marketing.

'Quit complaining and enjoy the show,' Badhrudin remarked, slapping Alegeshan on the back. 'And don't get too drunk or you will not be able to drive back home.'

'Got my driver,' Alegeshan remarked. 'Don't want to get into trouble with the cops. Too many checkpoints on my way back home.'

'Enjoy yourselves,' Rithu remarked, excusing herself. 'The show will start as soon as Mr. Mehra is here.'

Raghuram arrived a few minutes before seven, wearing a black blazer over gray trousers. He did not bother to either stop to talk to his team or any of the other employees who had already gathered at the venue. Except for a few known flatterers, headed by Sheon, none of the other employees bothered to approach Raghuram to greet him. Rithu tried her best to blend in with the crowd to ensure she was not spotted by Raghuram.

The chairman and managing director, Sandesh Mehra, arrived a few minutes after 7 p.m., by when the crowd had already started to crowd at the bar. Raghuram was quick to reach the gates to personally escort the CEO from the entrance to one of the reserved tables at the very front of the auditorium. Smartly dressed waiters moved amongst the crowd carrying food trays. Female employees of OTTER had already occupied most of the front tables near the stage. The sounds of clinking glasses and loud laughter could be heard around the hall.

The lights dimmed in the auditorium, and the booming voice of the master of ceremonies welcomed the gathering, urging them to make some noise. A loud cheer erupted, but the MC was not impressed. He goaded the crowd to raise the noise levels several notches higher. Some employees screamed and a few more whistled as the MC finally made an entrance onto the stage. More screaming with a few whistles followed as the crowd recognized the MC as a TV show host flown all the way from Mumbai.

Sheon smiled as if the crowd was rooting for him. He stood like a gladiator with his hands on his hips. He waved to imaginary friends around the auditorium.

The MC promised the crowd a good time with many amazing events fanned out for the evening and invited the Showstoppers, a local band to start the show. A side screen lifted to reveal the band seated behind it and the sound of drums and electric guitars filled the air. The female lead singer started with a song by Adele, from the movie *Skyfall*. The auditorium cheered in anticipation of a good recital, soon to calm down after the lady not only fumbled the lyrics but also the notes.

The second song, the old hit 'Hotel California' by a male lead, was much better, and a nervous Sheon started to breathe much more easily. The crowd started to relax after the third song, which was the cue for the MC to intervene and say a few words about the company and the reason for the celebration. He urged the crowd to cheer more for OTTER and most employees who were not at the bar counter or looking out for waiters with trays cheered loudly.

At the exclusive table laid out for the leadership team, Raghuram seemed visibly pleased with the proceedings. He had ensured that he sat flanking the CEO. He kept chatting up Sandesh Mehra to ensure the boss was kept engaged.

One after the other, performers walked on and off the podium, entertaining the crowd. The crowd cheered for some and booed at some. And then all of a sudden, the lights in the auditorium were dimmed and the lights on the stage were switched off. An uneasy silence descended abruptly in the auditorium for just a couple of moments. A soulful tune played on violin started playing out at low volume and gradually a cimbalom and bass sounded out as the music got louder. The crowd gasped as a woman appeared out of nowhere, her face covered in a thin veil. She wore a floral gown, which was slit all the way up to her waist, exposing a pair of thin long legs. The halter top she wore exposed her milky-white skinny shoulders. They covered her long arms up to her forearms, which she moved with grace to the accompaniment of the music. A matching bandana tied tightly across her forehead added to the Gypsy effect.

As the music grew louder, she slowly danced her way to the center of the stage and from thin air, produced a crystal ball the size of a soccer ball. The crowd let out a collective gasp and clapped. The lady bowed gracefully and proceeded to unveil her face. Again a collective gasp could be heard when the crowd saw the face. She looked like she was in her early thirties, but what was unmistakable were those two beautiful eyes sparkling like two precious diamonds. Unlike the complexion of her shoulders, her face was dark and long, with high cheekbones. As she smiled, she exposed a long and deep dimple that ran all the way from her eye to her chin. She moved gracefully as she danced to the tunes, sometimes flipping her body backwards like an ace gymnast even while balancing the crystal ball. The crowd clapped feverishly. She stopped to let the ball float in thin air and brought it to a standstill in front of her at waist height.

'Lads and lassies, there are some idiots who will tell you that the future is not important,' she announced. Her voice had a certain gruffness to it, which again took the audience by surprise. 'They lie. Because people who don't think of the future are only afraid of what it holds for them.'

The crowd listened attentively.

'You have to know your future because that is where you will spend the rest of your lives,' she continued. 'So? Who wants to know their future? Step forward and I shall tell you what dangers lie ahead of you.'

Nobody moved. She waited silently, rolling her hands over the crystal ball. If the audience was expecting something to happen, nothing did. They continued to wait in suspended anticipation.

'What is the matter, no one here believes they have a future?' she asked again. Some people laughed nervously.

'*You*,' she said aloud, pointing to someone in the crowd, 'don't be a coward, step forward. Haven't you heard that fortune favors the brave?'

All eyes fell on John, a junior executive in the marketing team, as someone pushed him forward. He tried to fight his way back to reclaim his place back in anonymity. After the initial struggle, he gave up the fight as John found himself being tracked by a follow spotlight. The Gypsy had picked him for his two minutes of fame. The little resistance he had, gave way as he soon heard the crowd chanting his name. '*John, John.*'

John smiled nervously and made his way to center stage. John was all of four feet seven inches including his spiked hair. As he neared the woman, he made her look gigantic, though she was only close to five feet ten.

'Three cheers to Long John,' the lady said loudly and people laughed aloud because Long John was his nickname in his department.

'So, John,' the lady started, 'you belong to the racketing department, right?'

'Marketing,' John answered, his voice hardly audible.

'That is what I said,' the lady said and the crowd laughed aloud. 'Let us cut it *short*, John.'

The crowd laughed again at the intended pun.

'What would you like to know from the crystal ball? Remember, neither the Gypsy nor her ball ever lies,' she said, 'so ask and be careful of what you ask.'

John looked around nervously and someone ran to hand over a cordless microphone to John. John fiddled around with it for a few seconds.

'Tell me what you see for me in this company,' John asked, sounding as if it was a very intelligent question.

The Gypsy woman contemplated on the question for a second.

'Growth,' she answered and the crowd understood the joke only after a couple of seconds. They started laughing and someone screamed, 'Growth for Long John.'

John looked around nervously and, after a few moments, almost as if on cue, exited the stage.

Slowly, the auditorium settled into an uneasy calm again.

'Who wants to know their future, step forward,' the Gypsy lady announced again, continuing to roll her hands over the crystal ball and looking at the audience.

A couple of people started to queue near the small stairway that led to the dais.

Ram, one of the team leads, pushed his way through and scrambled up the stairs. He tripped on the last stair and, in an attempt to break his fall, tried to hold on to a steel rod nearby and ended up with a half-torn sleeve. The Gypsy looked at Ram as he staggered towards her in a half-drunken stupor.

'What's the *tearing* hurry, honey?' she asked as the crowd laughed again. 'Aren't you the dancing queen?' she asked, holding her hands high in the air and shaking her hips.

The crowd laughed again because Ram was nicknamed the dancing queen in the office. Ram would always be the first one on the dance floor every time the music played. He considered himself a good dancer, but everyone in the office would have begged to disagree. They loved his dance only because he made a buffoon of himself.

'The dancing queen with two left feet,' the Gypsy announced loudly, 'and if he is not careful today, he will have no feet left.'

The crowd started to boo. 'Ram, get out . . . Ram, get the hell out.'

Ram lost his nerve and forgot why he had come on stage in the first place. He hardly waited for another moment and left the stage with the same speed that he had come in. He descended the stairs and headed straight for the bar.

Rithu watched the proceedings, amused. She was happy that the crowd was enjoying the show. Sheon had managed to pull it off after all. She glanced at the table that seated the top management of the company. Sandesh Mehra was enjoying the fun, no doubt. Raghuram sitting beside him was talking animatedly to Sandesh Mehra. Badhrudin was preoccupied with his cell phone, replying to email, and Alegeshan sat upright in his chair, engrossed with the proceedings on stage.

All of a sudden, Alegeshan got up from his chair and moved towards the stage. A lady was about to put her foot on the first step when Alegeshan reached the stage and pulled the new participant back, almost a repeat of Ram's act. He climbed the steps and briskly proceeded towards the Gypsy woman, who was all the while watching Alegeshan approach with a bemused expression.

'Ah, the money man,' the Gypsy exclaimed, 'takes care of the money of the company, but is careless with his own.'

The audience clapped in encouragement. Unlike Raghuram, Alegeshan was popular with the crowd. Alegeshan stood before the Gypsy silently until the commotion died down, contemplating his next move. He looked around for the second microphone and gestured for someone to fetch him one. In a couple of moments, the mike was in his hands.

'I am not careless with my money,' Alegeshan retorted once he was sure the mike was working.

'In which case, Mr. Cash Cow,' the Gypsy said, 'can you lend me ten rupees from your purse?'

'Only if you will convert it into a hundred,' Alegeshan said, laughing. The crowd chuckled in unison.

'I am a poor Gypsy woman,' the Gypsy stated, 'not the Reserve Bank of India. Give me ten rupees first and then see the magic.'

Alegeshan shoved his right palm into his trouser back pocket and froze for a moment. He couldn't find his wallet. He tried both the front pockets of his trousers and still drew a blank. He started to run his hands over his trousers and his shirt, searching for his wallet. The Gypsy laughed and produced a wallet from behind her for the crowd to see. The crowd burst out laughing, confusing Alegeshan even more.

She waved the wallet in front of the crowd and then held it in front of Alegeshan and asked, 'Is this what you are looking for?'

Alegeshan was visibly embarrassed and grabbed for his wallet. 'How did you—' he started to ask when the Gypsy held up a finger in front of her lips.

'Are you a magician or a Gypsy?' Alegeshan asked, bewildered.

'I am just a poor Gypsy who can tell you your fortune,' the Gypsy remarked.

'How do we know that you are not a fraud?' Alegeshan asked, regaining his composure and his sense of humor.

'You dare call me a fraud?' the Gypsy woman laughed. 'Oh sweet god of destiny, give this man a sign that I am not a fraud, at the count of three.'

The Gypsy woman held up her finger in front of her lips to silence the crowd. 'One,' she shouted. The crowd fell deathly quiet. 'Two,' she continued.

'Two and a half,' someone shouted from the crowd.

'And three,' the Gypsy woman said out loud. A moment later, there was a loud sound of crashing cutlery. Everyone turned around to look at a waiter who had slipped and was lying on the floor dazed. All around him lay pieces of soup bowls and wine glasses. People laughed nervously, not sure if this was part of the act or a real accident. The audience was even unsure if they could laugh at the poor chap's predicament.

'Is that sign good enough for you?' the Gypsy woman asked, smiling.

'Accidents happen all the time,' Alegeshan remarked.

'Yes, they do,' the Gypsy woman laughed. 'You joined this company by accident; your marriage was an accident. Ask your parents and they will tell you that even you were an accident.'

The crowd was not sure if they could laugh at this one joke.

'And,' the Gypsy woman continued, 'do be careful, you will be involved in one more tonight. Now go,' she commanded Alegeshan. Alegeshan laughed as he walked away from the stage and walked straight to Rithu.

'Was the waiter tripping a part of the act?' he asked Rithu.

'I don't know,' Rithu confided. 'I can find out for you.'

'Strange,' Alegeshan remarked. 'Not many people know that I came into this company by accident and that my wedding was by accident.'

Rithu did not want to ask if the Gypsy was right about his birth too.

'Who will be the last one to know their future?' the Gypsy said. 'I have traveled miles to meet this one person.'

Someone from the back of the auditorium shouted out, 'Raghuram, she has come for you. Go say hi to your sweetheart.'

Again the crowd laughed nervously. Raghuram turned around to see who the drunken joker was.

'Come, Raghuram,' the Gypsy called out. 'Where are you? I have traveled miles to just meet you.'

'Your lover waits for you, Raghuram,' another voice shouted from the back. 'What is the matter? Afraid of being sexually harassed by the Gypsy?'

Chuckles erupted from the crowd. There were a few whistles and a few catcalls. Rithu noticed Sandesh Mehra amused by the whole happening. Badhrudin was coaxing Raghuram to get up on to the dais, and Raghuram was shaking his head vigorously.

'We want Raghuram, we want Raghuram' chants reverberated in the auditorium. Sandesh Mehra placed his hand and gently prodded Raghuram to get up. Raghuram got up slowly, not wanting to displease his boss. A few people screamed their approval. Rithu noticed Sheon was shaking with fear.

Raghuram slowly approached the dais, absolutely unsure if he should be doing this at all. However, by the time he reached the last step, he was holding up his arms much like Sachin Tendulkar would have after having scored a century.

'Come on, my dear,' the Gypsy woman said. 'So you are the one. Not very popular, are we?'

Raghuram just smiled in response.

'What would you like to know?' the Gypsy asked, more to the crowd than to Raghuram directly.

'What is the future of this company for the next five years?' Raghuram asked, never one to lose an opportunity to create an impression in front of the big boss.

'Shouldn't you be more worried about your future?' the Gypsy asked.

'Yeah, yeah,' the same drunk joker, his voice now unmistakable, shouted. 'Tell us when he will die. He has been a real pain, you know.'

Raghuram turned around to look at the crowd. If only he could get his hands on the funny guy.

'Seriously,' the man shouted again, 'tell us how he will die. Will someone from our office kill him?'

Some people from the crowd laughed.

Raghuram, as hard as he tried, could not spot the troublemaker. He turned around to face the Gypsy woman again and was about to say something when he noticed her staring at his face. It was an icy-cold stare which made him nervous.

'I see a plane,' the Gypsy announced.

'What?' Raghuram asked, confused. Till now he was thinking this was all in good humor. Surely this lady was not going to predict his death just because a complete idiot had asked for it.

'I see a plane associated with your death and that shall come very soon,' the Gypsy announced.

Suddenly the whole auditorium became deathly quiet for a few moments. Raghuram stood before the Gypsy, baffled. He was totally confused, not knowing if this was supposed to be funny. He didn't find it funny. He wanted to lay his hands on two people: the loudmouth from the crowd and that idiot Sheon, for having such a brainless act in the program.

'You have been warned,' the Gypsy announced, her voice suddenly very hoarse. 'The Gypsy has to leave, for she has delivered the message she came to deliver.'

The music started to play again and drowned the voice of Raghuram as he said something in protest. The Gypsy had started to gyrate to the music. Slowly the lights dimmed even as Raghuram stood on the stage transfixed, not knowing what to do. The stage went pitch-dark for a second, and when the lights came on, the Gypsy woman was nowhere to be seen.

The music slowly started to play down, and the MC walked on to the stage and screamed, 'Are you having fun?'

The crowd, which had gone quiet, screamed back, 'Yes.'

'I don't hear you,' the MC shouted back and slowly guided a perplexed Raghuram away from the stage.

Everyone downstage was not sure how to react to Raghuram. Most of them ignored him or stayed away, faking great interest in the proceedings on stage. Raghuram walked towards Rithu, who was now standing nervously beside Sandesh Mehra.

'That was a stupid program,' Raghuram said half screaming at Rithu. 'Where is that idiot Sheon?'

Sandesh Mehra had intentionally turned away to avoid watching an overreacting Raghuram. Rithu scanned the crowd and saw a nervous Sheon looking at her. She beckoned to Sheon and he came scurrying.

'Where is the program chart? Who invited that stupid woman? Are there any more such stupid programs?' Raghuram screamed a volley of questions at Sheon.

Sheon stood paralyzed with fear. Even as Raghuram snatched the program sheet from Sheon's hands and scanned it, the MC requested Sandesh Mehra to come on stage and announce the names of the employees who had been promoted that year.

Raghuram turned to Rithu and asked, 'Can anyone tell me who that lady was? I don't see her listed here.'

Rithu looked at Sheon for help. Sheon seemed clueless. He kept looking back and forth at Raghuram and Rithu.

'Don't you know who that lady was?' Rithu asked Sheon again.

'Isn't her name there on the list?' a nervous Sheon responded.

'You tell me,' Rithu snapped at Sheon. 'Which category does that act fall under? I can see a magic show, a standup comic, and a Russian gymnast on the list. Where does the Gypsy fit in? The program before the R & R, which was live now, was the light-and-sound show and that ended almost twenty minutes back. Then who was this Gypsy woman and where did she come from?'

Sheon stood dumbfounded, looking at his copy of the program.

'Who the hell was the stoned idiot who kept passing those ridiculous comments, and how the hell did that lady manage to get in?' Raghuram thundered. A few people standing nearby turned to look at Raghuram and Rithu.

'I want you to go and find that lady, find out how the hell she got in here,' Raghuram screamed at Sheon. Sheon kept looking at Raghuram. '*Now*,' Raghuram barked. Sheon was more than happy to scamper off. Raghuram continued to glare at Rithu.

On the one hand, Rithu was secretly happy that someone had managed to fluster Raghuram. On the other, she was quite worried that someone, in all probability an employee of OTTER, had managed to pull off a fiasco knowing full well how incompetent Sheon was. She decided that this had to be an insider's job. It was pretty obvious that the person who had pulled it off knew a lot about the other employees. Rithu herself had no idea that Ram was referred to as the dancing queen in his department or that John was also called Long John. What baffled her was Alegeshan's comment too. And the waiter falling down—was it deliberate, accidental or just a mere coincidence?

She now worried and hoped that the rest of the evening would be incident free. Rithu turned her attention to Sandesh Mehra, who was announcing the names of employees who had been promoted.

One by one, the employees were walking up the stage, shaking hands with Sandesh, collecting an envelope handed out to them by the CEO, and leaving. The crowd was clapping as the names were announced one after the other. Rithu noticed that the crowds were slowly starting to relax. Even Raghuram, though still looking very agitated, was now focused on the proceedings.

'The next person on the list is', announced Sandesh Mehra, 'John from the marketing team.'

The crowd cheered loudly, but John was nowhere nearby and kept the CEO waiting.

'Wait a minute,' Rithu said, turning to Raghuram. 'John was not supposed to be promoted this year.'

'How can that be?' Raghuram asked. 'The CEO is reading from the list we gave him, right?'

'I believe so,' Rithu said worried that something was amiss.

'Don't tell me you guys messed up this one too,' Raghuram chided.

Rithu thought it best to just ignore the remark. It was typical Raghuram behavior anyway. She turned around to find the VP for marketing, Badhrudin, standing right beside her.

'How the hell did John get promoted?' Badhrudin demanded to know. 'As a matter of fact, we had agreed that he was to be put on performance improvement.'

John had already managed to reach the stage and was shaking hands with Sandesh Mehra. A photographer captured the CEO handing over the promotion letter to John, who was sporting a huge grin, obviously still not able to believe that he was getting promoted.

Rithu found Shriya standing on the stage looking perplexed. She gestured to Rithu to indicate she had no idea what was happening. One by one, the other employees were called, and to Rithu's relief, no other out-of-turn promotions were announced. As Sandesh Mehra completed the list, Shriya rushed across to him to take the list back from him. Rithu caught up with her a few seconds later.

'John's name was not in the list, Rithu,' she said, almost in tears. 'I have no idea how it cropped up on this list. It is not on my list or the copy I am carrying. I have no idea how it appeared in the CEO's list. God, I am so worried about the screwup, Rithu. Raghu is going to fry me for this.'

'Don't worry,' Rithu reassured Shriya, 'looks like someone is up to some mischief. Do you know that the Gypsy's act was also not on the program?'

'Don't tell me,' Shriya said, shocked.

Suddenly they heard a loud thud followed by a noisy commotion. There was a flurry of activity near the bar. People were shouting and Rithu heard someone call for an ambulance. She walked as fast as she could to the bar closely followed by Shriya. She tried to push her way through the people crowding the place, but there were too many people blocking her way. She heard someone wailing in pain.

Suddenly she heard someone shout, 'Hold his arms, pick him up slowly.'

'Hold his body, someone,' another voice called out.

Rithu saw Zia emerging out of the crowd and asked, 'What happened?' Just then, Sandesh Mehra, Raghuram, and Badhrudin joined her.

'Bloody freak accident,' Zia said, 'one of the huge speakers fell on one of our employees. Heavy piece of equipment just crashed on him. He was lucky it fell on his leg. Had it been his head, he would have been dead for sure.'

'Does it look bad?' Sandesh Mehra inquired.

'Looks pretty bad,' Zia replied. 'Maybe a broken leg.'

'Who was it?' Raghuram asked hesitantly.

Rithu, Badhrudin, and Sandesh turned in unison to look at Raghuram as Zia announced, 'Ram.'

'Oh God,' Raghuram said slowly, his face turning pale, 'the Gypsy's premonitions are coming true after all.'

'Don't be silly,' Badhrudin said, patting Raghuram on his back. 'This is just a coincidence. I am sure someone is trying to play the fool here. They just rigged John's promotion. Ram had been already drunk when he went on stage. I would have been surprised if he didn't break his leg.'

'You mean John was not supposed to be promoted?' Sandesh asked, surprised.

'No,' Rithu replied. 'If you don't mind me asking, who gave you the list?'

'I don't recall,' Sandesh replied. 'I thought your team handed it over to me.'

'Where is Alegeshan?' Raghuram asked, suddenly interrupting. He seemed shaken with the series of events unfolding.

'He left fifteen minutes back,' Badhrudin replied. 'Don't worry, he should be home by now. He has a driver, and a safe guy, for that matter—'

Badhrudin's phone rang and he fetched it from his shirt pocket. 'Speak of the devil,' Badhrudin remarked, 'that's Alegeshan on the phone.'

Badhrudin pressed the 'call accept' button and held the phone to his ear. Within the next couple of seconds, Rithu saw him turn pale. He turned away from them and asked a few questions. Rithu looked at Raghuram and saw that he looked terrified. She turned her attention to the group which had managed to move Ram to a makeshift bed made out of tables. The company doctor was attending to him. Thankfully, Ram didn't seem to be in much pain now, probably because he was hopelessly drunk. Rithu heard Badhrudin close the call and turned to face him.

Badhrudin seemed to hesitate momentarily before speaking. 'That was Alegeshan,' he said, weighing every word with caution. It seemed to Rithu that he was trying his best not to alarm anyone, but the way he spoke was only making Raghuram even more nervous. 'He is absolutely fine.'

'Why don't you tell us what happened?' Raghuram said, losing his cool.

Badhrudin turned to Raghuram and said, 'There is no cause for concern. Alegeshan is absolutely fine.'

'Did he meet with an accident?' Raghuram asked.

Badhrudin again took some time to reflect on the question. 'You can't call it an accident. Another car crashed into his car as the driver got out to open the gate to his house.'

Raghuram looked downcast and kept looking at the ground. He looked up to find Sheon standing by his side and asked him, 'Did you find the Gypsy woman?'

'No,' Sheon answered. 'Nobody saw her leave and I searched the whole place. She isn't in here either. I swear I have no idea—'

Raghuram held up his hand to stop Sheon from talking.

'I have a morning flight to Bangalore,' Raghuram informed the group, almost as if saying that he had been condemned to the gallows. The others nodded silently.

'What time is your meeting?' Badhrudin asked. Rithu found it strange that everyone had readily accepted Raghuram's fate.

'Evening,' Raghuram said sadly.

'Why not drive down?' Sandesh suggested.

'Good idea,' Badhrudin chipped in. 'Start at five in the morning and you are there before lunch.'

Raghuram seemed to like the idea too. His eyes lit up for an instant as he asked, 'Before lunch?'

'Of course,' Badhrudin replied, 'I drove down just last month. Took me all of seven hours to cover the six hundred kilometers. Roads are smooth like butter. It's an amazing drive.'

'I can spare you my driver and the Audi,' Sandesh added. 'That way you can relax and not worry about anything.'

'I will take that offer,' Raghuram added quickly, not wanting to let it pass.

'I think we shouldn't be reading into this Gypsy business too much,' Badhrudin added as a parting shot. 'Forget the whole thing and let us get back to the party.'

Raghuram, however, could not get the Gypsy out of his mind that night. He sulked all through the night at the party, glaring at Sheon every time Sheon happened to look at him.

'I want you to find out who the drunken idiot was who kept making those smart-ass comments when I was on stage,' he kept saying to the rest of the team. 'If I lay my hands on him, I will squeeze out every drop of liquor he has consumed, through his sweat glands.' Raghuram continued to rant till the end of the party.

Raghuram did not wait for the party to end and left for home much before the DJ had taken over the proceedings. Once he had reached home, he ensured that he personally locked the gates and the main door of his home as if he expected a plane to crash in from the main door. Though he retired to bed soon after, he hardly slept the whole night as an air force plane ran sorties almost till early morning.

Every time he shut his eyes, the Gypsy appeared and kept repeating, 'I see a plane.' He switched on the television and kept surfing the news channels without the faintest idea of what he was hoping to see. He finally decided to leave his bed at 4 a.m. and showered, trying his best to keep the Gypsy away from his thoughts. He got a call from Sandesh's driver at 5 a.m., announcing his arrival. He went down to see the white Audi A4 saloon waiting with a uniformed chauffeur. The chauffeur soon collected his bags and placed them in the spacious boot of the car.

'Let us take the ring road,' Raghuram announced to the surprised chauffeur. 'I need to check on something,' he lied, knowing well that the new route would add another forty-five kilometers to the route. Taking the ring road, however, ensured that he avoided the local airport completely. He was not ready to take any chances.

The two-liter TDI engine ensured that the Audi was a comfortable ride, but Raghuram was too preoccupied to enjoy it. He kept looking at the sky for any signs of low-flying aircraft. The first break was not taken until they had cleared quite a distance from the city limits. It was almost two hours when they finally stopped at a coffee shop. Raghuram kept reading the morning newspaper he had bought at the coffee shop as he drank coffee.

He scanned the paper for nothing in particular, and the only one article that caught his eye was in the international section, about a plane that had crashed into a hangar in Santa Monica airport. He studied the news over and over again, wondering if it had any hidden clues to his own fate. Before they finally left the coffee shop, Raghuram had a quick chat with the owner to check if there were any airfields for the next one hundred kilometers or so. Once he was thoroughly satisfied of the nonexistence of any airfields, he continued on the journey.

Back in the car, he kept up his vigil of looking out for any low-flying aircraft. He finally fell asleep and dreamt of a huge Airbus 320 that kept chasing him across the corridors of his office. He woke up with a start and realized that he had been sleeping for quite some time. His throat felt parched from the humidity of the air conditioning.

'Let's stop for a bite,' he told the chauffeur and pointed to a small restaurant by the roadside.

Raghuram quickly finished eating a small meal and waited outside the restaurant for the chauffeur, who was only halfway into his meal, to join him. He looked around and saw that there were hardly any buildings nearby. There was a bus stop a little distance away where a few people from the nearby village waited for the bus to arrive. Some children were playing by the roadside. A tractor made its way lazily across the fields behind the bus stop.

He noticed a cigarette kiosk across the road and decided to indulge in a rare smoke. He walked across and purchased a cigarette and placed it between his lips to light it when he heard the distinct sound of an airplane. He froze for a moment and felt the fear grip him.

With the cigarette still unlit, he stepped away from the cigarette kiosk. He looked at the sky to locate the plane, but he couldn't spot it in the sky. He could still hear the low droning sound of the engines of the plane. A trainer aircraft, perhaps? He kept his eyes on the sky, looking around to spot the potential killer.

He suddenly felt the urge to look at the road ahead of him and spotted the lone truck headed towards him. It was coming in the direction of the bus stop. And the very next instant he saw a small child walk in the path of the truck to pick up something.

And the sequence of events that followed seemed to happen in slow motion to Raghuram. From the distance, Raghuram could clearly see the look of surprise register on the truck driver's face as he spotted the child on the road. The truck driver realized that there was hardly any chance of stopping the juggernaut in time to avoid running over the child. He did the next best thing, to swerve the truck away from the child, only to realize that the new maneuver would only make the truck head straight into the people waiting for the bus. The truck driver made another sharp turn on the steering wheel and just about managed to move away from the crowd. The last thing the truck driver expected was to see a man with an unlit cigarette standing right in his path with a dazed expression.

The last thing Raghuram heard was the loud screeching sound of the truck as the driver slammed the brakes and then he felt the impact.

'This was not how the Gypsy had predicted it,' he thought.

He landed back on the road a few feet away a couple of seconds later.

Raghuram managed to open his eyes for a few seconds with a valiant effort. He could see the blood dripping from his torn eyebrow. People were gathering all around him. He could taste a mixture of dust and his own blood in his mouth. He scanned the faces of the people gathered around him, hoping to see someone who could help him, though he knew this was the end. And then his eye fell on the small boy who had run across the road. In his right hand, the boy clutched the toy he had run across to fetch from the middle of the road. A small toy plane.

Raghuram took a last look at the mother who held the boy in a tight embrace. Unmistakably the icy stare of the Gypsy woman.

# THE BIRTHDAY GIFT

When she woke up in the morning, the first thing she saw was the tray with breakfast laid out on it. By the side of it, on the coffee table, there was a huge orange envelope with the words 'Happy Birthday, Sweetheart' written on it. She wondered how long ago it had been placed there. She hadn't heard him come in; maybe he had slipped into her room in the dead of the night. After all, she couldn't recall when she had passed out the previous night.

She took another couple of moments to look at the envelope. She had decided that she would not bother opening the envelope. She hadn't opened such envelopes for the past many years and yet she knew exactly what was in it. Undoubtedly, it was a birthday card with a few corny romantic lines written on it by that man. Oh! She so hated it. Nothing changed around here. The same nonsense, repeated year after year.

She looked at her desktop calendar. November 25th. One more year older and another year wasted. She sighed. She did not wait to check under the cloche to see what was on the plates laid out for breakfast either. She knew. Nothing changed much around here, you see.

She got up from bed and walked into the washroom. Finally, her eyes fell on something new. Laid out on a clean blue hand towel was a brand-new toothbrush with toothpaste on it. Even the toothbrush was blue and matched the color of the paste. Her favorite color. This had not happened before.

As she brushed her teeth, she looked at herself in the mirror. She pushed back the gray hairs that were visible at the temples. She stopped brushing her teeth to wipe out the dark circles from underneath her eyes but they wouldn't go. She washed her face and her mouth until she couldn't taste the mint aftertaste anymore. She wiped her face with the towel and checked her face in the mirror once again. She didn't like what she saw. She threw the towel into the overflowing laundry bag.

She walked back into the bedroom and lifted the cloche to look at the breakfast laid out on the plates. As expected, two fried eggs, sunny side up, lay on the plate with four slices of crisp toast like she always loved. God, he was getting so predictable. There was a lump of fresh butter in a cup and beside it a bottle of Orange marmalade. Agreed, she loved to eat each one of the items laid out on the tray. But couldn't he change anything? She looked at the breakfast without any feeling. A pot of steaming hot coffee with a cup of milk and sugar in a bowl all lay in the tray.

She picked up the toasted bread and spread the butter, all the time reflecting on the same day fifteen years back, her birthday. She had turned eighteen that day, full of enthusiasm and without a care in the world. She had been studying for a diploma in arts. She met him for the first time at a restaurant where her friends had planned a surprise birthday party for her.

She took the first bite of the toast. It was crisp and crunchy. 'I love my toast to be as crispy as a biscuit,' she had told him fifteen years back when they had breakfast at a small café. They hadn't been married yet and had spent their first night together.

'Just like the one I am eating now,' she said. He had reached out to snatch the toast from her hand and taken a bite of the toast to taste it. He didn't like it one bit and thought it tasted like sawdust. He just shook his head without showing any expression and said he would have preferred it to be much softer.

Having finished the toast, she now focused on the egg. She started eating the egg white first without disturbing the yolk. As always, at the end in one scoop, she put the whole yolk into her mouth. As she savored the gooey taste of the yolk, she thought everything had seemed so perfect fifteen years back. She placed the fork and knife back on the plate and looked at the large envelope and picked it up. She read the line over and over again: 'Happy Birthday, Sweetheart'. She placed the envelope back from where she had picked it up. She was not going to open it this year either.

There was a time many years back when she used to look forward to these cards from him. Now, she didn't care. Her mind wandered back to the birthday party fifteen years back. The restaurant had been full of people. Her friends had booked a corner table to seat six but could only find three people besides her to fill in the chairs. She didn't mind because it was the first time anyone was celebrating her birthday. The fact that it was a surprise party was a bonus.

She had noticed him from the moment she had walked into the restaurant. He was the one who had never stopped looking at her. He was not part of her table but just happened to be there at the restaurant. He and his friends were celebrating winning a basketball tournament. He had won the best player of the tournament award. The trophy was still proudly displayed on their table.

As her friends sang the birthday song while she cut the pineapple cake, it was evident that at least one of the invitees to her birthday party did not even know her name. But she didn't care because she was busy looking at him from the corner of her eye. She even caught him lip-sync the birthday song. She smiled and blushed. She didn't know she could have that kind of effect on anybody.

As her friends plastered a part of the cake on her face, she kept looking at him and hoped that the cream would not leave her face looking oily. After all, she was the star of the day and had attracted an admirer.

After quite some time, just as the birthday party was about to wind up, he conjured up the courage to walk up to her and wished her a happy birthday. She watched him walk towards her, but looked elsewhere on purpose.

'Happy birthday,' he said softly so as not to startle her.

'Thank you,' she said, turning around and looking at his smiling face. She was surprised at how handsome he looked from close quarters. His broad shoulders and muscled arms made him look much more powerful than the boyish looks she had noticed at first.

'Do I know you?' she asked coyly.

'Not as yet,' he said, smiling. 'But you will.'

They had hardly talked for a brief amount of time and so she was taken aback when he offered her a gift. A trophy.

'What is this?' she asked, surprised.

'That is the best player award I won,' he said, smiling. 'This is very dear to me. But I want you to keep it for me.'

She blushed and said, 'I am sorry, but I can't take it from you.'

'In which case, can I take you?' he asked.

'Excuse me?' she asked.

'I said, can I take you out sometime?'

She looked at him for a long moment. He clasped his hands, dramatizing a gesture of pleading.

'Please don't say no,' he said.

She smiled and said, 'Only if you promise you will behave like a grown-up.'

She would have agreed to go out with him even if he hadn't promised to behave. He hurriedly jotted down her home phone number on a piece of tissue paper, but didn't call her for almost a week. Every day she went back home, the first thing she did was check with her mother if she had gotten a call.

'Did anyone call for me?' she asked her mother.

'Yes,' her mother replied, 'there was a call from the local library, seems you are expected to return the books you borrowed.'

'Anyone else?' she persisted.

'Not that I know of,' her mother said, trying to recall.

'Were you at home the whole day?' she asked.

'Can I afford to do that?' her mother asked. 'Who were you expecting a call from?'

'Never mind,' she replied to her mother, disappointed.

Every time she was home and the phone rang, she ran, dropping whatever she was doing. She found excuses not to leave home and even sleep near the phone. But the call she was waiting for did not come. She worried that he had lost her number. She visited the restaurant three times that week on some pretext or the other in the hope of seeing him there again.

She cursed herself that she had not taken his phone number. She had been extremely confident that he would call.

And then a week after she had first met him, the call came.

'Why didn't you call me earlier?' she asked.

'You were waiting for my call?' he asked, sounding surprised.

'That is because I have my exams starting this week,' she lied. 'The exams run for the entire month and that means we can't go out anywhere. I have a lot to study.'

'Uh-oh,' he said, sounding disappointed. 'I guess we will meet after your exams then.'

She had hoped that he would put up a fight, come up with alternative solutions rather than give in so easily.

'No, wait,' she said, 'actually we can meet before the exams.'

'We can?' he exclaimed. 'When?'

'Tomorrow,' she said, 'but I need to get back home early.'

'What time can I pick you up from home?' he asked, excited.

'Not my home,' she said quickly. She didn't want him to come to her home and see her one-bedroom apartment. 'Let us meet at the same restaurant where we first met.'

'What time?' he asked.

'At 7 p.m. and I need to be back home by 9.'

'Six,' he negotiated. 'Give me at least a couple of hours to know you.'

'All right,' she said. 'Six. But I have to be home by nine.'

The next day, she wore her favorite dress, the same one she had worn for her birthday, and looked at herself in the mirror. For a couple of minutes, her mind was clouded in doubt. 'What exactly did he see in me?' she asked.

She reached the restaurant at 6.15 p.m. She didn't want to be there earlier than him. She wanted him to wait a few minutes for her. But when she reached there, she did not find him. She waited till seven. 'What if he waited for me and left?' she wondered. 'Or did I get the timing mixed up?'

She thought she should wait for some more time. At 7.30 p.m., when she found the other guests in the restaurant throwing curious looks at her, she decided it was time for her to leave.

She looked at the coffee pot lying in front of her. She poured herself a cup and added the milk and sugar. She picked up the cup and took a sip. She heard the door open, but refused to look up and see who was entering. She knew it was him.

'Happy birthday, darling,' he said as he walked in. There was no excitement in his voice. He said it in such a sad monotonous way that he could as well have been saying 'Did you notice our dog died this morning?' But then she was aware that he knew she hated him. Hated? Despised, loathed, and abhorred were better suited.

She ignored him and continued to silently sip the coffee. She visualized his disappointed face as being slighted and smiled inwardly. He stood for a few moments, hoping she would look up at him. She did not. He silently placed a big gift wrapped box on the bed beside her.

'I have made a lunch reservation at the Tulips as usual,' he said. 'I will be waiting for you outside by one. I hope you will not disappoint me.'

She did not look up, but waited for him to leave the room. She heard him walk out and close the door behind him. 'Tulips as usual,' she mimicked him scornfully. She looked at the gift he had placed on the bed. She reached for it and lazily started to unwrap it, again fully aware as to the contents of the box. She was sure it would be a dress. She opened the box and was surely surprised by what lay inside it: that beautiful gown she had so much lusted for, ever since she saw it advertised in that magazine. But how the hell did he find out? she wondered. Had she left the page open in the magazine?

The next box contained matching shoes for the gown. And then she noticed something else which she had totally missed the first time. A bouquet of thirty-three red roses lay beside the box. Had it been there all the time or did he just bring it in now? After all, he always thought that he had his way with roses.

She recalled the day she went back disappointed after waiting for him at the restaurant; she had cried for two full days. Her mother had asked her what the matter was and she had not disclosed anything. On the third day early in the morning as she was ready to leave to write her exams, he appeared at her doorstep, his leg in a cast, and a bunch of roses in his hand.

She wanted to take her mind off her marriage and focus on something else. She collected the tray with a couple of pieces of toast still lying untouched. She opened the door and stepped out. She saw him sitting on the couch, speaking on the phone. He hadn't noticed her stepping out of her room.

'Yes, doctor,' he was saying. 'I did get the medicine.' After a long pause, he continued, 'I am trying my best, doctor, but nothing seems to be working.'

She waited near the kitchen sink, straining to hear the conversation. 'I understand, doctor. I know how important it is,' he reassured the person, and again after a couple of moments, he added, 'Trust me, I am at my wits' end, not knowing what else to do.'

She heard him reassure the person a couple of times more before he closed the call. 'Good day, doctor. I will keep you posted.'

Must be the psychiatrist, she thought. She placed the tray in the kitchen sink and looked at the bottles of whisky lying empty near the sink. She picked up one of the bottles, and for a moment, she pictured herself sneaking up behind him and smashing the bottle on his head. She visualized the shocked look on his face as he turned around, blood draining from his face and a scream escaping from his mouth. 'Depressed wife hits the bottle' would have seemed like a likely headline in the local newspaper.

She resisted the temptation and placed the bottle beside the sink. She walked back into her bedroom as silently as she had stepped out. She closed the door and walked to her wardrobe to find something to wear for the lunch. She decided that she would not wear the new blue gown. All her past birthdays, she had worn the new attire that he had brought her. Today she wouldn't.

She found a red top with bright yellow flowers. It had been quite some time since she had used the top. It was badly wrinkled and the color looked faded. That would do just fine. She picked out the first skirt that she could lay her hands on. Bottle green. It looked gaudy, but what the hell, she thought. 'I don't want to look attractive to him.' She selected a pair of black shoes to go with it. Nothing matched. Great. She wanted to embarrass him as much as possible.

Next stop, the shower. She undressed and walked into the shower cabin and opened the taps to let the icy-cold water hit her face. As she stood under the shower, she thought of their first visit to the psychiatrist. The interview had gone for more than an hour. The psychiatrist was a no-nonsense hard-nosed jerk. Hardly listened. Psychiatrists are supposed to listen, aren't they? That is what they get paid for. Bloody idiot. He had a stupid look on his face which screamed, 'I don't believe a word of what you are saying.' But then, can't blame him. Who would have?

All the time she spoke, she saw the shrink shake his head, his spectacles slipping down the bridge of his nose. He seemed to be taking notes all the time. What the hell was he writing? A novel?

She tried to clear her mind and think of something else. She tried to think of her mother. The day the doctor broke the news to her. The oncologist had also seemed so distant. There had been absolutely no expression on his face as he told her mother that her mother had only a few days left. Are these people real? Don't they understand feelings?

She closed the shower taps and continued to stand underneath the shower, catching the last trickle of water that dripped from it.

Much as she tried not to think of her husband, her thoughts kept going back to him. She remembered the time she had caught him speaking to her friend Rita near the library.

'Why do you have to speak to Rita?' she had questioned like a jealous lover.

'Rita just wanted some info about basketball,' he had defended himself.

'Don't give me crap,' she screamed. 'Rita doesn't play basketball.'

'She doesn't, but her brother does,' he retorted angrily. After a while, he sat beside her and held her hand. 'Look, you cannot get jealous every time I speak to a girl.'

'I can't help it,' she said. 'I fear you might leave me and go.'

'I will never leave you and go,' he replied and, after a moment, laughed and said, 'Good housemaids are hard to find.'

She punched him hard on his arm as he laughed and tried to evade her blows. She had chased him all around the park. If the psychiatrist had been one of those people who had witnessed them in the park, how the hell would he believe what was happening now?

She reached for the towel and dried herself. She went back to the bedroom and looked at the blue gown lying on the bed once again. It was indeed beautiful. She picked it up and tried it on. Even though the size was an XL, she had to struggle quite a bit to fit into it. She turned to admire at herself in the full-length mirror. Someone else would have looked beautiful in it. She removed it and settled for the skirt and top.

She looked at the alarm clock on her bedside table to check the time. It was five minutes past one. She could wait a few more minutes before she stepped out. 'Let him wait,' she thought.

She did not bother to put on any makeup. She just brushed her hair and looked one last time in the mirror. She looked pathetic and it suited her just fine. On her way out, she picked up the bunch of roses and dumped them in the wastepaper basket by her bedroom door.

When she closed the door and walked out of the house, he was waiting by the car. She saw the disappointment register in his face on seeing that she hadn't worn the blue gown. But he quickly recovered and walked to open the front passenger door for her. He still walked with a slight limp, a broken leg from the basketball game fifteen years back. Back then, he used to lean on her for support.

Even as he stood with the door open, she opened the rear passenger door and sat down. This time she saw the disappointed look linger for a longer time. She felt a sense of gratification. He closed the door and walked to the driver's seat.

The next twenty minutes of the drive were spent in silence. He looked at her in the rearview mirror a couple of times. Every time their eyes locked, she just turned her face away to look at the traffic. At one of the traffic signals, she saw a man with his leg in a cast being helped across the road by a young woman, and she was hit by a fresh torrent of memories.

After he had come to her house the first time, she had asked him how he knew where she stayed.

'You think I wouldn't have found out?' he asked, smiling. 'You are aware of my existence only for a week. I have been looking for an opportunity to meet you for so many months now.'

They went out the first time that evening. He was struggling on his crutches for most part of the evening as they went back to the same restaurant where they had met first. He wanted to go to a movie later, but she insisted that she had to go back home and study for the next exam. He insisted on dropping her back home, though she felt he had to get back home for some rest.

'Can we meet again tomorrow?' he asked her.

'I have to study,' she said reluctantly. She hoped he would be persistent.

'Can I watch you while you study?' he asked as she laughed, relieved.

'You will distract me,' she complained.

'I promise I won't,' he said, placing his hand on his heart.

'Don't you have to study?' she asked him.

'Yes,' he smiled. 'You?'

'No. Seriously,' she said, 'aren't you going to prepare for your exams?'

'What for?' he asked.

'You need a job. You need to earn money. You need to eat,' she laughed.

'Love is enough to see me through this life,' he laughed. She just marveled at his attitude.

He waited to hand over the car to the valet and saw her walking in without waiting for him. He walked briskly, wincing in pain even as he caught up with her. The doorman saluted as they reached the door. He smiled and patted the man on his back. She just ignored the doorman and kept walking.

Quite a few heads turned as they entered the restaurant. At 6' 3", his drop-dead handsome looks had that effect on people. But today was different. The patrons at the restaurant were quite curious to see the smartly dressed man accompanied by a sloppily dressed woman troop into the restaurant. Quite a few of them were amused when he walked to an empty table and pulled out a chair for her to sit and she ignored him and picked a different chair to settle down. He was aware that people had noticed. He quietly sat on the chair he had offered her.

'Ah, Mrs. and Mr. Rishi Verma!' the captain exclaimed, walking up to them. 'We are so delighted to have you back. Mrs. Verma, please accept our greetings for your birthday.'

'Thank you so much,' he replied to the captain. She couldn't understand the excitement in the captain's voice. *After all, they had met every year on the same day for quite a few years now.*

The captain did not wait for an acknowledgement from Mrs. Verma. He hadn't got one in the last so-many years. He knew he was not going to get one today either.

Shortly after, the captain personally ensured that his special guests were served the finest items on his menu. Curious guests, every once in a while, stole a glance at the odd couple eating their lunch in silence. Occasionally he would say something to her, only to find her totally disinterested and looking out of the window by their table. He kept serving her across the table and she neither refused nor acknowledged the servings. She left quite a bit of the dessert untouched.

Finally, when the bill arrived, he paid by credit card and ensured he had added a generous tip for the maître d'.

'Will we see you again next year same day, Mr. Verma?' the captain asked as they made their way out.

'Hopefully,' he replied to the captain, looking at his wife who was already walking towards the exit.

The next stop was the usual jewelry store on Park Street. As usual the sales manager greeted them by name and wished Mrs. Verma a happy birthday. He was greeted by the same stony silence that he always got in return. He led them to the section which housed the latest collection.

They were comfortably seated near the counter that displayed necklaces of different kinds by the usual salesman who had always attended to them in the past few years. The display window showcased necklaces with huge diamonds, some with precious stones embedded and some that took your breath away because of the sheer exquisite designing that had gone into making them.

The salesman removed the necklaces one after the other from the display cabinet and placed the jewellery on the table in front of them. As was the practice, the salesman would then wait for Mr. Rishi Verma to inspect them closely before showing the ones that caught his fancy to his wife. Mrs. Rishi Verma showed absolutely no interest in the proceedings and was more interested in the closed-circuit camera in the distance.

She speculated at this exercise in futility. Within the next twenty-four hours, the same jewelry would find its way back to some jeweler in the city, the money spent on a fanciful distraction.

He set aside a few pieces that looked interesting to him. He picked one of the necklaces and admired the craftsmanship before proceeding with the intention to place it around his wife's neck. At the last moment she turned her head away abruptly on purpose, of course, leaving him mortified, his hands still in the air.

He just looked around to check if anybody had noticed, quickly realizing that the salesman had purposefully looked away and got busy with adjusting the jewelry trays. A couple of other customers too looked away swiftly and got preoccupied with their own assortments.

'I wish you would choose one of them,' he said without looking at her. 'If not, we will spend endless hours here.'

She turned to look at the trays in front of her. Like him, she too wanted to end this charade as soon as possible. The salesman observed her as she picked a piece that looked the grandest of them all. Four layers of chains, every alternate layer embedded with rubies and diamonds. The message was clear. When it came to gold, she was choosing quantity over quality.

He turned to the salesman and asked, 'How much is that piece?' Any other customer would have flinched at hearing the price, but not him. After all, his father had left him an inheritance that would cover buying a similar piece every day for the next fifty years.

The set was gift-wrapped and handed over to the customer after he paid the amount partly by cash and the rest by credit card. By the time he signed the merchant's copy of the credit slip, she had already reached the exit.

The next stop was the movie theater not far from Park Street. In fact, with all the traffic on the road, they could have reached the theater faster on foot than by car. The usher led them to their designated seats. She would have preferred to sit somewhere far away from him, but the theater was full.

As soon as the lights went out, she took the opportunity to close her eyes and catch some sleep. Fifteen years back, they would have used the opportunity of sitting in a dark theater more productively. When she woke up, it was nearing intermission. The lights came on a few moments after she woke up. Much to her relief, he did not try to make small talk with her. He got up and left her sitting alone in her seat. He walked in after the movie had started, empty-handed. Some things have changed for sure. On earlier birthdays, he would have walked back with a bucket of corn and offered it to her. She wondered if he was finally giving up on her. She had not known him to do that.

She recalled two incidents that had happened before they got married.

The week her mother died of cancer, she had informed him that she had to go to Bangalore as she had landed a job there.

'Why do you need a job?' he had asked.

'You have a family inheritance,' she had reasoned, 'but my father left me nothing. I need the job. My mother was the only relative alive. Now that she is gone, who will take care of my needs?'

'You will live with me,' he had said. 'You won't need the job.'

She had refused to relent and had gone to Bangalore. Two days later, he showed up at her working women's hostel unannounced.

'What are you doing here?' she asked, a bit embarrassed as the other inmates came out one after the other on some excuse or the other just to take a look at him.

'I came to fetch you,' he said. 'Come back with me, you don't need to live here.'

She protested and he persisted. He rented a room in the starred hotel across the street. Every day in the morning, he showed up at her room and walked with her to her office. He took her out for lunch and tried to talk her out of her decision. In the evening, he was waiting for her outside her office to walk her back to the hostel.

Then one day he invited her to his room for dinner. She accepted with a resolve that she would convince him to return home.

'Why don't you understand that this job is important for me?' she asked as they had dinner in his room.

'And why don't you understand that I need you back home?' he asked.

She looked at him for a long time and asked, 'Will you ever give up on me?'

Early the next morning as she looked at him sleeping peacefully holding her hand, she decided to return with him.

A week after their return, she had wanted to meet his mother.

'I don't want you to meet my mother,' he had said. 'She will never approve of you.'

'If we get married, it will only be with your mothers' approval' she had insisted.

Two days later, she boarded a plane for the first time in her life after he had reluctantly agreed to take her to Jaipur, where his mother stayed in their ancestral home. All the way from the airport to his home, she kept asking him about his mother. His replies were either evasive or in monosyllables. It was very obvious that mother and son did not enjoy a loving relationship.

She wondered if she would be meeting his biological mother or his stepmother. However as the car entered the huge gates and rolled towards the palatial house across the acres of well-maintained lawns, she forgot all about his relationship with his mother and focused all her attention on trying not to show her astonishment.

She walked through the maze of corridors and rooms in a state of disbelief. The rich paintings, tasteful chandeliers, and wooden staircases made her stay appear surreal. Every night, the dinner at the huge dining table with numerous butlers trooping in and out, with the dishes she had only heard of and never tasted, made her wonder if she would wake up suddenly disappointed.

Every night, as she lay in his arms in his bedroom, she wondered if she should ask him what it was that he had seen in her. The only reason she stopped herself from asking him was that she was afraid he would realize what a mismatch they were. Early in the morning as she left his room, she was aware of the curious looks of disapproval the maids gave her.

Though she stayed at his home for three days, she never got to meet his mother for the first two. The first day, he took her to see his sprawling estates. The second was spent waiting in the hope that his mother would summon for her. His mother finally agreed to meet her on the third day, a few hours before their planned departure.

She had visualized meeting a plump stately woman with an arrogant attitude. She had seen the wedding album pictures of his mother, where his mother had looked quite on the healthier side. She was shocked to meet a frail old woman who turned out to be quite pale and weak. There was obvious tension between mother and son when they met. But the old woman had been quite polite to her.

'Don't marry him,' the old woman had said. 'You will regret it.'

How prophetic those words had turned out to be. They got married a week after his mother died.

She watched the movie from the intermission. It didn't take a genius to figure out the plot though. The female lead was having an affair without her husband's knowledge, or so she thought. The husband had all along been plotting to murder his unfaithful wife without her getting suspicious. He was taking her to fancy restaurants and buying her costly jewelry. She wondered if the movie had been deliberately selected to give her a message. However, she liked the ending because in an attempt to kill his wife, the husband ended up in a coffin. She almost broke into a jig when he slammed his fist in disappointment when the male lead died in the accident. Obviously he had not been expecting it and was totally disappointed by the twist in the tale.

For the first time in the day, she smiled openly because after the movie ended, she found many men brooding and women smiling in the theater.

She returned to the back seat of the car. Dinner was a takeaway from McDonald's, which she ate in the car itself. She felt thankful that the farce was finally coming to an end when he parked the car in the porch. She hurried to her bedroom and was about to close the door when he appeared at the door. She just left the door open and he walked in. He stood by her bed for what seemed to be a long moment to her. She looked at him with disdain as he struggled to say something. He was having trouble, not knowing how to start.

He changed his mind and decided to say 'Happy Birthday' instead. He had hardly finished saying it when his eyes fell on the roses lying in the dustbin. The usual responses of disappointment that she had seen appear so many times that day registered once again on his face. This time he did not make any attempt to conceal it, however.

He then looked at the orange envelope lying by her bedside. He picked it up to see that it was still unopened. He walked towards the dustbin and put it in along with the roses. He again paused for a moment after he reached for the door. She expected him to turn around and look at her. He didn't. He just walked out, closing the door softly behind him. She walked to the door and placed her ear on the door. She heard a door close in the hallway. Things could have been so different.

She lay down in bed, trying to clear her mind of the day's incidents. His mother kept appearing in her mind.

'Don't marry him,' the old woman had said. 'You will regret it.'

She did not know when she fell asleep.

She woke up with a stinging pain in her stomach. She opened her eyes to see him towering over her. She cuddled up to avoid the next blow and caught a glimpse of the alarm clock. It was 12.01.

'Bitch,' he screamed, raising his hand to strike her again, 'your birthday is over. Get back into the kitchen and clean up the mess.'

# DOUBLE WHAMMY

I f I had had any inkling of how the day would turn out, I would have stayed in bed.

I woke up on Saturday morning with a migraine. It must have been the party that I attended the day before. The music had been extremely loud, and though my wife suggested we leave early, I stayed around. I had kept away from parties for quite some time and getting to hang out with some old friends after a long time was the incentive. It was almost 3 a.m. by the time my wife finally managed to drag me away.

The drive back home was not very joyful. My wife, who usually never enjoyed these parties, was not at her cheerful best. I did try to make small conversation by asking a few questions, but most of the answers were in monosyllables, and that too with her looking out of the car window made me wonder as to whether I was sitting inside or outside the car.

And so that morning, I decided that discretion was better than disclosure and refrained from telling her of my splitting headache. I was relieved that it was the weekend and I did not have any pressing commitments outside my home. I did, however, silently curse myself that I hadn't heeded her warnings to make an early exit. I drank my morning coffee in silence, reading the newspaper, and it just didn't help that my son had the music channel on in the living room, listening to Bruno Mars, who was wreaking havoc in my mind.

I asked my son to tone it down a few decibels but nothing happened. My wife was obviously aware of my predicament and decided that a cheap thrill was better than a show of sympathy. She sat across from me, enjoying the show, faking interest in the magazine section of the newspaper.

I would have had to raise my voice several decibels above my competition, a certain Mr. Bruno Mars, to attract the attention of my son. I was certain that my wife would have been more than happy giving me an earful if I did so, and both Bruno Mars and I would have been no match for her in the vocal department.

I decided to suffer silently in the bedroom rather than live dangerously in the living room. I figured that a good afternoon siesta would hopefully cure me or there was always an early night retreat I could resort to. And so when I heard the phone vibrate, the rational part of me told me to resist the urge to check who was calling. The truth is I would have been richer than Bill Gates and stronger than Arnold Schwarzenegger if I only listened to my saner part. All right, I am exaggerating. At least I wouldn't have been suffering this damn headache if I had preferred to listen to the saner part.

The exploratory side won and I picked up the phone to check who was calling. It was not a number listed on my phone which intrigued me even more. Because of the weekend, I was sure no credit card or phone company was trying to sell me something I just didn't want. I took the bait as I accepted the call by sweeping my thumb across the display screen.

'Thank God, you picked up the phone,' a male voice said. 'I was wondering if I had offended you in any way.'

'Excuse me?' I asked, taken aback. 'Who is this?'

'Raj,' the caller introduced himself.

'Raj who?' I asked. I knew a hundred guys with the name Raj.

'Rajeev Chowdhary. St Anthony's School,' the caller announced.

'Bloody hell, you son of a gun!' I said, excited. 'Where the hell have you been, Raj? It's been over six years since I last saw you. And how the hell did you get my number?' I rattled on.

'One question at a time, mate,' Raj said, 'or would you rather have me answer them to your face?'

'You are in town?' I asked, surprised.

'Not exactly,' Raj said, 'but I will be reaching your city this evening. Do you know that there is a school reunion planned for tomorrow morning?'

'No,' I confessed. 'Nobody actually told me about any such plans.'

'That's because you don't keep in touch with any of your school friends,' Raj chided. 'It's on Facebook too.'

'I will check that out,' I replied.

'Are you in touch with anyone from school?' Raj inquired.

'Just Chaks,' I replied.

'Good old Chaks,' Raj said, a smile evident in the way he said it, 'still trying to lose weight, is he?'

'Lost the battle of the bulge long time back,' I laughed.

'Good.' Raj added, 'Let us meet up this evening then. Call Chaks too. Will SMS you the venue and time.'

Even before I managed to say 'Sure', the line went dead.

I smiled recollecting my last encounter with Raj. It had been for a schoolmate's wedding. Raj as usual had been in his element and had everyone splitting their sides, narrating our school escapades. He mimicked our English teacher to perfection as he recited his own version of *Romeo and Juliet*.

Only after I had put the phone down did the next predicament hit me. The smile quickly vanished from my face as I tried to figure out on how the hell I was going to convince my wife that I had another party to attend in the evening. Tell her the truth? Oh sure! Tell me more.

The more I thought of it, the throbbing in my head increased in intensity. I decided I would put it away for later. I reasoned that Raj was probably not really serious about the get-together. What if he forgot all about it and got busy? It had not happened before, but what if it did happen? No point making devious plans for a getaway now. I was anyway not good at scheming, at least not when I had a throbbing headache. I searched for my migraine tablets but couldn't find them in the medicine cabinet. Damn. Maybe my wife hid them to teach me a lesson.

The next thing I did was to text Chaks on Whatsapp. I thought it best to keep him prepared. The message I sent was 'Raj wants to meet us for dinner tonight.'

I got a message back from Chaks within a couple of seconds. 'Raj?'

I was typing my response and before I could press the send button, I received his next message. 'I get it. Rajeev from school. Venue?'

I had to erase my response before replying, 'No idea. Will keep you posted.'

I set the phone on my bedside table and pulled the window shades to block out any sunlight streaming into the room and lay down on my bed. I figured I could catch some shut-eye for an hour and hopefully the migraine wouldn't be there when I woke up. I wanted to take my mind away from the pain. I shifted my focus back onto Raj. Nice guy. He would treat everyone with a lot of respect and was ever ready to help anyone. Impeccable manners . . .

I woke up with a start. My wife was pulling the shades away, making as much noise as possible in the process. The sunlight streaming into the room made it hard for me to open my eyes. I blinked a hundred times to adjust my vision to the sudden brightness of the light. I slowly turned my gaze to the clock on the wall, still trying to adjust my vision—3 p.m. Damn, I had slept for a full four hours. I remembered that I hadn't had breakfast or lunch. My wife continued to move about the room, doing nothing in particular, at the same time making as much noise as possible. I was sure she was there with the sole purpose of waking me up. She did not look at me even once though, which made things worse. I could judge from the way she went about tidying the wardrobe that she was upset. I was sure that even a tiny whimper from my side would open the floodgates. Why do women overreact to everything? I was the guy suffering the headache after all.

I picked up the phone from the side table and looked at the display. Seven missed calls. Four of them were from Raj, two from Chaks, and one from my brother. There were also six messages. I decided to check the messages before returning calls.

The first one from my brother wanted to know why my wife was not taking calls on her mobile. I decided not to reply.

The next message was from Citibank stating that they had sent the latest bill with the amount and due date mentioned. They wanted me to please pay the minimum amount before the due date. 'Oh sure,' I muttered, which made my wife turn around and look at me for a second. She went back to attacking her wardrobe, disappointed that I was not making any attempts at a conversation with her.

The next three messages were from Raj. The first one was a link on Facebook to the school reunion. Half an hour later, he had messaged me 'Most flights delayed. Will keep you posted.' The last message was sent a few minutes back: 'Made a reservation at the Pavilion, time 7–10 p.m. Be there. No excuses.' I figured that his calls were obviously to inform me of the developments. They did not qualify for a call back.

The last message was from Chaks. 'Where are you? Why are you not picking up the phone? Call me back'. This qualified for a callback.

I got up from the bed and staggered to the washroom. My wife, I was sure, was watching me from the corner of her eye. I splashed some water on my face and realized how hungry I was. I stepped out of the washroom and silently proceeded to the dining room to find something for me to eat. There was nothing. I searched the refrigerator and the kitchen. Zilch. My wife was surely creating opportunities for me to go back to her and plead for forgiveness. Very soon I would have to devise some strategy to break the news to my wife that I would be partying alone one more night. I found some biscuits and bit into one of them. They tasted musty, nothing compared to the verbal onslaught my wife was waiting to dish out for me. Suddenly the biscuits tasted much better. I ate three of them quickly. I proceeded to call Chaks on his mobile.

'Why are you not answering calls?' Chaks asked 'Do you owe me any money?'

'Would I call you back if I did?' I countered.

'No,' he laughed. 'Where are we meeting?'

'I got a message from Raj saying he has made a table reservation at the Pavilion,' I replied.

'The Pavilion?' Chaks gasped. 'That bloody place is so damn costly. Are you paying?'

'No way,' I replied, 'I would be out of my mind. Maybe he will pay. Maybe we will split the bill.'

'Raj couldn't settle for something cheaper like the Garden Retreat or the Fern House?' Chaks said, a tad irritated.

'I think he chose the Pavilion because it is the closest to the airport,' I replied.

'How does that make a difference?' Chaks asked, surprised. 'We are not catching a plane to go meet him.'

'We are not, but he is,' I said. 'He is arriving only in the evening.'

'I see,' Chaks seemed to agree. 'What time?'

'The message said seven to ten,' I averred. 'I guess it means we meet by seven and leave by ten. That would be preferable.'

'Fine then. I will be there by seven,' Chaks said before cutting the call.

I walked to the bedroom, where my wife was still mauling her wardrobe. I pretended I was still on the line with somebody and continued talking to no one at the other end.

'I see your point,' I said to the nonexistent person, 'but can't we meet him some other day? Today seems difficult.'

I knew I had my wife's attention. Whatever it was that she was doing, her movements slowed down to eavesdrop on my conversation.

'That is a pity,' I said again, avoiding looking at her. 'He is leaving tomorrow early morning? So I guess we have to meet him today. All right, I will be there by seven. Bye,' I said, closing the nonexistent call. I looked at my wife. She plunged right back into the wardrobe and now she was managing to make enough sounds even by throwing some clothes around. I spent the rest of the day working on my laptop. That way, I could keep away from her glaring eyes.

By around half past six in the evening, the tension in the house had gotten worse. Unable to get back at me, my wife was picking on my son, who had the look of a fatigued soldier scampering for dear life from sustained enemy firing. He had a totally confused look, not knowing if he was getting fired at for something he had done or not done. My migraine had greatly reduced, probably in anticipation of the evening get-together.

I figured it was best to make a silent getaway from home and went about getting dressed without much fanfare. My wife had left the poor wardrobe alone and was now sitting on the bed with a book in her hand. I wondered if she was reading a book called *Ambush*. We were both aware of the slightest of moves we were making in the bedroom. She was watching me much like a patient hunter watches his prey before deciding on releasing the arrow.

I reached the door and made a loud statement to nobody in particular, 'I have an important meeting, I won't be home for dinner.' I quickly closed the door behind me and rushed out of the main door. I was quite relieved by the time I reached the elevator to go down. I got into the car and headed for the Pavilion, which was a good half-hour drive from my home.

The Pavilion is a lounge bar within a five-star hotel called Marquee. The Marquee is situated about a ten-minute drive from the airport, on a seven-acre plot of land. By the time I turned my car into the driveway, I noticed that there was a stream of cars already queuing to reach the porch of the Marquee and a majority of them were the high-end Jaguars, Audis, BMWs, or Mercedes. Surprisingly, even the cabs plying in and out of the hotel seemed to be high-end SUVs. Even a Land Cruiser or a Škoda Superb would have stuck out like a sore thumb in the parking lot. I was driving a Honda City and was well aware of sneering looks thrown in my direction. The valet who approached me to take charge of my Honda City gave it a contemptuous look, almost as if he would have to be rushed to the hospital for a tetanus shot just for touching my car. I was, however, smiling imagining the plight of Chaks as he drove in his immense bulk in a Suzuki Alto.

I entered the Marquee and found myself in a lobby which seemed more like a palace. To the left was the front desk and to my right was an open coffee shop. There was a life-size bronze statue of two horses at the center of the lobby. One of the horses was looking directly at me while the other busied itself grazing. Right behind the statue was an array of lifts, the ones you could see go right up to the topmost floor. The roof must have been a hundred feet up with a magnificent skylight. It certainly was the most impressive lobby I had ever seen in my life. I imagined that the effect must have been even more dazzling at daytime.

I found it rather strange that though there were many people in the lobby, they were talking in whispers. Since this was my first visit to the Marquee, I had to approach the front desk for directions to the Pavilion. I walked towards the front desk and waited for the assistant to acknowledge my presence.

'The Pavilion?' I asked and heard my voice boom across the lobby. I managed to attract unwanted attention. So that was the reason people were whispering in the lobby, I figured. Stupid place.

The assistant only pointed towards a huge door at the far end of the lobby. I noticed the huge signage just beside the door with the directions to the prestigious lounge. I had no idea how I had missed the board. I walked through the door and was greeted by a short flight of marbled stairway which led into a corridor. The stairway was flanked by a brass handrail, which seemed to have been freshly polished.

I managed to find my way through a maze of corridors and finally reached the Pavilion and was approached by the captain, who interrupted my passage into the restaurant.

'Do you have a reservation?' the captain asked.

'There is booking in the name of Raj. Table for three,' I said.

'Yes, sir,' the captain said, checking a log in front of him. 'Mr. Raj is waiting for the pleasure of your company.'

'You don't say,' I wanted to respond, but I didn't.

I walked into the restaurant and was struck by the opulence of the place. Each and every piece of furniture seemed to have been shipped in from Italy or Germany or wherever they made such fancy furniture. The walls and the furniture were bathed in just two colors of white and blue. Each and every light fitting should have cost a fortune, but it all seemed like money well spent.

I saw Chaks sitting on a settee facing me, his bulk unmistakable. He seemed to be putting on a few pounds every other time I met him. As I walked towards him, I spotted Raj seated comfortably opposite Chaks. Unlike Chaks, he hadn't changed much since the last time we met. He continued to look much younger than his age. Lean and fit, as most of the girls in school (or later, college) had described him.

I reached the table and Raj got up to greet me with a handshake.

'How are you doing, man?' he asked.

'Can't complain,' I replied. 'How about you?'

'I have seen better days,' Raj replied.

I laughed because that wasn't Raj's standard reply. I recalled the day he had broken his arm in a football match and we had gone visiting him at the hospital. 'Awesome,' he had replied when we had asked him how he felt. The day he flunked his math exam, the day our science teacher had caught him kissing a girl in one of the classrooms at the college (for which he later got suspended for three days), and the day someone stole his motorbike on the first day of work—the answer was always 'Awesome.'

I took my place beside Raj. There didn't seem enough space for me to sit beside Chaks anyway. I suddenly realized how hungry I was and asked, 'Have you ordered anything to eat? I am starving.'

'We were waiting for you to arrive,' Raj said and looked around for the maître d'.

I looked at Chaks, who was desperately trying to attract my attention with a short wave of his hand. He gestured to me with his eyes to take a look at the menu, made a quick gesture of scratching his index finger with his thumb, and widened his eyes. I understood that he was referring to the prices on the menu card. I nodded to him that I understood his concern and picked up the menu card and opened it to glance through. Chaks was bloody right. The damn place seemed two to three times more expensive than the costliest five-star restaurant in town.

As the maître d' appeared, Raj did not consult us on our preferences and made his own decisions on the choice of food. This was for me an encouraging sign as it meant that he would pick the tab. I was still unsure if Raj understood the implications of this daredevilry. Chaks too seemed to pick the signal as he quickly opted for a costlier whisky. I settled for a mojito. 'All the taste of the mojito without the alcohol,' the menu card described. A safe drink after a night of misadventure, I decided.

We discussed common friends and a few of our school adventures as we sat around, having our first couple of drinks. I noticed that Raj had a Cartier watch strapped to his wrist. Sure signs of affluence. Once the maître d' had departed, having served us a fresh round of drinks, I turned to Raj and asked, 'Where the hell did you disappear all these years, mate? The last time I remember we met must have been around six years back. It was for Joshua's brother's wedding, right?'

'Nope,' Raj replied, 'the last time we met was when we bumped into each other at that mall, I don't remember the name of the mall, and it's at that intersection near the Volvo showroom.'

'Disney mall?' I asked. 'I can't seem to recall that meeting. How long back was that?'

'Maybe five years back. Anyway, don't bother. We did meet quite a long time back,' Raj said, dismissing the topic. That was when my phone rang. I checked to see who was calling. It was my wife. Surely she had thought of something nasty to say. I was in two minds on taking the call.

'Isn't it strange . . .' Raj said, leaving the sentence hanging, waiting for us to react.

'What is strange?' Chaks questioned.

'Well, somebody travels a thousand miles to meet us, the mobile phone rings and our first instinct is to answer the phone.'

'So what do you suggest?' I asked, laughing.

'Next couple of hours you guys spend with me, the mobile phones remain switched off,' he said and proceeded to fetch his own Apple phone from his pocket. I watched Chaks as he reluctantly brought out his Nokia phone. It almost resembled a Mexican stand-off scene from a Hollywood movie, each of the three holding his phone and slowly placing it on the table after switching it off. We looked at each other and laughed.

'So what have you been up to?' Chaks asked Raj, eager to be the one to start off a conversation.

'Nothing much. Have been traveling the world. Been there, seen that, and done everything, kind of boring life,' Raj said, trying to sound as modest as possible. 'What about you?' he asked Chaks.

'I have my own business now,' Chaks replied, akin to a schoolboy showing off his new bicycle. 'We have a pharmaceutical dealership.'

'Great,' Raj replied, 'what were you doing earlier?'

'I had another business dealing in plastic furniture,' Chaks replied a bit sheepishly. I knew that Chaks had been moving from business to business for quite some time now. Not much had been working for him, primarily because he had involved too many of his relatives in the businesses. He had tried his hand at quite a few things from real estate to auto parts dealerships. He was plain lucky that his wife had inherited a fortune from one of her maternal uncles.

'And before that?' Raj persisted.

I was not sure if Raj was getting cheeky at Chaks discomfiture or he was genuinely interested.

'What do you mean by traveling the world?' I butted in, much to Chaks' relief. 'Six years back, you were working for a multinational bank in Delhi.'

'Quite a story,' Raj replied. 'Will tell you more in some time. How about you?' he asked, turning to me.

'I am a trainer,' I replied.

'That's good,' Raj said.

'Not exactly,' I replied. 'Training is much like insurance. When the revenues are down, the first things companies do are cutting down on training. So our corporate training division isn't exactly on fire.'

Raj just nodded sympathetically.

'We also do a lot of public programs,' I quickly replied, not wanting him to think I was struggling. 'That keeps the fire burning. Anyway, that is only part of it. I am on the verge of finishing my book.'

'A book?' Raj asked, pleasantly surprised. 'What is it about? Self-improvement, motivational stuff, I presume.'

'Not exactly,' I replied. 'I am writing fiction. Short stories, in fact.'

'That's nice,' Raj replied. 'What sort of short stories?'

I paused for effect. 'Sort of thriller meets supernatural stuff.' I was not sure I was making sense.

Raj nodded in appreciation. 'So you write thriller-meets-supernatural stuff. Hmm.' He was merely repeating what I had said.

However, I soon spotted Raj suppressing a smile. Chaks too noticed it.

'What is it?' Chaks asked.

'Nothing,' Raj replied, biting his upper lip. 'I was just wondering if I should share a real-life story of mine. Maybe it will become a story in your book.'

I noticed Chaks' eyebrow rise up high on his forehead and realized that my expression was quite similar.

'Caught your interest, didn't I?' Raj laughed, looking at us both.

I was again unsure if Raj was leading me or he really had an interesting tale to tell.

'Try me,' I replied. 'I am always a sucker for good stories.'

Raj looked at Chaks, almost as if he was taking Chaks' permission to tell the story.

'Is this a ghost story?' Chaks asked 'As in supernatural stuff?'

'What is supernatural?' Raj retorted 'Some people say there is a scientific explanation for everything. There are a hundred different concepts in the supernatural. Which ones have you heard of?'

'I have heard of ghosts, spontaneous combustion, moth man, Yeti, little people, alien abduction, and so many more.' I added, 'There are new ones being identified just about every other day.'

'I had an uncle who claims to have missed an entire day in his life,' Chaks contributed. 'He had no memory of what he did that day. To date, we haven't found out what happened.'

'Interesting,' Raj averred. 'Actually, I am not surprised. The way we lead our lives, we sometimes have no idea what we did for an entire week.'

'So what is your story about?' I persisted, 'Ghosts? Or something else?'

'You decide,' Raj replied. 'I am not sure what name you could give to this story: ghost story, paranormal story, supernatural story. All I know is that this is a true story and it revolves around a certain Rajeev Chowdhary.'

'Can I take some notes while you tell us the story?' I asked 'You never know when a good story comes by.'

'Will I get a royalty from your sales?' Raj asked and laughed. 'I was just joking. By all means, do take notes.'

I looked around, searching for tissue paper to scribble on but the Pavilion only laid out fabric napkins of the satin variety.

I signaled to the maître d' and requested a few sheets of paper. I wondered if they would bill us for the paper too. As we waited for him to return with the paper, I turned to Raj and asked, 'How the hell did you get my number?'

'Somebody gave it to me,' Raj said, waving his hands to dismiss the topic.

'Who?' I insisted.

'That is not important,' Raj replied. 'Actually, the truth is I forgot where I got your number from.'

I figured Raj was not too keen to continue the conversation. He clearly did not want to tell me where he got my phone number from. I wondered why.

'I visited the link and registered,' I told Raj, hoping to change the subject.

'Which link?' Raj asked, surprised.

'The Facebook link on tomorrow's school reunion invite,' I reminded him. 'Aren't you coming?'

'Of course the school reunion,' Raj replied. 'Yes, I am indeed coming.'

'I also sent the link to you,' I told Chaks. 'The reunion is tomorrow morning at eleven. At the school itself.'

The maître d' returned with three A4-size sheets and placed them in front of me. Raj took the opportunity to order another round of drinks for us.

'Where is the food?' he questioned the maître d'.

'Will be here in a moment, gentlemen,' the maître d' replied before moving away.

I spread out the sheets in front of me and waited for Raj to speak, much like a reporter on a first assignment, waiting for some juicy tidbits from a movie star.

'Can't wait, eh?' Raj asked, punching me in the arm.

'We might as well get it out of the way,' Chaks informed him.

Raj looked at his glass and took out the remainder of his drink in one gulp. I wondered if narrating the story was making him nervous.

'If it is something you are not comfortable sharing, then it's okay,' I said softly.

'No. Not at all,' Raj laughed. 'I was just wondering where to start and how to narrate the whole incident.'

Our next round of drinks arrived and Raj ordered a repeat.

'While you listen to the story, I just want you to go with me and not ask any questions,' Raj said, 'because if you interrupt me, then the flow will be lost. So just bear with me,' he requested.

Chaks and I just nodded in agreement.

Raj picked up his next glass of liquor, looked at it lovingly, brought the goblet up to his nose, smelled the aroma, and proceeded to down it in one go. Chaks gasped because this time, he had not added any water or ice to the drink. It must have really burnt his throat. But Raj did not even flinch for a moment. Two things struck me. One, Raj seemed a tad bit nervous, and more importantly, to me it was seeing 1,500 bucks disappearing in one gulp.

'Remember, I was working for this multinational bank sometime back?' Raj started and, without waiting for an answer, continued, 'I was heading the division for secured and unsecured loans. This would include loans given out under various categories like home, vehicle, personal, etc. It also included the credit cards.'

I quickly started to jot down some of the important points for my future reference. Raj was considerate enough not to keep rattling his story and wanted to give me time to take notes. The next round of drinks had arrived and Raj signaled for a repeat of his drink. I marveled at the speed of service at the hotel. Chaks did not want to be left behind and started gulping down the remainder of his drink. He too ordered for his next round, much to the glee of the maître d'. The munchies too had arrived to my great relief, but the quantities seemed hardly enough for three people to feed off a single plate. The bloody restaurant was turning out to be a rip-off.

'You understand the responsibility associated with the job?' Raj asked and, again without waiting for an answer, continued, 'The portfolio was worth millions of rupees. Earlier I told you that I had been to places, this story is exactly about that. Six years back . . . do you mind if I tell you this story as a third person would?' Raj asked.

'As with?' I asked.

'I will narrate it as if I am one of the characters in the story. I will not refer to myself as "I" but as "Raj". That way the story will be clearer and if you do intend to include this story, it will be much easier for you to narrate it,' Raj said.

'Anything that suits you,' I replied.

'Thanks,' Raj said and started. 'Raj was about to complete his seventh year at the bank with a couple of months to go.'

'Raj, as in you?' Chaks asked, sounding a bit confused. I thought the drink was getting to him.

'Yes,' Raj continued, happy that we were getting the drift. 'The seventh year is an extremely important milestone at the bank where Raj worked because as per the company contract, on the completion of the seventh year, Raj stood to gain a huge amount as a loyalty bonus. Also, the company would be obliged to give a huge increment in the salary and perks. However, there were a few clauses relating to profitability and stability of the bank, which had been incorporated in the work contract. Raj had ensured even these were under control. And so it came as a surprise when the management without a warning filed a legal case against Raj a few days before Raj completed his seventh year.'

'Hold it,' I said, quickly capturing as much as I could on the paper. 'Could you repeat that last part again?'

'The bank filed a legal case against Raj,' Raj repeated.

'But that is you,' Chaks said, confused, still not getting a grip of the narration.

'Yeah, yeah,' I replied, trying to silence Chaks, 'why did the bank file a legal case against Raj?'

'But he is Raj,' Chaks said, pointing to Raj and taking a big gulp from his glass. The next round of drinks arrived.

'First indications pointed to foul play on the bank's side,' Raj continued. 'Raj was immediately suspended from his job pending investigation. Raj even approached one of the best lawyers to represent him. The case was pertaining to disbursement of lakhs of rupees in loan on the basis of fraudulent documents or in some cases no documents at all.'

'How can that happen?' I asked.

'Some policies of the bank were questionable,' Raj said, sipping from his fresh supply of whisky. 'In some rare instances, the bank relied on completing the paperwork after the loans were disbursed. This was especially done for customers who had a proven track record with the bank.'

'Is that permitted?' I asked.

'Not exactly,' Raj said, 'but every bank does it. There is a lot of competition out there and time is money. If one bank doesn't oblige, another will.'

'Sad,' I reflected.

'Why?' Raj asked. 'What is wrong with that?'

'I said sad because every time I went for a loan, banks have found reasons to increase the paperwork and reject the loan on flimsy grounds.'

Raj laughed. 'However, what really came as a shocker was that Raj had approved a huge number of credit cards and personal loans for the employees of a certain BPO which had no previous history of any transactions with the bank,' Raj continued. 'The company in question was a rank newcomer with absolutely no credit history whatsoever with any bank. Evidence pointed to a scam pulled off by Raj in collusion with a fraudulent corporate.'

'What was the evidence?' I questioned.

'Can we continue after I visit the porcelain goddess?' Raj asked.

'Visit whom?' I asked.

'The good old loo, my friend,' Raj laughed. 'And while I am at it, mind ordering us a couple more of the drink?' he said, pointing to Chaks and himself.

'I will have a couple more too,' Chaks said, his voice rising a bit. The people from a nearby table turned to look at us. I was embarrassed, but Raj seemed to be enjoying the show.

As soon as Raj left, I ordered each of them a drink, but Chaks insisted that Raj had asked for two and so requested the maître d' to double the order.

'Watch out, Chaks,' I cautioned. 'I think you have hit the limit.'

'You have no idea of my limit,' Chaks argued. 'I can drink a whole bottle and still be as steady as a rock. It is that guy I am worried about.'

'Who? Raj?' I asked. 'But he seems perfectly okay to me.'

'Then why does he keep referring to himself in the third person?' Chaks asked. 'Moreover, he didn't even recognize me when I met him here. I had to tell him who I was.'

I was not surprised. Anyone who had met Chaks five years back wouldn't be able to recognize him. Actually, even two years was enough. The alacrity with which he was putting on weight month after month and year after year was disturbing.

'I had to repeat my name four to five times for him to remember me,' Chaks continued. And that got me suddenly wondering what Chaks' real name was. I scratched my head to recall his real name. We had called him Chaks all our life and it stuck. Even fifteen years ago when there were no mobile phones and I had to reach Chaks on his office landline, I had just said I wanted to speak to Chaks and he came on the line. The problem was that his name was a tongue-twister. No wonder Raj must have got truly confused.

Raj returned a few moments after the next round of drinks had arrived. He straight away downed one of the glasses before even saying a word. Damn, he must have been dehydrated with the short walk to the washroom. He saw my surprised look and said, laughing, 'Never dilute a good whiskey.'

'The story,' I reminded him as he carefully selected a piece of butterfish and nibbled at it.

'On the face of it, everything looked like Raj was involved in a huge financial scandal,' Raj continued, 'but surprisingly the allegations did not stick. The signatures were proved as frauds though the management did argue that no two signatures of the same person ever tallied and all that stuff. Pending investigation, Rajeev Chowdhary was reinstated with full honors.'

I was a tad disappointed with the story.

'So, what is so surreal about this story?' Chaks asked. 'Somebody suspected you of forgery and couldn't prove it.'

'The story continues, my friend,' Raj said, smiling. 'Because Raj was the head of the division, his job entailed travel all over India. Raj traveled close to twenty days every month. Nothing untoward happened for close to two months and then all hell broke loose. A series of allegations broke out across the country. Raj had approved a loan in Mumbai and then Kolkata, Chennai, Bangalore, Jaipur, Jamshedpur, Cochin. Every place Raj had visited in the previous two months, there were allegations flying about how Raj had defrauded the bank. The modus operandi was the same. Raj would approve a loan for an unknown company without any documents. In a couple of cases, there were eyewitnesses who claimed that Raj had personally approved the file by signing in front of them.'

'How—' I started to ask, but Raj held up his hand to remind me of our agreement not to ask questions.

'Raj visited each and every one of these places to investigate the allegations. He discovered that there was indeed a pattern to all the cases. The cases were approved on the day Raj was leaving for the next town. In fact, a few minutes before closing hours. Signatures were a close match; however, there were a few minor differences—a dot here or a line there, which never appeared in any of Raj's genuine signatures. People argued that they might have been put in there deliberately by Raj to mislead later investigations.'

I requested that Raj pause so that I could take notes. Raj took the opportunity to down another drink, and I had lost count of the number of drinks he had already taken. Chaks had sensibly decided not to compete with Raj and was now taking smaller sips of his brew.

I looked at the notes I had scribbled and, reasonably satisfied that I had captured most of it, said, 'Please continue.'

'Luckily for Raj, there were gaps in every allegation that was leveled against Raj,' Raj continued.

'How can that be?' I asked. 'You said some people claimed Raj signed approvals right in front of them.'

'That is what makes this case interesting,' Raj smiled. 'People who claimed that they had seen him sign documents were unable to produce the signed documents. In most other cases, there was no evidence to track it back to Raj. No money trail. Zilch. The companies which were the beneficiaries simply vanished without a trace. The bank checked on Raj's lifestyle for any anomalies. They found nothing. No fancy cars, no new asset purchases. Nothing.'

My gaze unconsciously fell on the Cartier watch Raj was wearing. As a reflex reaction, Raj immediately covered it up with his shirt sleeve. It was an embarrassing moment for both of us.

'The losses were estimated to be in the range of crores of rupees,' Raj continued, quickly recovering from the momentary awkwardness. 'The first thing Raj did was to send out a memo to all the branches under him with a list of strict dos and don'ts on the loan documentation policy. As an afterthought, he added a postscript stating that should he even personally recommend a case, the files were to be cleared and the funds disbursed only after following the required protocols.'

Raj paused again for me to take notes. I knew the story had more to come. I waited for Raj to continue.

'It took Raj three months to clear each and every case, which included face-to-face interviews with people involved and tons of paperwork. For a couple of months, things seemed to fall in place and then came the clincher.'

I braced myself in anticipation as Raj paused to sip his drink. Chaks was feigning keen interest in the proceedings. I realized that he was not able to follow most of what was being narrated by Raj.

'Raj took a holiday to visit Singapore,' Raj continued. 'As was his usual practice every time he visited Singapore, he made a courtesy call at the Singapore branch of his bank. One month after his visit, an audit threw up a curious case. A check for 10,000 Singapore dollars was detected to be a fraud. The bank clerk clearly remembered Raj personally encashing the check in the branch. The clerk knew Raj as a high-level employee who worked in the Indian division of the bank and claimed to have met Raj numerous times. He recalled that Raj had stated that the account belonged to a close friend of his and the teller had matched the signatures and found nothing amiss.'

'If everything was in order, then what was the fraud all about?' I asked, sitting up.

'The account holder did not authorize the withdrawal,' Raj said. 'The instrument itself was forged.'

'My God,' I said.

'The bank immediately contacted the Indian operations head and alerted him of the situation. It seemed they had clear evidence this time of Raj's involvement. The closed-circuit cameras installed in the bank captured Raj's interaction with the teller and the bank clerk. The final nail in the coffin was images of Raj collecting the 10,000 dollars and placing them in his wallet.'

I had stopped writing for the last few minutes. I looked at Raj and wondered where this was all heading. There was no mention of ghosts or anything supernatural. At best this seemed to be a confession from Raj. I waited for something to build up and it came suddenly.

'There was a twist in the tale though. The transaction took place on the 15th of September evening. Raj was in Singapore from the 12th to the 19th September. He had visited the bank the first time on 14th September. However, on 15th September, Raj was involved in a minor accident. He had come out of his service apartment and was crossing the street when a cab rammed into him, fracturing his right leg. All through the day, Raj was in the Raffles hospital on the North Bridge Road. He also had the police records to back it up as a police constable was with him during the entire time.'

'Then how the hell did all this happen?' I asked.

'You tell me,' Raj said, smiling. 'You are the expert on paranormal stuff.'

'Multiple personality disorder?' I asked.

'Is that bad?' Chaks asked eagerly chipping into the conversation.

'Not if all of them are earning,' Raj laughed. 'No. Multiple personality disorder cannot account for one person being in two places at the same time. That too, almost fifteen miles apart.

However, I have heard of something called a doppelgänger or fetch.'

'What is that?' Chaks asked, surprised.

'A doppelgänger is a person's exact double,' Raj informed him. 'If you research, you will see enough of it mentioned in paranormal blogs. Several people have claimed to see a person in one location when the person was in a different place altogether. There are a few such incidents when the double displayed characteristics or behavioral traits in direct contrast to the original.'

'Unbelievable,' I said.

'Isn't it?' Raj asked. 'Do you know that some people have actually had the experience of having seen themselves. Imagine you saw the next person who walked in through that door,' he said, pointing to the entrance, 'looked exactly like you.'

I looked at the entrance and shrugged. I wondered if there was my exact double lurking out there somewhere. Seemed highly improbable. Even if he was there and my wife happened to meet him, she would have ensured that he ran away.

'In fact, your doppelgänger might just be sitting right behind you' Raj said to Chaks. Chaks turned around to check. I wondered what Chaks' mirror image would be like. The thought, I should admit, was mildly amusing.

'Is there any proof for this stuff?' Chaks asked, equally disturbed from the talk of doppelgängers.

'Abraham Lincoln, Guy de Maupassant, Queen Elizabeth I, and an English poet, Percy Bysshe Shelley, have claimed to have seen their own doppelgängers. John Donne claimed to have seen the doppelgänger of his wife, while the owner of Penguin India, Ravi Singh, claimed to have seen one of the author Ruskin Bond,' Raj said.

'No. I meant is there proof of your doppelgänger?' Chaks clarified.

'The images captured on close-circuit cameras in the bank at Singapore,' Raj informed him, 'I guess that is the proof. Interestingly, though doppelgängers were originally believed to have been evil, none of the recorded experiences seem to suggest anything sinister about them. A word of caution, however, is that seeing one's own doppelgänger is a harbinger of death.'

'Quite an amazing story, I must agree,' I said, 'so how does it end?'

'Mr. Raj quit the bank six months back,' Raj said. 'Don't you think that is a decent ending?'

Chaks shook his head in agreement. Raj smiled and looked at his watch. 'Time to go,' he informed us. 'Dinner?'

I felt quite full with all the munchies I had been gobbling down all evening. 'Not for me,' I informed him.

'I have dinner waiting at home' Chaks announced.

Raj called for the bill. I guess that was the signal Chaks was waiting for. Chaks got up and excused himself to go to the washroom.

I looked through the notes. There was definitely a story in those pages.

'So we meet tomorrow morning,' I said to Raj. 'Just in case I need some more clarifications to include in the story, can I get them tomorrow?'

Raj just nodded his head and asked, 'So you decided to include it?'

'Let us see how it develops,' I said. That is when the bill arrived.

A few minutes later, I went to the washroom. I switched on my mobile phone and waited for it to boot as I too worshipped the porcelain goddess, as Raj would have put it. As I walked back to the table, both Raj and Chaks were ready to leave. We walked to the entrance as Raj dialed someone on his phone. I heard a few message alerts sounding on my phone.

'Main entrance and make it fast.' Turning to us, he said, 'That was the cab driver I called.'

'I assumed that you were staying in this hotel,' I told Raj.

'You must be out of your mind,' Raj said, laughing. 'This place is too damn costly.'

By the time we reached the entrance, Raj's cab was waiting for him. He said a quick goodbye as Chaks and I handed over our valet tokens to the valet.

We saw Raj getting into the cab and driving away. I took out my phone to check the messages.

The first one was from my wife.

I cringed as I read it. 'Thank you for forgetting my birthday,' it said. Bloody hell. That explained why she had been so upset since morning. I did not even wish her a happy birthday, forget buying her a gift. That, I thought, had made the night so much nastier.

And then Chaks, who was still looking at Raj's cab making its final turn near the gates, turned to me and said, 'Do you know, he fell short of money to pay the bill? I loaned him ten grand, which he promised to pay tomorrow.'

I froze in shock, not knowing how to react. Which news do I break first? The fact that I was the one who paid the bill amounting to 25,672 with my credit card, because Raj had said that he had forgotten his wallet, or the message that I had received on my phone? I read it once again in sheer disbelief.

'Tried to call you. Your phone was off. My flight is canceled. Will meet you tomorrow. Take care. Raj.'

# THE OUIJA BOARD

'What, according to you, will be evidence that the Ouija board is not a hoax?' Parvathi asked, gritting her teeth.

'You tell me,' Kyra challenged. 'You seem to be the one wanting to so desperately prove it.'

'I don't care a damn whether you believe in it or not,' Parvathi said. 'I am not here to convince you.'

Rahela and Nadia exchanged nervous glances. This was the third time this week that an argument had started between the girls. It was only Wednesday and it seemed like it was going to be a long week ahead.

'Girls, come on, everybody is watching us,' Rahela said, looking apprehensive.

Parvathi kept glaring at Kyra. Kyra broke eye contact to look around and found Rahela was right. Quite a few of the students gathered at the symposium were looking in their direction.

'You both fight at the slightest provocation,' Nadia said.

'I can't help it' Kyra said, avoiding Parvathi's glare. 'She does come up with a load of crap these days ever since she started playing silly board games.'

'The Ouija board is not just another silly board game,' Parvathi contested. 'It is just that you don't have any understanding of it.'

'Listen, Parvathi,' Kyra said finally, locking eyes with Parvathi. 'I know you had a couple of tragedies in your life—'

'Let's not talk about that now,' Rahela pleaded, knowing very well that it was an invitation for a full-fledged assault.

'Rahela is absolutely right,' Nadia asserted, ensuring Kyra backed down.

'Whatever!' Kyra said, putting her hands up in frustration. After all, she thought that she was trying to help Parvathi to cope with her issues. A couple of minutes of uncomfortable silence followed.

'Let us finish with the symposium first,' Nadia said, taking the lead to break the silence. 'I believe the speakers are good.'

In the auditorium, Parvathi and Kyra ensured that Rahela and Nadira were seated between them. This ensured no further clashes ensued during the short breaks.

Seeing the persistent icy stares Parvathi and Kyra were giving each other in the auditorium cafeteria, Nadira broached the topic again.

'Look, this can't go on,' she said, looking at the girls. 'We have one more year of our postgraduate studies left, and if we keep fighting like this, it won't be fun, I promise you.'

'So what do you suggest we do?' Kyra asked. 'Accept blindly that the Ouija board is for real?'

'Nobody said that,' Nadira interjected quickly, not wanting another unnecessary complication. 'I suggest we experience the Ouija board firsthand.'

Rahela looked at Nadira, wide-eyed.

'Are you serious?' she asked, half amused, half apprehensive.

'Yes,' Nadira replied.

'I am ready anytime,' Parvathi said.

'I am not,' Kyra said. 'I don't believe in this and—'

'Then quit talking about it, chicken head,' Parvathi mocked.

'Enough,' Nadira said, turning to Kyra. 'If you don't believe it or experience it, you have no business to comment on it.'

Kyra considered the comment. She looked at Rahela, who was waiting eagerly to see how Kyra would react.

'All right,' Kyra responded cautiously, 'I accept on one condition. It should be a wager.'

'Wager?' Nadira and Rahela asked in unison. Kyra saw that she had interested Parvathi too, only Parvathi was not willing to show it.

'Yeah,' Kyra said. 'If Parvathi wins, I will never say a word again when she talks about the Ouija board. On the other hand, if I win, she should publicly acknowledge that the Ouija board is a hoax.'

Rahela and Nadira now turned their attention to Parvathi, who seemed to be seriously considering the proposal with pursed lips.

'Why should only I publicly acknowledge my defeat?' she asked, looking at the three of them. 'If Kyra loses the wager, even she should publicly acknowledge defeat.'

'Fair enough,' Rahela said as Nadira nodded in approval. 'Let's make it more interesting. The loser gives us a treat,' she added, laughing.

'Bull,' Kyra and Parvathi said in unison, finally agreeing on something.

'So, how do we go about this?' Parvathi asked.

'Simple,' Rahela said, already excited at the prospect of experiencing the Ouija board, 'ask a question about the future and if you get the answer for it, we agree that the Ouija board is not a hoax.'

'I suspect it is not going to be as simple as that, Rahela,' Nadira said, looking at Kyra and Parvathi.

Parvathi did not offer any suggestions. She knew that Kyra would come up with something that would be as comprehensive and complicated as it could be made out. She was waiting for Kyra to speak.

'I need to think this over,' Kyra said. 'Give me a day and I will work this out.'

Parvathi smiled in anticipation. She couldn't wait to see what Kyra would come up with.

'I understand that you already know how to do this Ouija board thingy?' Nadira asked Parvathi.

Parvathi nodded.

'Do you have one of those boards?' Rahela asked, excited.

'Yes,' Parvathi smiled, looking at Rahela's infectious excitement.

'So that is settled,' Nadira said, bringing the discussion to a close, 'we meet tomorrow to discuss the finer details.'

Rahela and Parvathi decided to walk back to their homes and Kyra offered to drop Nadira back home on her scooter.

'I am so excited,' Rahela screamed, jumping to try and grab the branch of a nearby tree after Kyra had left with Nadira.

'Shh,' Parvathi said, trying to calm her down, 'calm down, and never pull the branches of a tree. It hurts them.'

'You really mean it?' Rahela asked.

'Yes,' Parvathi replied, 'even trees have feelings. They are very sensitive.'

Rahela turned and started to talk to the tree. 'I am sorry, my dear tree. I didn't mean to hurt you. I hope you understand that.'

Parvathi laughed and gently pulled Rahela to walk with her.

'That was more for you than the tree,' Rahela said, turning to Parvathi and studying her face in the streetlight's illumination. 'I know you are very sensitive, Parvathi. I like that quality in you. I think you are extremely sweet.'

Parvathi laughed and placed her hand over Rahela's shoulder to draw her close.

'The feeling is mutual, sweetie,' Parvathi said. 'But I am not too sensitive when it comes to Kyra, I am sure.'

'I am sure she doesn't mean bad,' Rahela said. 'It's just that she has been brought up that way. She has her problems. I heard her parents are headed for a divorce.'

'I understand,' Parvathi agreed, 'though I doubt she does. I bet she thinks that I hate her. She will be disappointed when she finds out that I don't dislike her.'

'I know,' Rahela said. 'However, she shouldn't have been so insensitive talking about your past like that.'

The mention of her past made Parvathi stop in her tracks for a moment. She gulped hard and looked away from Rahela, not wanting Rahela to see her eyes moisten. Rahela realized that she had touched some raw wounds.

'I am sorry, Paru. I truly am,' Rahela quickly apologized. 'My intention was not to hurt you, dear.'

'That's okay,' Parvathi said, quickly getting back in her stride. 'It's just that . . .' Her voice trailed away.

For a few moments, they both walked in silence.

'So,' Parvathi asked resuming the conversation, 'why are you so excited about the Ouija board?'

'I have so many questions I need answers for,' Rahela said. 'I have been so lost in the last couple of years. Dad's business isn't doing well. I am worried if it will get any better soon. It has been three years since I saw Dad smile. He is my hero, Paru, and I hope things get better. My own future is dependent on things getting better, you know my plans, right?'

'Everyone has problems, Rahela. You are not alone,' Parvathi said, comforting Rahela by placing her hand on Rahela's shoulder. 'Have faith in yourself, your future is in your hands. It has nothing to do with his business doing well or not doing well.'

They walked the rest of the distance to their home without much conversation. They both had mixed feelings of the day.

The next day, they hardly got to speak during the first two sessions in college. The first session was organizational behavior, which Nadira was too engrossed in and Rahela just couldn't grasp. An open-book assignment was announced in the second session in Labor and Industrial Law. Since the test was totally unexpected, the students ran around to lay their hands on their manuals for the first five minutes and, once they got hold of these, kept flipping the pages to find the right answers for the balance of forty minutes.

It was only halfway through the third session that the four girls decided to sneak out of the class even as Prof. Ramachandran explained in detail competency development and its applications in present-day HR.

'Did the Ouija board prepare you for the exam today?' Kyra asked Parvathi, attempting to annoy her.

'Why don't you wait for the results to find out?' Parvathi replied.

'Peace,' Nadira said, holding up two fingers in a V-sign.

'That is the sign of victory,' Rahela laughed out, and Parvathi and Kyra joined in the laughter.

Nadira smiled. She was trying to lighten the mood and did not mind the joke being on her. They settled down near the soccer ground on lush green lawns of the college. They would have chosen the dining hall, but that was the first place the principal usually searched for students bunking off classes. The soccer ground was behind the main campus and on lower grounds, which made it difficult for anyone to see from the ground floor of the main campus, where the principal's room was located.

Once they had settled down, Nadira pulled out a pack of KitKats and passed it around.

'Did you have time to think it over?' Rahela asked Kyra.

'Sort of,' Kyra replied.

'Shoot,' Nadira said as the four girls moved closer to each other.

'I was thinking of three rounds,' Kyra said, producing a sheet of paper from her backpack. She did not spread it out for the others to see since she did not want to give anything away to Parvathi. She was keen to observe Parvathi's every reaction.

'I think the first question', she started, 'should be about something for which only we know the answer.'

Parvathi started to object, when Kyra held up her hand to silence her. 'Let me finish the three rounds and then we can have the clarifications and work out the finer details of it.'

Parvathi hesitated a moment before giving in.

'The second round should be about the present,' Kyra continued, 'about the here and now.'

She looked around for effect. Rahela seemed to be silently absorbing the conditions, Nadira was also listening intently, and Parvathi was already readying her objections or maybe her own set of conditions, Kyra deduced.

'The last can be about the future,' she concluded.

'Will it be the best of three?' Rahela asked.

'What is that supposed to mean?' Kyra asked. Parvathi and Nadira were as puzzled.

'I mean what if two answers out of three is correct?' Rahela explained. 'Does that count?'

'What do you think this is? Rock, paper, scissors?' Kyra asked, amused. 'We are supposed to be talking to a spirit. Not the finance minister of India.'

Even Parvathi smiled at the joke.

'Actually, we will never know if the third one is right or wrong,' Nadira added. 'Only time will tell if the answer to the futuristic question is answered correctly or not.'

Everyone nodded in silence.

'Can I speak if you are done?' Parvathi asked.

'Yes,' Kyra replied.

'What if the spirit answers both the questions, about the past and the one on here and now correctly,' Parvathi asked, looking at Kyra directly, 'but one of you cheats and does not accept it to be the right answer?'

Though the question was generic in nature, there was no doubt in anyone's mind as to whom it was directed at.

'Why would we do that?' Nadira asked, trying to sound as if the question was not directed at anyone in particular.

'What if', Parvathi repeated, 'you do not accept the right answer?'

Nadira and Rahela looked at Kyra nervously.

'You have my word,' Kyra said, placing her hand on her chest.

'Word is not good enough,' Parvathi said.

'What do you have in mind?' Kyra asked, knowing very well that Parvathi was not going to give in very easily.

'We write down the answers beforehand,' Parvathi said.

'And hand them over to each other?' Kyra asked 'Not done.'

'There is no need to hand it over to anybody,' Nadira intervened. 'This is how we will do it: we will write the answers and put it in an envelope before we come. The envelopes will be placed in a bowl where we can all see them. In case of dispute, we can open the envelopes and check.'

'Fair enough,' Rahela agreed. She was keen to get into the thick of action. She was already clear about the three questions she would ask.

'Only in case of dispute, we will need to open the envelopes,' Parvathi repeated, looking at Kyra.

Kyra felt there was something in this condition. She only felt she hadn't figured it out. Whatever it was, she would think of something to outsmart Parvathi, she figured.

'Okay by me,' she finally said.

'Cheers,' Rahela squealed, obviously excited that they had made a lot of headway.

'Next clarification,' Parvathi continued. 'No trick questions to be asked.'

'As with?' Kyra asked.

'Questions which are controversial in nature or questions for which no one has the answer,' Parvathi replied.

'Is your spirit media shy?' Kyra laughed. Nobody else laughed. Kyra consoled herself thinking they didn't see the joke.

'Give me an example,' Nadira clarified.

'Let me put it this way,' Parvathi replied, 'hmm, for example, who was responsible for the death of John F. Kennedy?'

'I thought it was plain clear that it was Oswald,' Nadira said.

'Killed, maybe Oswald. Actually, even that is in question,' Parvathi answered. 'But who is responsible? Maybe only the CIA knows the right answers.'

'If the CIA knows it,' Kyra said, 'then even your spirit should know it.'

'Agreed,' Parvathi replied, 'but will you accept the answer without dispute?'

'Absolutely fair,' Nadira averred. 'So it is agreed, no controversial questions.'

Rahela and Kyra nodded in agreement.

'So how do we go about the whole thing and when?' Parvathi asked.

'Let us do it as soon as possible,' Rahela cried out.

'Okay,' Nadira agreed 'This weekend . . . Saturday the 13th okay with all of you?'

Nobody had any objection.

'"Where?" is the million-dollar question,' Nadira said.

'Not my house,' Kyra informed them. 'I have enough issues to . . .' She left the statement incomplete.

'Not mine either,' Nadira stated. 'My mom is having a kitty party, and if I am at home, I will have to keep running around.'

'What about mine?' Rahela asked. 'Let's do it at my home.'

'We can,' Parvathi laughed, 'but remember, if the spirit refuses to leave at the end of the ritual, then you have to live with it in your house for the rest of your life.'

'Noooooooo,' Rahela said, covering her mouth with her hands, her eyes wide with fear.

'Don't scare the kid,' Kyra admonished.

'Okay, do you have a place in your apartment where we can do it?' Parvathi asked.

'No,' Rahela answered, already thinking it was a bad idea to invite them home for this activity, 'we have only two bedrooms and . . . I don't think we can do it there.'

'What about your home?' Nadira turned to Parvathi and asked. 'You have your own bedroom on the first floor and it has a separate entrance from the side of the building.'

'And best of all, my parents are not in town and that means we have the whole house to ourselves,' Parvathi informed them.

'So that's settled then,' Nadira announced. 'Parvathi's home. We meet by 6.30, start at 7 p.m., and we wrap it up by 9.'

Kyra felt that Parvathi had all along wanted the experiment to be conducted at her home. Lure the bait to the den. That was the whole idea behind giving Rahela the jolt. And the dumb kid fell for it, Kyra thought. If only the damn kitty party was not the same week, they could have had it at Nadira's home. It would have been a perfectly neutral territory. Now, she was sure, Parvathi would do something to prep the house. What could it be? Closed-circuit camera? Nah, she dismissed the thought. That would be too much money and effort for such a dumb exercise. But there had to be something.

'Forget it,' she thought to herself. 'There's nothing much I can do about it anyway.'

'Anything else?' Kyra asked, looking at the three of them.

'Just one small detail,' Parvathi said, smiling at Kyra, 'within how many days of the activity will you publicly accept defeat?'

Parvathi's choice of words amused Kyra.

'Let us see who will have the last laugh,' Kyra said, sneering. 'Whoever accepts defeat will do it on the 18th. There is a literary festival starting on that day, remember?'

'Get your speech ready,' Parvathi said, pointing to Kyra.

'And you, yours,' Kyra said, pointing to Parvathi.

The rest of the time she spent in college, Kyra kept scheming on how she would go about outsmarting Parvathi. She wondered what cheap tricks Parvathi would pull to win the wager. She wondered why Parvathi had manipulated the group to finally narrow down the selection of the venue to her home. There was something about the venue that Parvathi would use to her advantage, Kyra was sure. Kyra decided that her plan of action had to be foolproof. The second thing Kyra suspected was that Parvathi would try and play the fool with respect to the answers in the envelope. Parvathi had insisted on it and so she would somehow try and find the answers. But, how?

Kyra was even more disturbed to see Parvathi totally relaxed at college. Even if she was nervous, she cleverly disguised it. Either Parvathi had her modus operandi worked out or she was a damn good actor, Kyra thought.

Kyra decided to ignore what was beyond her circle of influence. She decided that she would have to work on different levels to throw Parvathi off guard. She was not yet sure how, but she was sure she would come around to it eventually. It was only Thursday and she had almost forty-eight hours to come up with a solid plan.

By Friday morning, Kyra had a rough idea figured out in her mind. With a pen and paper in hand, she sat down to write a list of all possible questions and scenarios that she could conjure to get cracking. After an hour poring over it, she still felt something missing. She sat there for the next five minutes, massaging her temples with her fingers to come up with more ideas. Within the next fifteen minutes, she felt exhausted and thoroughly frustrated that nothing new emerged.

Early afternoon, she walked into her father's study and her eyes fell on a Jeffery Archer book of short stories. She looked at the cover and decided to incorporate the book's title into her little scheme: *The Red Herring*.

She went back to her plans and spread the sheets she had been working on the table. She wrote down a single word on the sheet—Diversion. She smiled, thinking how she would set the ball rolling on a plan which she figured would send Parvathi into a tailspin. She deduced that the questions should not be something very hard for Parvathi to track the answers for. It had to be juicy bait propped in front of Parvathi, and the moment she took it, Kyra had to know about it.

Kyra also figured that Rahela was the most intimate friend of Parvathi. Rahela had to be the unsuspecting bait if her plan was to succeed. The most crucial factor Kyra was depending on was Rahela's innocence. No, stupidity, Kyra corrected.

She called Rahela on her mobile to set the plan in motion. After indulging in college chitchat for a couple of minutes, she asked an unsuspecting Rahela if she was prepared for the next day's experiment.

'I always knew what questions I would ask the spirit,' Rahela chirped. 'I think even you can figure it out.'

'Really?' Kyra asked. The truth was she didn't care a damn about what questions Rahela would have in mind. 'Did you tell Parvathi which questions it would be?'

'No,' Rahela replied, 'but I am sure she will not be surprised.'

'Let me guess, it must be about the marks you are going to get in the final exam,' Kyra suggested, knowing pretty well that it was not.

'I thought you would ask me about the questions I was planning to ask in the past and present category,' Rahela replied.

'Yeah of course,' Kyra said. 'Then it must be about your childhood crush.'

'I never had a childhood crush actually,' Rahela corrected. 'But never mind, go ahead and give it one more try.'

'Is it about . . .' Kyra said, thinking hard about which other question she could come up with that would sound credible. 'Let me think . . . the name of your best friend in school.'

'Wrong again,' Rahela sounded triumphant.

'Beats me then,' Kyra said, trying to sound defeated. 'Would you tell me your question if I told you mine?' she asked.

'That sounds fair,' Rahela said satisfied that Kyra was not able to figure out the questions.

'I will tell you mine, then,' Kyra started. 'You know my cousin Rini? She is in the second year in our college.'

'Yeah,' Rahela concurred, 'we all know her well.'

'It so happens that Rini goes for private music classes,' Kyra said, sounding secretive. 'I am going to ask Parvathi for the music teacher's name and phone number.'

Rahela giggled at the suggestion.

'My god, Kyra,' she complimented, 'you have really come up with a tough one.'

'If you fail to plan, girl, then you plan to fail,' Kyra said. 'And my question about here and now will be to guess the last message I received on my mobile phone.'

'That is truly amazing,' a wonder-struck Rahela said. 'You want to hear mine?'

'Yes, tell me,' Kyra said, sounding excited and listened to Rahela's questions with a smirk.

After Kyra disconnected the call, she called her cousin Rini on her mobile.

'I want to know if Parvathi calls asking for your music teacher's name and phone number,' she informed Rini. 'On second thoughts, let me know if anyone asks you the same information anytime from now to tomorrow evening.'

'Why?' Rini wondered aloud.

'Just let me know, please,' Kyra said 'I will tell you the details when we meet at college on Monday.'

The bait had been laid for both the questions. Kyra smiled in anticipation.

Kyra did not go to college that day. She texted Nadira that she was bunking off classes because she was not keeping well. She wanted to prepare for the war and allow Parvathi to interact with Rahela without her foreboding presence at college. She loved the wager.

As Saturday evening approached, Kyra was ready for the action. She had made three sets of envelopes with answers written on A4 sheet papers. These sheets were in turn folded and refolded until they were the size of a visiting card. This was placed in an envelope which in turn was placed in yet another envelope. She didn't plan to use this unless absolutely needed. She was waiting for a reply to a text message she had sent her uncle in the morning. If the reply came, the envelopes would be discarded.

There were other preparations she had done too. Since morning, she had been searching the whole house for near-empty perfume canisters. She managed to find two from her mother's closet, and spent the next ten minutes making absolutely sure that she sprayed out the remaining residue. After she was satisfied that the cans were empty, she placed them in her backpack.

Around 4 p.m., she received a call from her cousin Rini. Kyra answered it enthusiastically, expecting to hear what she had anticipated.

'I don't know if this is connected to what you asked for,' Rini said, sounding bored. 'You remember Raghu from second year, my classmate who broke his leg in an accident two months back?'

'Yes,' Kyra confirmed. 'What about him?'

'He called saying that someone told him I was going for music classes,' Rini said. 'He wanted the name and phone number of the music teacher.'

'And you gave him?' Kyra asked, excited.

'I wasn't supposed to?' Rini asked. 'Oh my god, I went ahead and gave him the name and number. You didn't tell me anything about not giving him the number,' Rini complained.

'That all right,' Kyra replied. 'You did well.'

'What is this whole shady stuff about Kyra?' Rini asked.

'Nothing,' Kyra reassured Rini. 'You will find out by next Friday even if I don't tell you.'

'You are sounding very mysterious,' Rini complained.

'It's nothing. Don't bother,' Kyra said, disconnecting the line.

After she cut the call, she wondered how Raghu knew Parvathi. Anyway, it didn't matter.

At 6 p.m., Kyra texted a reminder to her uncle and, within minutes, received a reply with the name 'Wen Lui' followed by an angry-face emoticon. She smiled, realizing it must have been 5.30 a.m. Saturday morning in Chicago. She ran a couple of errands for her mother before leaving her home at 6.45 p.m. She wanted to be sure that she arrived a few minutes late as part of her plan. When she finally parked her scooter in front of Parvathi's home, as expected, she had a couple of messages waiting on her phone. She was happy that everything was going as per plan when she opened the messages to see one from Parvathi.

'Where are you? Waiting for you.'

The second message received a couple of minutes earlier was with the same content sent from Rahela's mobile. She entered the gate to find the main door open and walked in. Just as she entered the formal living room, she saw Parvathi typing a message on her mobile.

'Hi,' Kyra announced her arrival.

'Oh shucks,' Parvathi replied. 'I just sent you a message asking where you are. I pressed the send button and saw you enter.'

Kyra smiled at the thought that her plan was working. The answer to the 'last message on my mobile' query was being adequately taken care of.

Nadira and Rahela were already inside the house, waiting for Kyra to arrive. They were seated on the living room couch with the TV on. It didn't look like they were particularly interested in what was going on in the television.

'What took you so long?' Rahela complained.

'Traffic,' Kyra lied. 'Now that I am here, let's get started.'

Parvathi, who had joined them in the TV room, started setting the expectations about the ritual that was about to take place without wasting any more time.

'We will enter the dining room in a few minutes from now and that is where we will be conducting the ritual,' she said, making Kyra wonder why Parvathi made it sound as if it was a sacred ceremony. This was the second time she was referring to the experiment as a ritual.

'I have already set up the place for the ritual,' she continued.

'*I bet you have,*' Kyra thought to herself. '*I only wonder what technological gizmos you have placed in there.*'

'Once inside, we shall invoke the spirit who shall enter this medallion,' she said, producing a silver medallion about two inches in circumference. The medallion had a hole about an inch in diameter in the center. The medallion was passed around and Kyra took extra time inspecting it. It weighed a little over 100 grams, Kyra guesstimated.

'There will be a board on the table, with letters and numbers. There is also a separate YES and NO marked on the board,' Parvathi continued. 'We shall place the medallion on the board and wait for the spirit to enter the medallion. At all times our index finger will have to be placed on top of the medallion.'

She placed the medallion on her left palm and placed her finger lightly on it to give a demo. She waited for everyone to place their fingers on the medallion.

'Not so hard,' she said, looking at Kyra, who immediately reduced the pressure her finger was exerting. Kyra was waiting for opportunities to unsettle Parvathi and she found one soon enough.

'As soon as the spirit enters the medallion, he will make his presence known by moving the coin,' Parvathi said. 'After which we will proceed to ask the questions one after the other.'

'How will we know it is not your finger moving the medallion?' Kyra asked.

'You will only know when you get the right answers to your questions' Parvathi shot back.

'Anything else we need to know or do? Nadira asked.

'One last thing,' Parvathi replied, 'do not scream or squeal once the ritual has started. If anyone wants to back out, now is the time.'

She looked at each one of the girls, spending a couple of extra seconds eyeing Kyra. Kyra assumed that these were mind games that Parvathi was playing or, at best, these were setting up the mood. She bit her upper lip to stop herself from saying anything. The bemused smile on Kyra's face was not lost on Parvathi.

'Hand over your envelopes,' Parvathi said, not taking her eyes off Kyra. Nadira and Rahela immediately produced their envelopes. Kyra considered her next course of action.

Everything was going quite predictably. She was not sure if that was good news or bad news. She knew Parvathi was a smart girl, and things being so predictable was a little bit unsettling.

She dug into her trouser pocket and pulled out her mobile.

'My answers are on the phone,' she said and noticed a faint smile on Parvathi's face.

'In which case you will have to switch it off and hand it over,' Parvathi said.

Parvathi and Kyra had been locked in a staring match for quite some time now.

'Are you worried as to whether a phone call or message will disturb the spirit?' she asked, emphasizing the word 'message'.

'You can imagine so,' Parvathi replied, handing the phone back to Kyra. Kyra checked her messages and found the last one sent by Parvathi still unread. She didn't bother to read it, switched off the mobile, and handed it back to Parvathi. Parvathi placed the mobile along with the other two envelopes in a tray.

'Let's go in,' Parvathi said.

She carried the tray as she led the others into the dining room. The three girls followed her and Rahela gasped at the effect in the room. The room was almost dark except for the light emanating from a couple of candles which had been placed on the table. Thick curtains were drawn across the windows to block any streetlight that could have been bright enough to enter the room. The air conditioning was evidently on, as the room was cold and the humming sound of the compressor was the only sound that could be heard. Kyra wondered if the room was dimly lit to conceal some equipment in the room.

To one side of the room was a circular wooden table with four wooden chairs surrounding it. The table had been clearly moved to ensure that the breeze from the AC did not blow out the candles. In the center of the table was the Ouija board Parvathi had mentioned earlier. The candles were placed on candle stands at diagonally opposite corners to give clear visibility of the board.

Parvathi took her place first on the far side of the table, making Kyra wonder if it was strategic placement. Nadira sat to the left of Parvathi and Kyra quickly took the seat opposite Parvathi. She wanted to be able to observe Parvathi's every move and facial expression directly from the front.

'Are we ready?' Parvathi asked softly, placing the medallion on the board.

The three girls nodded and Kyra could see Rahela was clearly nervous. Parvathi placed her index finger nimbly on the medallion and the others quickly followed, imitating her action.

'I shall invoke the spirit now. Please remain quiet,' Parvathi ordered.

The room was engulfed in silence. Kyra looked at Parvathi, who had her eyes closed and seemed to be meditating. Kyra looked around the room and saw the shadows of the other girls cast on the walls. Slowly the shadows seemed to dance as the candles started to flicker. The flickering got stronger and Kyra worried if the candles would altogether blow out. However, the candles held on until the wick started to burn bright again.

'He is here,' Parvathi said softly and the girls noticed the medallion moving slowly. Kyra looked closely to check if Parvathi was exerting any more pressure than the other three participants. She couldn't be too sure.

The medallion slowly moved to a black dot on one corner of the board. Kyra looked at Parvathi, who was gazing at the board and caught her smiling. Parvathi suddenly looked up at Kyra, and their eyes locked for just a moment. Kyra noticed a sudden change in Parvathi's expression, but was not able to read it.

'Who wants to start asking the questions first?' Parvathi asked, keeping her voice just about audible.

'I will,' Nadira volunteered.

'Go ahead,' Parvathi said as the other girls nodded their approval.

'Give me the name of my fifth-grade math teacher,' Nadira said, looking at the medallion intently.'

The coin started to move slowly, stopping at one letter after the other. Kyra felt the cool breeze of the air conditioner softly stroke her back.

'P-R-I-Y-A,' Parvathi read out slowly following the trail of letters the medallion was pausing at.

'Priya?' Parvathi asked. 'Is that name right?'

Nadira just nodded her head.

'Wow,' Rahela exclaimed.

'Your next question, Nadira,' Parvathi prodded.

'Give me the names', Nadira asked, 'of any two persons attending the kitty party at my home tonight.'

The medallion waited almost as if processing the question like a computer does and then started moving. Kyra observed closely once again.

'L-E-E-L-A,' Parvathi said and interpreted it for the benefit of those in the room. 'He says Leela is one and . . .' She focused her attention back to the board. 'S-A-I-R-A, the second one he says is Saira.'

Kyra caught the term 'he' again. *'Deliberate misdirection?'* she wondered.

'Are they the right names?' Parvathi asked.

'I am not sure,' Nadira said, which sounded like music to Kyra's ears. The whole list is in the envelope. We can check it later.'

'No,' Kyra interrupted, 'let us check it now.'

'Fine,' Nadira said and reached for the envelope with her name on it. It was not sealed and so she managed to open it without much ado. She pulled out a sheet with names written on it and she proceeded to check the names.

'I can see Saira aunty's name,' Nadira said, 'I can't find Leela though.'

'Can you check once again?' Parvathi said before Kyra could jump for joy.

Nadira referred back to the sheet. She was obviously having difficulty reading the sheet as the lights were quite dim.

'Nope,' she said, 'not here.'

'Any other name she is known by?' Parvathi sounded a bit desperate. Kyra was enjoying the show, sitting on the sidelines.

'How silly of me,' Nadira said, 'her name must be under Krishna Leela. Let me check again.'

Nadira went back to the sheet as Rahela looked at her anxiously.

'There!' she said. 'It is under Krishna Leela.'

Rahela gave an audible sigh of relief, Kyra cursed under her breath, and Parvathi smiled silently.

'Your last question about the future,' Parvathi asked Nadira.

Nadira hesitated a moment before asking her last question.

'When will I meet the love of my life?' Nadira asked, looking at her friends nervously. Rahela covered her mouth to stifle a giggle.

'D-E-C-E-M-B-E-R 1-4,' Parvathi said, following the medallion. She was aware of Kyra's eyes following her every move. She tried to ignore Kyra's prying eyes.

'Which year?' Nadira asked.

'T-H-I-S Y-E-A-R,' Parvathi said to a smiling Nadira.

'Are you satisfied with the answers?' Parvathi asked Nadira.

Nadira nodded a silent agreement.

'Who is next?' Parvathi asked, turning to Kyra and Rahela.

'I will go last,' Kyra informed the group.

'Fine,' Parvathi said as if she had expected the answer.

'Okay,' Rahela said, clearing her throat as if she would break into a song any moment, 'I want the spirit to tell me the name of the only pet I ever had,' she said, addressing Parvathi.

Kyra was stunned at the stupidity of the question. The day before, when Kyra had talked to Rahela on the phone, the question had been totally different.

The coin started to move slowly, stopping at one letter after the other.

R-U-F-F-U-S

'Why would you want to ask that?' Kyra whispered to Rahela loud enough for all to hear. 'We all know your dog's name was Ruffus.'

'We all did,' Rahela reasoned. 'But how could the spirit have known it?' she asked innocently making Parvathi and Nadira smile. Kyra looked skywards and groaned in helplessness.

'I hope you have a better question to ask for the here and now,' Kyra asked in her normal tone.

'Shh,' Parvathi said, silencing Kyra. Kyra gave a look of bewilderment.

'Your next question?' Parvathi asked.

'I am going to think of a person,' Rahela said again, addressing Parvathi directly. 'I want him to tell me who I thought of.'

'*Him?*' Kyra wondered. '*Now Rahela is referring to the spirit as "him"? That's cool, Parvathi has managed to brainwash Rahela. At least this time, she has come up with a better option than the name of her mongrel.*'

'Go ahead,' Parvathi said.

Rahela closed her eyes and hid her face with her hands. She shook her head a couple of times almost as if trying to shake away a thought. She removed her hands and gave a puzzled look to the group.

'Any problem?' Nadira asked, concerned.

'No,' Rahela said, still looking lost. 'Let's continue.'

'Finger on medallion,' Parvathi reminded. Everyone placed their fingers right back on the medallion.

'Y-O-U-R F-A-T-H-E-R'

'He says that it was your father you thought of,' Parvathi reiterated.

'That's a wonder,' Rahela said, wiping away a tear that had formed in her eye.

'Why is that a wonder?' Kyra asked 'I would have guessed that even without the so-called spirit.'

'It's a wonder because I was originally planning to think of Barack Obama,' Rahela said, 'and that is what you will find if you open my envelope. Somehow I just couldn't finish the thought without recalling my father's face.'

Nadira placed her hand on Rahela to comfort her. They all knew how attached she was to her father.

Kyra found that absurd. Her mind raced to find answers.

'That's impossible,' she thought, 'unless this whole thing is a prank they are pulling on me. Yes. That is the only logical answer I can think of and it fits perfectly. Rahela and Nadira are a part of this scam.'

She looked at Nadira and Rahela through this new revelation. She replayed the cycle of events that had happened since the ritual started. *'Nadira's and Rahela's questions could have been agreed upon before the session started,'* she thought. *'That could have been the reason I already found them here when I arrived. Now I need to play my cards close to my chest.'*

'Your last question about the future,' Parvathi said, looking at Rahela.

'Ask him if I will make it to the United States?' Rahela asked, all excited.

Kyra was lost in her own thoughts, but she snapped back when she saw something interesting happen. The medallion made a tentative move towards 'NO' and stopped. As Kyra watched closely, she clearly saw Parvathi's finger press down on the medallion exerting extra pressure on it. Parvathi looked up to see if anyone had noticed. Rahela and Nadira were closely watching the medallion, but Parvathi knew Kyra had noticed because Kyra quickly looked at Parvathi with a 'There, I caught you with your hands in the cookie jar' look. Parvathi quickly looked away, embarrassed but trying hard not to show it.

'Yes,' Parvathi said. 'It says yes.'

Rahela yelped in delight and found it hard to contain her excitement.

'Ask when?' Rahela said hurriedly.

Kyra again observed closely as Parvathi's finger pressed harder than the other participants of the ritual.

Parvathi said, '2 Y-E-A-R-S'.

'How will I make it there?' Rahela had a rejoinder.

The usual pressure was applied. In fact Parvathi was not even doing a good job of covering it up anymore.

'S-P-O-N-S-O–R,' Parvathi said. 'You will find a sponsor.'

'His name?' Rahella continued.

'Maybe later,' Parvathi said firmly and turned to look at Kyra.

Kyra had an amused expression on her face. She was sure that Parvathi had guided the medallion. But she still couldn't prove anything.

'*Even if I do bring it up, they will gang up and never accept it,*' she thought. '*The best way is to prove that the Ouija board is a scam. They still expect me to bring up the questions on the last message on my mobile and Rini's music teacher's coordinates. Time to spring the surprise.*'

The three girls were now looking at Kyra expectantly.

'I am only going to ask two questions,' Kyra started. 'I don't care much about the future question. Nor do I want to know anything about the past. I am only interested in the here and now. So I have two questions pertaining to only that.'

Parvathi nodded her understanding. 'Changing the rules of the game?' she asked.

'Is there a problem?' Kyra asked and looked at Parvathi closely to check for any signs of disappointment.

'No,' Parvathi said. 'Go on.'

'My first test', Kyra said grandly, 'will be this: I will go to the next room and hide something I brought with me. Your spirit has to tell me what I hid and where?'

Again Kyra watched closely to read the expression on Parvathi's face. Parvathi did not give anything away. Rahela started to say something, but let it go. Nadira had an amused expression.

'All right,' Parvathi nodded.

Kyra picked up her backpack and walked to the living room. She ensured that she closed the door behind her before taking out the empty perfume canister out of the bag.

She pressed the nozzle letting out a stream of plain gas. She made sure she walked to every corner of the room with the nozzle pressed. The hissing sound was much louder in the room now than when she had tried it at her home in the morning. There was nothing she could do about it now if anyone in the room had heard it. On second thoughts, this didn't seem such a bright idea now after all. It seemed dumber than Rahela's question.

She put the can back in her backpack, feeling extremely disappointed with herself. She walked back into the dining room where the group was waiting for her.

'Done?' Nadira asked, a smile playing on her lips.

'Done,' Kyra replied, trying to put up a brave face.

'Finger on the medallion,' Parvathi reminded. Everyone placed their index finger on the medallion.

'Ask your question,' Parvathi told Kyra.

'What did I hide in the living room and where?' Kyra asked, frustration evident in her tone.

Kyra watched as the medallion slowly started to move.

'A-I-R  A-I-R  E-V-E-R-Y-W-H-E-R–E', the medallion moved slowly across the board.

'I don't understand this,' Parvathi said. 'You will have to say if this makes any sense to you, Kyra.'

Kyra nodded her head in acceptance. She did not sit down to explain her experiment. It was a pointless exercise. She now had just one chance at redemption. Her uncle's neighbor Wen Lui was the only person who could save her now.

'The last one', Kyra said, 'is for your spirit to give me the name of my uncle's neighbor in Chicago.'

Kyra looked intently at Parvathi's face. Parvathi's face did not register any change of expression. Kyra started to worry a bit. She looked at the board and slowly placed her index finger lightly on the medallion. She watched with elation as the medallion moved towards R instead of W or L.

'R-I-C-H-A-R-D M-A-R-T-I-N-E–Z,' Parvathi said as she looked up at Kyra. Kyra was beaming with joy. She had finally made a breakthrough. She held back her grin and exclaimed, 'Your spirit is wrong.'

'Wait,' Parvathi said, holding up her left hand to silence Kyra. 'There is more.'

Kyra watched as the medallion started to move again under their fingers: '1-1-2-0'. After a pause, it started to move again: 'M-A-R-I-A E-D-W-A-R-D 1-1-3-1'.

Kyra watched in amazement as she continued to follow the medallion: 'A-N-D W-E-N L-U-I 1-1-2-2 E-L-M-W-O-O-D P-A-R-K'.

She continued to look at the board in disbelief with her mouth open.

'Is that right?' Parvathi asked.

Kyra stood up not saying a thing. Her mind was a myriad of confusion. She didn't know what to say.

'Wow' was the only word that escaped Rahela's mouth.

'So, you accept that the Ouija board is not a hoax?' Nadira asked Kyra.

'I need some time to think this over,' Kyra replied, not looking at anyone in particular. She felt that there was a loophole she hadn't found out about.

'Don't forget the wager,' Rahela remarked.

'Just forget the wager,' Parvathi interjected. 'There is no need for any public apology or acceptance.'

'I need to leave,' Kyra said, picking up her backpack. She turned around abruptly and left the room.

Parvathi, Rahela, and Nadira watched as she stormed out of the room like a sore loser, not even waiting to say a goodbye.

Nadira and Rahela stayed back for a few more minutes discussing the incidents of the night.

'I am so excited,' Rahella said, hugging Parvathi. 'I was so worried about my future. We should do this again sometime soon. I have so many unanswered questions.'

'Time to leave,' Nadira said, dragging Rahela away from Parvathi. 'Thanks, Parvathi, that was fun.'

Parvathi walked both the girls to the door and watched as they walked away laughing and excited.

Rahela and Nadira walked a few steps when Nadira stopped in her tracks. She turned to Rahela in shock and put her hand on her forehead. 'Oh my God,' she exclaimed, 'we need to go back.'

'Why?' Rahela asked, worried.

'We forgot to send the spirit back to where it came from' Nadira said.

'Oh my God' Rahela screamed.

They turned around and dashed towards Parvathi's home. They reached Parvathi's home and found the front door open. The door to the dining room where they had conducted the ritual was slightly ajar.

Rahela was about to call out Parvathi's name when she saw Nadira hold up her finger to silence her. They heard Parvathi speaking to someone. Nadira gestured Rahela to stay where she was and walked silently to the door leading to the dining room and peeped inside.

The room was exactly as they had left it a few minutes back. The lights were still off and the candles were burning. Nadira could feel the cool air from the air conditioner wafting out of the door. Parvathi was sitting on the chair facing the door. She seemed to be smiling and speaking to herself.

'But, you are getting very insensitive these days,' Parvathi said aloud. 'We both know that Rahela will not live to see the next year. But do you have to see the girl die heartbroken?'

Nadira watched in horror as she saw the medallion move all by itself all across the Ouija board: 'I W-A-S J-U-S-T T-E-L-L-I-N-G T-H-E T-R-U-T-H H-O-W W-A-S I T-O K-N-O-W T-H-A-T Y-O-U D-I-D N-O-T W-A-N-T R-A-H-E-L-A T-O K-N-O-W T-H-E T-R-U-T-H'.

Parvathi smiled and said, 'Come, it's time to go to bed' and she blew out the candle.

# Unnoticed

In many ways, I have found myself trapped in an inconsequential life.

All my life, I led a life of mundane existence. I was born the sixth child amongst nine in a farmer's household. Added to my woes were the fact that my parents lived in a joint family and so I grew up unnoticed amongst the twenty-four other children in the family, who fought for everything from food to our parents' attention. My parents hardly even put in an effort to come up with a name that would have stood out in such a household, for I shared my first name with four other children of the vast family.

At the government school, I studied, I struggled to be noticed amongst the hundreds of other children. I neither possessed uncanny intelligence to excel in academics nor was I exceptionally talented to excel in sports or in the literary arenas. I was just another roll number—58. In fact the teachers at school referred to me as just that—roll number 58.

I was never romantically involved, nor did any girl at any point of time ever express any interest in me. It probably had to do with my looks. I was not what could be described as tall, dark, and handsome. At best I was unnoticed.

After I completed my graduation in arts, I left home to find a job in the city. I doubt anyone even felt my absence back at home. And that includes my mother. She would have probably noticed an extra plate with untouched food during mealtimes.

I came to the city, to find a job of my dreams where I could achieve everything a dreamy youngster would aspire for. Three months and a week of hunger later, I was ready to accept the first job that came my way. That is how I ended up joining a call center. The job had nothing to do with what I had prepared for in the past, and I seriously doubt if I had a future there either. I have been working there attending to phone calls for the last two years, logging in before the shift and logging out after the shift, with no life in between.

My life usually followed a pattern depending on which shift I was assigned. There were four shifts in all. The shifts started at 7 a.m., 9 a.m., 3 p.m., and 9 p.m. All the shifts were for a duration of ten hours. My favorite shift usually was the 9 p.m. shift. The calls were less and so was the queue to the washroom. No matter which shift I was in, I had to be at the bus terminus an hour before my shift started. The ride to the office was usually forty minutes in the morning and a little over an hour on my return back home. Once I reached the office, I would punch in my code into the Avaya phone and log in to the web portal to mark my attendance. This would then start the process of routing incoming phone calls of our client Wave TV to my extension number.

Wave TV was a direct-to-home digital broadcast satellite television provider. I worked for their outsourced BPO called Bandwidth Communication. I would have preferred to call the company Bandit for that is what they were, a bunch of thieves. All the dreamy promises that had been sung out before signing on the dotted line had remained just that—dreams. The 45-minute lunch break had been cut short to 30 minutes. The 15-minute breaks had been shortened to 10. The fancy incentives never came unless you achieved a call quality score of 95 and above. You never achieved these scores because the quality analysts who audited your calls were jokers who had never talked to a customer in the last two years and were far removed from reality.

The other promises included a professional work experience (whatever that meant) and a state-of-the-art recreational facility with a sports center, a library, and a gym. The sports center only had board games like snakes and ladders and ludo. Can you believe that? Ludo, for Christ's sake! And for some strange reason, all the white pieces of the only chess set that was available had gone on strike. The knight resurfaced every once in a while in the curry they served in the canteen. The canteen in itself was a gambling den. You never knew what you were eating even after it had been served on your plate. Hell, you never knew what you were eating even after you tasted it.

You could read a few comics and magazines that were at least three months old in the library. That is because the magazines, as soon as they arrived, were circulated amongst the top management staff, who would take them home. There was a notice that warned patrons that the magazines were not supposed to leave the library. But that notice was for people like us. There was a gym on the terrace, but all you ever found there was the skipping rope without the handles.

They had also promised a friendly working atmosphere. Friendly? The last time my team leader even smiled at me was two months back. I seriously doubted if he even knew my name because most often he referred to me as number 144, the seat number I had been allotted. Added to all these were a list of strict dos and even stricter you-better-not-dos that were updated from time to time. Don't wear a collarless T-shirt, don't be caught chewing gum, don't carry a book and pen to your desk, don't carry your mobile to your workstation, don't eat at your workstation. I wondered when I would find a 'Don't breathe at your workstation' notice at the notice board near the canteen.

All in all, I was reconciled to the fact that my life would one day be summed up in one word: unnoticed.

And then one day something dramatic happened.

That week I was in the 9 a.m. to 6 p.m. shift.

The day had been an especially busy one at the call center. The European Premier League had started and calls were streaming in back to back from subscribers interested in adding the sports channel. I never knew football was so popular in India.

All day long, it was the same opening lines that I repeated over and over again, 'You have reached Wave TV, your world of entertainment. What can I do for you today?' and the same closing, 'Thank you for calling Wave TV. Happy viewing.'

By 7 p.m. I was more than ready to log off and head back home. As I logged out of my Avaya phone, I noticed for the first time the girl sitting in 146 had been crying. I had never noticed her earlier and assumed that she was a new recruit who had experienced one of those nasty callers who thinks it is their right to abuse people like us as a means to distract themselves from their own frustrations.

I had myself been a target of many such callers, and had got used to the high-decibel abuses of some callers. I reassured myself that even this girl would get used to it and wound up for the day.

I walked to the bus terminus and waited for the first bus homewards. The bus arrived a short while later and I picked my usual seat by the window. I waited for the bus ticket collector to arrive and flashed my monthly bus pass at him even though he ignored me. I pulled out the newspaper to read any news article that might have missed my attention in the morning. Nothing caught my interest and I folded the newspaper and placed it back in my bag. That is when I noticed the same girl whom I had seen crying in my office earlier, seated one row behind me.

I smiled to her, and as expected, she ignored me. I noticed that she was yet to recover from her earlier teary look and wondered what request the customer who abused her must have called her for. Must have been technical troubleshooting, I deduced. That was always one hell of a call. The steps were confusing and required the caller to conduct a series of difficult maneuvers to reboot the set-top box using both his hands while speaking to the call center employee all at the same time. The problem was that most times the caller had to wait several minutes to be sure the problem was rectified. Added to that, the troubleshooting also at times added new problems like erasing programs from the favorite lists and, every once in a while, blocking a few channels for twenty-four hours which usually left the caller highly irate.

I recalled handling a troubleshooting call a month back. The caller had been an old lady who had her set-top box placed at a raised platform and had to climb a chair to reach it. The call went on for forty minutes and finally ended when she fell off the chair, with the set-top box landing on her head. A service engineer who went to visit her the next day discovered that she had a broken arm and six stitches on her forehead.

The team leader had screamed at me for being responsible for the accident. I should have scheduled a service engineer visit, he chided me. I quickly reminded him about another case, just a week prior to this incident, wherein I had scheduled a service visit for another old customer. I had been screamed at that day too, because I had not even attempted a basic troubleshooting on the call. I was accused of being insensitive to cutting costs. They had treated me like a terrorist for a whole week, barging into my calls or listening to my calls, silently waiting for me to make the smallest mistake. For one full week, I lived in the mortal fear that Navy SEALs would show themselves near my workstation to take me down.

I looked at the girl again and felt the deep urge to empathize with her.

'It happens,' I said. 'We do come across rude people. We need to learn to ignore them.'

She preferred to ignore me instead.

I thought of what I could say next. Something funny to cheer her up? Share some experience when I had got shouted at, perhaps? The hot favorites with the agents were to abuse the team leader, or better still, the organization. But I deduced that since she was new, she wouldn't probably agree with me. I decided to empathize with her by saying something nasty about rude customers.

I kept thinking of something really funny and smart to say. As I turned to her, I found her sobbing uncontrollably. I could see tears streaming down her eyes and it was making a mess of her eye shadow.

'What the hell did you tell her to upset her?' A smart aleck, who had been obviously observing us for some time, asked me. He was sitting in the seat across the aisle from her.

'I didn't say anything,' I said, shrugging my shoulders. I tried to look as innocent as I could.

'You did and I saw that you did,' he insisted.

I looked at the girl for some form of support. She continued to cry.

'I want you to apologize to her this instant,' the smart aleck demanded.

'Listen, brother,' I said, defending myself, 'I want no trouble. I swear I didn't say anything offensive. Ask her.'

The bus ticket collector who had been witnessing the exchange walked towards us.

'What is the problem?' he asked.

Even before I could say anything, the smart aleck remarked, 'I think he was verbally abusing her. Look, she is crying.'

'Hello?' I asked, shocked at the sudden turn of events. 'Verbally abusing? What do you mean verbally abusing?'

'Do you know her?' the ticket collector asked me.

'She works in my office,' I replied, still trying to get a grasp of the situation. By now a couple of other passengers were evincing keen interest in the proceedings.

'Is that true?' the ticket collector asked the girl. She looked at the ticket collector, confused for a moment, and shook her head. 'No.'

I was taken aback by her reply. Then it struck me that the girl had probably not seen me in the office.

'That's not true,' I said. 'Look at my office ID card.' I pulled out my official ID, which was hanging from my neck, suspended on a band, and held it up for the ticket collector, the girl, and the smart aleck to see. I don't know why I showed it to the smart aleck, but it seemed like the right thing to do then.

The ticket collector took a close look at the ID, the girl went back to crying, and the smart aleck got back to glaring at me. Some of the other passengers had started to look at me like I was a pedophile.

'What did you tell her?' the ticket collector quizzed me again.

I was regretting the unwanted attention I was getting for the first time in my life. I so desperately wanted to be unnoticed again.

'Look, all I told her was that it happens and we do come across rude people. We need to learn to ignore them.'

'Why did you say shit happens?' the smart aleck asked.

'I didn't say shit happens,' I said, my voice turning squeaky and starting to sound like a boy who had just hit puberty. 'I said *it* happens.'

The ticket collector gave me a long hard look. I ensured I was putting on one of my most innocent looks.

'I don't want trouble,' the ticket collector said, continuing his tough look. 'If you even look at her, I am throwing you out of the running bus.'

The smart aleck let out a snigger. He started telling the other passengers what a scumbag I was. I felt like boxing his face, but I had already got into more trouble than I ever had in my life. I pulled the newspaper out again and hid my face behind it. I didn't look up until the bus pulled up at my stop.

I was planning to slip out of the bus as quietly as I could. I had barely put one leg on the pavement when I saw a blinding light followed by the sound of a huge explosion. I felt a wave of hot air gushing towards me and then I blacked out.

I woke up a few minutes later at the sounds of blaring sirens. There were ambulances and police cars surrounding the place. I looked at the restaurant across the road from where I had alighted. It was in flames and the smell of acidic fumes filled my lungs. A huge crater had formed on the pavement beside me. I tried to move, but it was seemingly impossible. There was a huge sheet of metal lying on my leg. I did not feel any pain.

People were screaming all around me. Some were screaming for help and others to attract attention. Some people were moving injured people from all around. I tried to raise my hand to call for attention but couldn't. I tried to call out for help but realized that hardly any words were stemming from my mouth. My throat felt parched and my skin burnt.

One paramedic rushed towards me. He looked at me for a moment and shouted out, 'There is a man alive here, there is a man alive here.'

A couple of other paramedics arrived, followed by a policeman. A paramedic held my hand near the wrist. 'Yes, he is alive,' he shouted back.

'He looks bad,' one of them said, and I hoped they were not referring to me. They lifted me and I was thankful that they had attended to me. I tried to say thanks by holding up my hand and touching one of the paramedics.

'Don't say anything,' the paramedic replied. 'Just relax, we will rush you to the hospital.'

The last thing I saw was the ambulance door closing.

I have no idea how much time passed before I woke up again. As my eyes opened, I got aware of people shouting instructions all around me. It took my eyes some time to adjust to the lights in the room.

'We have two more injured people coming in,' someone barked.

'Where is the IV stand? Nurse, I want the IV stand,' another one screamed

'Hand me the gauze tape,' someone who seemed not so stressed said in a calm voice.

I opened my eyes slowly and tried to feel the pain in my body. As before, I could not feel any pain.

'Have you sedated this one?' I heard a man ask. The confidence in his voice hinted that he was probably a doctor.

'Yes, doctor,' a female voice replied, confirming my doubts.

How much time before it wears off? I wondered. My hands and legs felt numb. I tried to take stock of the situation.

This was a casualty ward, I reckoned, or some sort of an emergency room. I was lying on a stretcher and not on a cot, I figured, because every time someone moved close by, the bed I was lying on moved. If it had been a cot, it wouldn't have moved.

From where I lay, I could see the entrance of the room. There was chaos everywhere. People were rushing in and out of the room. There were injured people still being carried into the room. The doctors and nurses were moving from one bed to another, attending to patients. A couple of them seemed extremely stressed by the sheer magnitude of the incident and were shouting impatiently. There were a lot of people lying around in various stages of treatment; quite a few of them were in stretchers. The hospital had not been able to find enough beds to accommodate all the injured, I deduced. I saw the girl who had been crying in the bus lying in a bed nearby. She was still crying. I could see a tear slowly roll down her temple as she lay facing the false ceiling in the emergency room. She had patches of blood on her face. I saw that her hand was bandaged.

I thought of all the trouble she had put me through a while ago, and felt like walking up to her and slapping her. Somehow the fact that she was going through all the trouble gave me a secret sense of satisfaction. That feeling was with me until I looked at the stretcher that lay directly opposite me. The ticket collector was looking directly at my face. For a moment, I thought he was dead until he asked me, 'What are you staring at?'

'Nothing,' I replied, remembering his last threat of throwing me out of the bus if I so much as looked at her. I didn't want to be thrown out of the emergency ward now.

I turned my gaze away from the girl.

'The bomb was in the restaurant,' I heard one of the doctors telling another.

'So it was a bomb,' I thought to myself. Strange how you see these kinds of things in the news channels and think it will never happen to you. And when they show you all those nameless and faceless people that get killed and injured, you never feel for them. Not until it happens to you.

A nurse came within a little distance. She was carrying a lot of medical supplies in her hands.

'Excuse me, nurse,' I called out. I guess my voice got drained in all the chaos. She didn't even turn around to look at me. She got busy attending to a patient lying in the bed nearby.

And then a scary thought hit me. This did look like a corporate hospital. I waited for the nurse to turn around. She had the emblem of a corporate hospital on her apron. Did we have to pay an advance to get medical attention here? This is a bomb blast and they should be providing emergency care anyway. What does the government policy covering private hospitals have to say about this? I tried to recall any one of the news articles that appeared in the newspapers about this. All I could recall was that the government had announced an ex-gratia payment of a pittance amount to the injured in a similar case a few months back. First aid has to be given, I asserted.

I looked at the ticket collector. Nobody was attending to him either. Did the hospital staff know that we did not have money? Maybe people who traveled by public transport didn't have rights. Maybe we were not important citizens.

The ticket collector looked at me.

'Why aren't these people attending to us?' I asked.

'Is there anyone in your family who has been informed?' he questioned back.

'I don't know,' I replied. 'I have no one here in town that can come for me. What about you?'

'I saw them taking my purse out for identification,' the ticket collector informed me. 'I think I lost my cell phone in the blast.'

I wondered how they would react to this news at home. The only person I had talked to in the last two years was my mother. She had never referred to anyone inquiring about me. How would they even inform her? Her phone number was not written anywhere. Maybe they would get in touch with my company. I wondered if the crooks would even acknowledge that I was an employee there. Not if they would have to pay the hospital bill. The last time I had cut my finger at work, the HR did not want to part with a Band-Aid and convinced me that some wounds need to be left open.

Suddenly there was a flurry of activity near the door. A familiar face walked in. He stopped near the entrance to absorb the scene around him.

'Hey,' I shouted. 'I know that guy. His face seems familiar.'

'He is the home minister,' someone remarked near me. I turned to look. It was Mr. Smart Aleck, who was lying on another stretcher. His shirt was all torn off to the right. The left part of his shirt was soaked in blood.

'He has come to ensure the media doesn't hound him later,' Smart Aleck replied. 'If that bloody fool did his job right, we wouldn't be in the hospital now.'

For the first time, I agreed with Smart Aleck.

'Now what?' I asked.

'Same bloody crap,' Smart Aleck said, sounding sarcastic. 'The minister will say he is shocked, the chief minister will say they will do their best to try and catch the people who planted the bomb, and the public will hold candlelight vigils for a couple of days. Everything will be forgotten within a week. The bomb blast will be on the front pages for a couple of days and slowly move into the inner pages. Nothing is going to change.'

'Don't be so cynical,' the ticket collector reprimanded him.

'Oh yeah?' Smart Aleck said. 'Don't you watch television every time something like this happened? You can't distinguish one bomb blast from another. It is the same thing that happens. Two days from now, a politician will die, or there will be a thousand-crore scam.'

I couldn't agree with him more.

'Worse still,' he continued, laughing. 'India will win the cricket world cup and all this will be history.'

I sighed in despair. Mr. Smart Aleck had a point. This was a regular. You couldn't fight the logic. Even worse, you couldn't fight the system.

I turned to look at the uninvited guest. The home minister moved from one bed to another, talking to the patients or the doctors attending to them. He walked up to the girl from the bus and talked to her. The crybaby started to sob again.

'Yeah, all right,' I said, 'why doesn't someone ask him what he said to upset her?'

'Oh, shut up,' the Smart Aleck said. 'You haven't figured it out yet, have you?'

'Figured out what?' I asked. I didn't get a reply.

The home minister consoled the girl and was even touching her hand. He looked around, spoke to a doctor, and walked away within a few minutes, hardly even bothering to look at other patients.

'Great,' I shouted, 'come back before the next elections. You just lost my vote, buddy.'

I heard the smart aleck laugh. It was a sarcastic snigger. Someone walked near my stretcher and in the process moved it. This helped give me a slightly better view of my right side. I was suddenly able to see below the ticket collector's waist. First, I thought I was imagining things, but a second look made me shiver in fear. The ticket collector's right leg was missing. The blast had ripped away his right leg from the knee downwards. I wondered if he had realized it. Do I draw his attention to it?

The ticket collector noticed the shock on my face.

'What is it?' he asked.

'Nothing,' I said, trying my best to look away from him.

'Can somebody move my stretcher, please?' I shouted out loud.

The stretcher moved again. Thankfully, I was not looking at the severed part of the ticket collector's body anymore. I tried to think of something else to take my mind off the ticket collector. I thought of office.

'You have reached Wave TV, your world of entertainment. What can I do for you today?'

'Let me hear some more excitement in your voice when you say "Wave TV",' my team leader would have said. 'Your voice should go up and down like a wave.' He would move his hands in an imaginary wave. 'Like that, see?'

And what were the other corny lines of his? 'Life is like a call center call. You get to interact with all kinds of people: the angry ones, the frustrated ones, the polite ones, the courteous ones. Each one has a need. You address his need and voila, you have a happy customer. Simple.'

Life is like a call center phone call! What a joke. Show me the troubleshooting stuff, Mr. Team Leader, and get me out of this mess. Bloody joker.

This was not helping. I was only getting even more frustrated. Every bloody jerk was taking me for a ride. The team leaders, Bandwidth Communication, this hospital, the stupid crybaby, the smart aleck were all hand in glove. This was a bloody nexus.

'Can somebody attend to me, please?' I said assertively. 'We call center employees have rights too, you know.'

A nurse looked towards me for a moment and turned away. Incompetent fools. Can't even handle a simple bomb blast. I had half a mind to walk away. I thought about the ticket collector. Why wasn't he screaming in pain? When you lose a limb, you scream in agony, right?

I tried to recall how they showed similar situations in movies. The hero gets up in the hospital bed and tries to get off the bed. Then he realizes he doesn't have legs. 'Where are my legs?' he screams before breaking down and crying. Maybe the ticket collector hasn't realized it yet. Maybe he is heavily sedated. What do they call it . . . local anesthesia?

Then a scary thought hit me. Could it be that even I had lost a leg? Or both? The ticket collector hadn't yet realized that he lost a leg. What if my leg was gone too? Maybe that is the reason the hospital staff was afraid to approach me. Maybe they don't know how to break the news. 'Sorry, boy, you lost a leg. You can never run again!' Scary. 'Sorry, boy, you lost both your legs. Forget running, you can't even walk again.' Damn scary. What could be worse? Going blind? Thank God I could see. Small comfort.

And then the girl started to cry again. This time she was wailing. I looked at her bed. Bed? Damn feminism at this hour. The guys get stretchers and the lady gets a bed? A couple of nurses rushed to her. This was getting to be too much. She cries and she gets the attention. What was that saying, 'the crying baby gets the milk'? The guys were fighting for attention and nobody was bothered?

'What the hell are you making a racket for?' I shouted at the girl.

'Oh, shut up,' the ticket collector shouted back at me. 'What is it between you and that girl anyway? Why were you creating all that trouble for her in the bus?'

'I didn't do anything,' I shot back.

I heard laughter from the back. Mr. Smart Aleck again.

'What are you laughing for?' I asked.

'Because of what happened in the bus,' he said, still laughing.

'What is so funny?' I asked.

'You guys have still not figured it out, have you?'

'No,' I said, 'what was so funny?'

'My God,' I heard Smart Aleck groan. 'You are a real idiot.'

I tried to recall the sequence of events. The first time I saw her crying was at the call center. I tried to picture her sitting there and crying. What was she holding? A mobile phone? She was looking at the mobile phone when she broke down. How the hell did she manage to get her mobile phone to her desk? Didn't she know the rules? All mobile phones stay in your locker. Never mind that. It meant that the reason for her agony had not been a rude customer. It was a personal problem.

And then I saw her on the bus. The first time I had seen her, she was talking to somebody. No, she was handing over something to somebody.

'Did you figure out why she was crying?' he asked again. He didn't wait for me to answer. 'She was crying because I broke up with her this morning. I was on the bus to take back the engagement ring.' I heard him laugh out loud as he finished saying it.

I flinched as I heard that. The worst part was the ticket collector joined in the laughter.

'Lucky woman,' the ticket collector added.

'Lucky woman?' I asked. 'Why lucky?'

'Oh my God,' the ticket collector said. 'What are you? A first-rate idiot? You still haven't figured it out?'

'No,' I said, perplexed, 'what is it that I am missing?'

'Don't tell him,' I heard the smart aleck say. 'Let's see how long he takes to figure it out.'

'Bloody loonies,' I said, 'keep your stupid secrets to yourself. What do I care why she is lucky?'

I really didn't care about the broken engagement or why she was lucky. I just wanted to know if all my limbs were fine. I would have been happy if somebody could just clarify my bloody doubts and attend to me.

And then I saw her. A young nurse. Must have been quite new to the job. She looked out of sorts and diffident. She was not sure what she was doing. She was attending to a patient. A senior nurse came by and grabbed the bandage from her hands, seeing her struggle to tie the knot. She moved away from the patient and looked in my direction. Our eyes met.

'Excuse me, nurse,' I called out to her softly, 'you mind stepping near me?'

She walked towards me with a cotton swab. She approached me and started to lightly dab at my forehead.

'Thank you so much,' I said. 'I can't feel a thing. I know I must be sedated. But could you do me a favor and tell me if I am all fine?' I asked.

That is when a senior doctor stepped beside my stretcher and asked, 'What do you think you are doing?'

'Doctor,' she replied in a sweet voice, 'this patient—'

'For heaven's sake,' he said, irritated, 'don't you know that the patients in the stretcher are the dead ones?'

I heard Mr. Smart Aleck and the ticket collector laugh out loud.

# A Miss-Placed Notion

I turned to take a second look at the girl Vinay was talking about. There was no doubt about it. She was one of the most beautiful girls I had ever seen in my life. Her long oval face was accentuated by high cheekbones. Her thin eyebrows arched above a set of smiling eyes. Her nose was thin, neither too long nor too short. She had just the perfect nose that so beautifully complemented her pink lips. The curls of her long ebony dark hair made her look a tad wild.

Even more reason why I was finding it hard to believe what Vinay was saying.

It was a sunny morning and there was no forecast of rain for another twenty-four hours. We had gathered for our informal meeting at the Taj Elegant, a fairly exclusive, but not so expensive, air-conditioned restaurant situated in close proximity to our office. The restaurant was mostly frequented by either college students who came by from the nearby university campus or young office-goers like us.

That day the four of us—Vinay, Aakash, Jai, and I—were following our daily routine of having coffee and breakfast before we started on our market visit. We all worked for a mobile phone company in the sales division as senior sales executives. Our job was to approach various corporate clients and sell bulk corporate connections. Business had been dull due to cutthroat competition, and it was two years since we had seen any hike in our salaries or the daily conveyance allowance. And so we had decided to pool resources as much as possible, and every now and then, we would piggyback ride on each other's bike.

Amongst the group members, I was personally close to Jai. He was the most senior amongst the four of us, having spent close to four years in the organization. He had a positive attitude and a great sense of humor. He took risks and believed in sharing knowledge. He didn't view me as competition and would be ready to give a helping hand when dealing with tough clients. He had taken up the onus of mentoring me and never hesitated in giving me feedback when I could have done something better. There was never a dull moment with him around. He hailed from a wealthy family and didn't need the job in the first place. He kept referring to the job as his training ground before he took over his family business. Jai was, however, prone to mood swings every once in a while. And during his bad days, he would prefer to clam up rather than showcase his caustic sense of humor.

Aakash, on the other hand, came from a middle-class background much like me. We both desperately needed the job and were there to build a career for ourselves. Aakash was an engineering graduate who decided to get into sales, much out of compulsion than by choice. Evidently he was not cut out for it as he was shy and struggled to keep a conversation going. He suffered from a huge inferiority complex because he felt he couldn't convince anyone to lend him a lifeboat even if his life depended on it. Add this to the fact that he was always looking to score with girls though he lacked any skills, and they made him quite an interesting character. I suspect that the only people he got along with were the three of us. We put up with him, more out of sympathy than any other reason, because he took every opportunity to remind us of all the dramatic issues he faced in life.

Coming to Vinay, I have often wondered as to how I would describe him. You see, the challenge has always been to find something nice to say about him. Just about everyone you talked to had something not very gracious to share about him. Penny-pinching, aggressive, manipulative, conniving, and flirty—and these were his better qualities! Most people had run out of words to describe his irritating persona. Personally, the most irritating trait I disliked was his audacity when it came to women. Of course I had many other nasty things to say about him, but the fact that he claimed to have romanced or loved and rejected every woman on earth, apart from Mother Teresa, was nauseating for me. Actually, just about everyone I knew, had a pet hatred when it came to Vinay. Jai had two, in fact. Jai couldn't decide whether it was Vinay's penny-pinching or his deceitful character he hated more.

But not everyone hated Vinay. All right, I knew one guy who didn't—Aakash.

Aakash found Vinay's company extremely uplifting and gratifying. I have often wondered why, and the only plausible answer was that both of them shared a common goal. They were both obsessed about scoring with girls. Every time Aakash had tried, he had failed.

The truth was that Vinay was a glib talker, all right. He did have the confidence to go and strike up a conversation with a girl at the risk of being rejected. With Aakash it was different. He couldn't even approach a girl, forget talking to her. Of late he had started to believe that if there was one person who could help him in his mission, it had to be Vinay. He truly believed that Vinay had the skills that would help him befriend at the least one girl. Vinay was going to be his messiah.

The last couple of years, the situation at the office had been quite bad. The sales reported by our team had been at an all-time low, partly because Vinay and Aakash had chased different figures from the ones Jai and I had been chasing.

Our office timings were from 9.30 a.m. to 5.30 p.m. Those were supposed to be the official timings, since someone from the admin department had put up a blue board with white letters to remind the management that everybody had a family to go to after office hours. The board served no further purpose than to remind us that we had to reach the office before 9.30 a.m. We would usually report back after our market visits and write our daily call report, which was then left on our marketing manager Vikram's table. I have no idea if Vikram ever bothered to go through the reports. Hell, I had not seen Vikram for the last three months! The last time I had met Vikram was in the washroom. I doubt he even recognized me.

Every once in a while, I found a bunch of my daily reports, sometimes unsigned, on my desk, with a terse 'For filing', scribbled on a yellow Post-it note. Most of my counterparts would just dump the reports in the bin. I ensured all my reports, or at least the ones that came back from Vikram, were chronologically filed in a box file.

There have been numerous days when I did not go back to my office in the evenings because it would have been extremely late, and no one even noticed. The truth was that no one bothered. The company had set us monthly targets to achieve, which we most certainly never did. If we reached close to 70 per cent of the assigned target, we believed that we had done a great job. Anything less than 50 per cent and we were extended the privilege of meeting Vikram.

The blundering executive then got to hear a few of Vikram's choicest expletives. And he did have a good assortment of them. He then would ask the failed candidate to stay back in office for the full week and give him a list of all his prospects, and their plans and just about any information he had about the market. Once that was done, Vikram would personally sit with his victim and review the list over a dozen times until sheer exhaustion took over. The problem is that by the time anyone was over and done with this activity, they were staring at another missed target for the present month too.

Thankfully, I had always stayed as close to my target as possible. Aakash wasn't that lucky and he had shared the experience with us.

'No less than a third-degree police torture,' he had said, recollecting the harrowing experience. 'Vikram will keep asking you the same question over and over and over again until he hears what he wants to hear. And all he wants to hear is that we have been loitering in the streets aimlessly.'

'Not a situation I ever want to find myself in again,' Aakash recounted with a shudder. Unfortunately for him, he has said this all the three times he went through the experience. He was the favorite whipping boy for Vikram. This month, I worried, I would have to brace myself for some persecution because it was already the 14th and none of us were anywhere close to even 30 per cent of our target. I did have a deal in the pipeline that would see me through, but it had been lying on the back burner for quite some time.

As a daily routine, considering I was way back on my targets, I made it a point to reach office before 9.00 a.m. and read the morning papers. I usually searched for information on new companies setting shop in the city. I would sit down to make a list of prospective client visits from the newspaper articles, and once done, I would run a customary brush on my blazer jacket. We had a strict uniform code and couldn't be seen visiting any of our clients without wearing the navy blue jacket.

I would then pick one of the ties lying in my draw and leave office to reach the Taj Elegant to have my breakfast and coffee. I can't seem to recall when or why the four of us had made it a ritual to meet at the restaurant every morning. It just started as a one off thing and became a routine. The discussions centered on cricket or the soccer game that was telecast the previous night or the latest movie we had seen. One thing we deliberately never discussed was any of our potential clients. The last time we did it two months back had resulted in a bitter fight between Vinay and me. I had discovered that Vinay had made a visit to one of my prospective clients and got twenty-two new connection forms signed by informing my client that I had quit the company. I never forgave Vinay for it ever. I had stopped meeting Vinay at the restaurant for almost two weeks and finally relented to his apologetic overtures later. I was, however, not ready to be tricked twice and so refused to disclose any of my clients in front of the group.

That fateful day, by the time I left for the Taj Elegant, none of the team members had shown up yet at the office, which was not unusual. By the time Aakash and Vinay finally did reach the restaurant, I had already finished eating my breakfast and was waiting for my coffee. There was no sign of Jai yet. As always, Aakash and Vinay sat at the same table as me, and continued their conversation about Sachin Tendulkar's imminent retirement. Vinay who, till the other day, was subscribing that it was time for Sachin to hang up his boots was now feeling nostalgic about how India would miss its favorite son on the cricket field.

I did not offer any opinion, because I had none, and focused on the coffee, which was much stronger and more bitter than the usual one they served. The restaurant was crowded as usual at this time of the day.

'I think the new kid Virat has a lot of potential,' Vinay was telling Aakash. Aakash just nodded his head in agreement. Aakash, it seemed lately, had no opinion of his own. He would readily agree with anything Vinay said.

'What do you think?' Vinay asked Aakash.

'I agree,' Aakash replied. Vinay was not very happy with the answer. He was looking for a debate and Aakash hardly stood up for a verbal duel in the recent past.

'What do you think?' he repeated and it took me a couple of moments to realize that the question was directed at me. I noticed Aakash looking at me with the same kind of expression an anxious judge would have when the defendant is questioned by the prosecutor for the very first time in a sensational murder case.

'I think Tiger Woods is better,' I replied.

Vinay and Aakash looked at each other briefly before giving up on me and going back to decide who, according to them, made the cut for the next world cup.

I was preoccupied with my coffee cup and quickly gulped down the remnants in it. I was concerned with my plan for the day. Usually, I would manage to prepare a list of seven to eight companies to cold call based on my cursory glance of the newspaper. That day I had just one. Most of my follow-up visits were not scheduled for the day. I reassured myself that I would come up with more names by the time I finished my only planned client visit. I didn't plan to wait for Jai and get further delayed.

I said a hurried goodbye to Vinay and Aakash, who seemed to be in no hurry themselves to hit the market. As I approached the exit door, I got preoccupied with the safety clip of my helmet and in the process did not notice the waiter suddenly open the door. I banged my head on the door and it took me a couple of moments to get over the pain. The waiter just smirked and suggested I wear the helmet even while walking. Bloody idiot.

I massaged my forehead with my fingers even while I walked towards my bike. I placed my bag on the petrol tank and strapped on my helmet. I had just about sat on my bike and turned the ignition key on, when I noticed a sharp shower of rain descend down on me. The rain was unexpected and I quickly grabbed my bag and dashed back to the entrance of the restaurant. I hoped for a quick end to the rain, but the rain only seemed to pick up momentum and vigor. I looked up at the sky and noticed a blanket of thick clouds that didn't seem to be disappearing any time soon. I figured I would be better off inside the restaurant and walked back into the restaurant.

When I reached the table, I noticed that Jai had joined the group. Strangely, I hadn't seen him enter the restaurant. He looked up to nod a greeting. I took my place on the only empty chair beside him.

'Looks like a thundershower,' I remarked to Jai, who moved the curtains of the nearby window and peeped outside. I removed my blazer and placed it on the backrest of the chair.

'They were expected,' Jai remarked.

'I thought the weather report predicted a clear sky with rains only expected tomorrow,' I remarked.

Jai shot me a curious look. 'Which news channel do you watch?' he asked. 'Anyway, it doesn't look like the rain will end anytime soon,' he remarked. Jai did not look his usual self and I quickly figured that this was probably one of those rare days when he was not in his element.

I found a pot of coffee on the table and poured myself a hot cup. I tore open the sugar sachet and added it to the cup. I looked at Jai toying with a piece of toasted bread. There were three more pieces begging for my attention and I didn't want to disappoint them. I dumped a lump of butter on one of them and turned my attention to Vinay and Aakash, who were involved in an animated discussion.

'I just do not know what it is in me that these girls fall for,' Vinay was telling an attentive Aakash. 'Do you know the reason why I broke up my previous relationship?' he asked, turning to the group.

He waited for an answer from us while sucking on an imaginary lollipop. He took turns to look at each one of us waiting expectantly for an answer. I had so many possible answers running in my mind that I could have offered to Vinay.

'*Your looks or the lack of them, your table manners, your painful attitude*' were a few thoughts running in my mind, but with Jai not in his element, I was not too sure of taking on Vinay all alone. I glanced at Aakash, but he was still looking at Vinay with abject devotion. I was afraid he would break into a devotional song any minute now.

'Go on, go on,' Vinay prodded me with enthusiasm.

'The recession?' I suggested, pushed to a wall.

'No,' Vinay replied, clearly not getting the sarcasm.

'Do tell, do tell,' Aakash beseeched Vinay.

Vinay smiled triumphantly. 'You take a guess,' he told Jai.

Jai took a good long look at Vinay and remarked, 'Whatever,' and got busy with his coffee. I looked out of the window. It was still pouring. There was no bloody way to escape the torture. I reached for the second piece of toast, spread some more butter, and picked up my cup for another sip of coffee.

'My girlfriend and her sister fought over me.'

As a reflex action, I spat out my coffee. A couple of people sitting on nearby tables turned to look at us. It just didn't matter to Vinay.

'I was about to be engaged to the elder sister, when the younger one proposed to me,' he continued. I was amused to see Aakash's eyes widen with surprise. I let out a soft groan and leaned back in my chair.

'Still don't believe me, eh?' Vinay asked. 'Tell you what. Anyone of you remember Roshni?' Vinay continued.

'Roshni?' Aakash asked.

'You wouldn't know her. She was our marketing manager Vikram's executive assistant some time back,' Vinay said, dismissing Aakash. It was obvious that he wanted to impress

Jai and me with his exploits. Aakash was already eating out of his hand.

'What about you?' Vinay asked me. 'You remember Roshni?'

'No,' I said tersely.

'When did you join the company?' he persisted.

'I don't remember. Around two years back,' I replied, showing no interest in the conversation.

'Date?' he asked. 'Do you remember the date?' he continued.

'How does it matter?' I asked, unable to conceal my irritation at being interrogated.

'Just tell me the date,' Vinay replied.

'Sometime around mid May,' I replied. 'Why?'

'Aha. I think Roshni quit in April the year before last,' Vinay added.

'I joined much before that. There was no one called Roshni even then,' Jai made his first genuine contribution. He ensured that he looked at his coffee all the time just in case we misunderstood that Vinay had got him interested in the conversation.

'Looks like you don't remember her. Can't blame you, she just worked with us for two or three months,' Vinay said.

'What about Roshni?' Aakash asked enthusiastically.

'Yes. She joined in November and quit in January,' Vinay continued as if he hadn't heard Aakash. 'How could I forget? I still remember the New Year's Eve party we went to. It was at Novotel. I paid ten grand just for the two of us.'

'The Novotel got inaugurated only last March,' I reminded.

'Then it must have been the Marriott,' Vinay barked back. 'Does it matter which hotel it was?'

'Not if the devil isn't in the details,' I remarked.

'The name of the hotel isn't important,' Vinay insisted.

'If you insist' I replied.

'Are we discussing hotels here?' Aakash asked me, irritated, and turning to Vinay said, 'You were telling us about Roshni.'

It was evident that Aakash was the only guy interested in the conversation. I looked out of the window again. Some jobless idiot had started floating paper boats on the road outside. I looked at the boats as they got caught in the wheels of a two-wheeler parked carelessly on the road.

'The New Year's Eve party in Radisson's was going for . . . eight grand,' he said thoughtfully. 'Yeah, eight grand. Correct. That's because I remember telling Roshni, "What is two thousand bucks for a night of happiness?"'

I still had no idea why I was putting up with the torture. I started reflecting on my value system. Maybe I am a sucker for pain, I contemplated. The real reason was that I usually don't like to be curt with people. I believe in being polite, even in the face of extreme pressure. Maybe I felt the need to be liked by people. Even people like Vinay.

Vinay continued his blabber. 'I remember, Vikram patted me on the back and said, "I always knew you were the best",' he said and started patting Jai, who in turn gave an irritated shrug.

'Yeah? Good. But you still didn't complete the bit about Roshni,' Aakash pleaded.

'Roshni?' Vinay asked. 'Oh yeah, Roshni. Cute kid. Curly hair. Dimpled cheek, always wore modern outfits.'

'That's nice. But what happened between both of you?' Aakash insisted on knowing.

'Well, that is a long story,' Vinay smiled, 'but I will tell you nevertheless.'

'As if we had a choice,' Jai retorted.

Vinay just glared at him and then looked at me to check my interest level.

'I need to go to the washroom,' I said quickly, getting up. 'Don't wait for me, please do continue.'

I felt relieved to even get away from the table and walked leisurely to the washroom. I was in no hurry to get back to the table and did my best to keep myself occupied in the washroom by looking out of the washroom window for a long time. I quit after one of the customers gave me a 'you seem so unemployed' look. I ensured I spent a lot of time patting my hair down, washing my hands with soap, pulling my shirt out and neatly tucking it back again a couple of times, and unknotting my tie and tying it back up all over again. Certain that there was nothing more to do, I looked out of the window once again to still see the rain pouring down. Disappointed, I strolled back to the table. En route, I looked at my watch to check the time. It was close to 10.45 a.m. and the date was shown as 15th instead of the 14th.

I removed my wrist watch and fiddled with the crown to change the date back by a day. Back at the table, nothing had changed. Vinay was still holding Aakash's undivided attention.

Jai glared at me as I approached the table and asked me privately, 'Where the hell were you? How the hell can you leave me with these loonies?' I just shrugged helplessly.

'The last time she met me, she said, "I wish I could continue working with you, Vinay."' Vinay was concluding his story grandly.

'So touching.' Aakash said, visibly moved. I remembered that Vinay had started his story with an argument that two sisters had fought over him. I wondered if that had been covered in conclusion. But I was not going to risk asking him anyway.

I sat down at the table, feeling helpless at my situation. The fear of being way off my targets and the fact that I didn't seem to have an inventory of prospects was only making me feel worse. The futile chatter between Vinay and Aakash made me feel trapped in an inglorious existence.

I desperately needed something that would cheer me up, something that would make me thank God, a signal that not all was lost, that there was hope . . .

That is when I saw her just outside the glass door of the restaurant.

It would be an understatement to say that she was the most beautiful woman I had ever seen. As she waited to wipe away a few raindrops from her face with her handkerchief, I felt my heartbeat race. The whole world seemed to come to a standstill; actually it looked as if the world didn't exist in the first place. As she entered the restaurant, the place just lit up as if someone had just opened the blinds for the sunlight to come right in. Her face seemed so familiar, as if I had known her for ages. Something about her was so familiar, so endearing. I felt so much lighter and felt my arms just drop by my sides.

She opened the glass door and walked the first couple of steps into the restaurant and I saw her hair bounce as if to an inaudible beat. The light streaming in from behind her seemed to create a halo around her head. As she entered the restaurant, the restaurant was enveloped in a respectful silence. I realized that each and every one of the customers sitting there had stopped doing whatever they were doing and was looking at her. The men were admiring her with abject devotion and the women in sheer envy.

It was obvious that she was used to creating this effect wherever she went, for she just looked around as if to search for known faces. She was hardly disturbed by all the attention she got, and for a brief second, her eyes met mine as she looked at the group I was sitting with. She gave an excited smile of recognition and waved in our direction. It must have been a reflex action that my hand automatically sprang up to wave back. It remained there for a few moments until a sudden realization hit me that probably the girl hadn't waved to me but someone else in our group. I forced my hand down and looked at my colleagues to check who the lucky guy was that she could have waved to.

I spotted Aakash with his mouth open and just short of drooling. Jai, like me, had his hand up acknowledging the wave. It was Vinay, however, who stumped me. He was standing up and waving back to the girl.

The girl, I hoped, would walk over to our table. She smiled at us before quickly turning away and walking to an empty table on the far side of the restaurant.

We watched for a moment and I was suddenly aware of a few appreciative glances directed at us coming from people sitting near our table. I looked around at my group. Aakash still had his mouth open, Jai had gone back to sipping his tea and Vinay was still on his feet looking in the direction of where the girl had headed.

From where I sat, I could continue to see the girl. 'Wow' was all I managed to say as Vinay sat down

'And that gentlemen, is the girl I am dating now,' Vinay said triumphantly.

'What?' the three of us asked in unison. I was sure I had heard it wrong.

'I said I am seeing her now,' Vinay said with a proud smile.

'We all saw her now,' Aakash said.

'No, you idiot,' Vinay said, irritated. 'I said that is the latest girl in my life. We are *dating*.' He laid special emphasis on the last word.

'Are you serious?' Jai asked, shocked.

'For the first time, I must admit I am. So is she,' Vinay replied, still full of himself.

'How do you know her?' Jai was suddenly curious.

'You will find this interesting,' Vinay said, 'but I just met her yesterday.'

'Yesterday?' I asked, shocked. 'I am not sure I understand. You just met her yesterday and both of you decided that you are *on* to each other?'

'This, as I said, will be an interesting story,' Vinay said.

'Please do tell,' Aakash pleaded.

Vinay looked around at us for approval to go ahead with his story. Jai was noncommittal but I must admit my face would have disclosed my keen interest to hear more. For the first time, I was keen to hear Vinay speak. I was not sure if anything he said would be the truth, but he had got me interested anyway.

'I will tell you, provided you do not interrupt me,' Vinay said, the statement more or less directed at Aakash.

Aakash ran his index finger on his lip in a gesture of zipping up and waited.

'Yesterday morning, I was making my routine field visit when I came across this office called Helois Developers,' Vinay started.

The name suddenly seemed very familiar to me. I couldn't readily recall where I had come across the name. 'Was it in the newspapers today?' I wondered. Maybe Vinay was using my technique to source prospective clients.

'I walked into this office and at the reception asked for the admin department,' Vinay continued. 'I was asked to wait for a few minutes by the front desk executive, after which he informed me that most of the admin staff were not available and asked if I could meet with their admin executive. I was not keen, because you know that an admin executive hardly ever gets to take any crucial decisions. However, since I did not have any more calls planned for the day, I thought what the hell, so be it.'

That seemed very unlike Vinay. He would not meet anyone unless he was sure he would manage to squeeze some business out of the person. I did not comment.

'I walked into the admin department,' Vinay continued, 'and that is when I saw this girl for the first time. To be honest, I have seen many a beautiful girl in my lifetime, but she just was so exquisite and different.'

I saw Aakash shaking his head heartily in agreement. I couldn't disagree on the point myself.

'The first time she smiled at me, I felt as if I was in a garden, in the midst of beautiful flowers with delicate butterflies fluttering their wings around me. I was bathed in wonderful sunshine and felt surrounded by positivity all around me,' Vinay said with a dreamy look on his face.

As I sat there listening to Vinay, I was sure that was exactly the effect the girl had on me when I first saw her. I was still feeling the warmth of her gaze on me when she had looked at me for that one instant. I knew I would never ever forget that smile in my entire life.

'She greeted me warmly and asked me for the reason of my visit,' Vinay carried on. 'Trust me, guys, when I say that her voice was so melodious that for a moment all I could hear was the soulful sound of music. I just wanted to stand there and keep looking at her till eternity.'

I noticed Jai watching the whole exchange with a bemused look on his face. Aakash was getting bored with the poetic descriptions. He wanted to get straight to the action.

'All right, what happened next?' he prodded Vinay.

'Hold on, buddy, I am getting to that,' Vinay snubbed Aakash 'I obviously turned on my irresistible charm and told her the reason for my visit. She heard me out attentively and said I was just the person she was looking to meet. To tell you the truth, the way she said, it sounded like she was looking for a life partner and I was just the one she had been waiting for.'

Aakash let out a groan. Obviously he was frustrated. I could relate why. Vinay was pathetic when it came to handling romance. It was not the words, it was the way he said it, especially his body language and the tonality. They were all a big letdown.

'Anyway, I asked her what she meant by saying that I was just the person she was looking to meet,' Vinay continued where he had left off without getting into a verbal duel with Aakash. 'She told me that since she had just moved into town a week back, she was looking for a new phone connection and wanted to know if I could help her with it. I of course was quick to seize the opportunity and handed her a new connection application form and asked her to fill in the details. She asked me if I would want to pick up the forms later, but frankly, I couldn't imagine being anywhere else but near her. I offered to wait as she filled in the form. I kept looking at her as she filled in the details. After she had finished filling the form, I asked her for her photographs to be attached to the form. She searched her bag and couldn't find one.'

I studied Vinay closely as he narrated the story. Thus far it seemed to be a credible story, though predictable. I was worried that the whole story would turn out credible. Somehow I just didn't want the story to be true. You don't go to a movie to see the scoundrel marry the heroine.

'I was quite disappointed that she was unable to find a photograph,' Vinay continued, 'but soon my disappointment turned to joy when she asked if I could take her down to the nearby mall which had a photo studio. I almost jumped for joy and instantly agreed. We both drove down to the mall on my bike, and for me the time just seemed to stop when she held me as I drove the bike. I don't remember the traffic; I don't remember the potholes. All I remember is the fragrance of her breath as she spoke to me with her face so close to my ear. I don't remember anything she said, only the softness of her grip on my shoulder.'

The way Vinay said it, I felt as if I had been going through the experience myself. It seemed all so surreal.

'After we reached the mall,' Vinay said, 'we walked to the photo studio and had her pictures clicked. The studio assistant told us that it would take twenty minutes for him to give us the pictures. She asked me if I was busy and I said no. She asked me if I would like to have a cup of coffee with her at one of the cafés in the mall. I was more than happy to agree and we walked to the cafe on the second floor. Trust me; I was getting quite a few envious glances from the visitors at the mall.'

Now that was a profound statement from Vinay. Every time he had ever talked about a relationship with a girl, it was always about him. How the girl was madly in love with him and how the girl was lucky to have him, blah-blah-blah. For the first time, I heard him say that he was the one getting the envious looks from people. Well, I didn't doubt that after seeing the girl. She was indeed exquisite. But the marked change in his usual spiel was distracting. Was he finally saying something true? Or was this deliberate diversion?

'We ordered coffee and got talking,' Vinay chatted on. 'I asked her if she didn't have to get back to office and she said that as per her office policy, she could take the day off to search for a permanent accommodation as she had been transferred to the new location. We kept chatting on a few things like the nature of her job and I have never felt so good talking to someone for the first time. It almost seemed like we had been friends for a very long time. Though our interests were different and we hardly had anything in common, I found myself wanting to be with her for a longer time. The topics shifted from movies to music and a lot of other things. I think we spent more than an hour talking when we finally realized that we had to get up and go to pick up the photographs. The photographs were ready and she handed over a thousand-rupee note for the sixty rupees the studio assistant had charged for. The studio assistant did not have the change and so I offered to pay for the photographs. I took two photographs out of the six and handed the envelope back to her.'

'Two?' Jai quizzed 'But you need just one to process a new connection.'

'I wanted to keep the other one,' Vinay said sheepishly, 'but she took the envelope and put it back in my blazer pocket, saying that since I had paid for it, she couldn't take it until she had paid for it.'

I had a strange feeling about the story Vinay was telling me. I couldn't put my finger on it. Was it the fact that I couldn't imagine such a beautiful girl being wasted on a scumbag like Vinay? Was it that Vinay must have been cooking up the whole story? On the face of it, it seemed quite real. And as he said it, I could visualize the whole thing, almost as if it was me who had gone through the entire experience and not him. I decided to continue listening to Vinay without commenting.

'As we walked down the stairs, she asked me if I had any other pressing commitments. I asked her what she had in mind and she replied that, she had noticed a supermarket on the first floor and that she would have loved to buy a couple of things and in the process also return my sixty bucks. I told her that the sixty bucks were not important, but she insisted. So we went to the supermarket. The time we spent in the supermarket was one of the most memorable times in my life. To start with, we walked in the aisles looking for nothing in particular. Whenever she saw something that interested her, she would hold it for me to see and explain the product in detail. Do you know this toothpaste has salt? Do you know that if you use a mix of this spice with tomato puree, you get a tangy taste and so on and so forth. Other customers kept looking at us as if we were a newlywed couple. In fact, she actually noticed it and mentioned that we looked like newlyweds.'

'Was it Cajun? I interrupted.

'Sorry?' Vinay asked.

'The spice that she talked of, was it Cajun spice?' I asked.

'I think so,' Vinay said. 'Why?'

'I don't know,' I replied 'I have heard it before that tomato puree and Cajun spice does give a tangy taste. Maybe it was in *MasterChef Australia*.'

'Is that important now?' Vinay asked, a tad irritated. I just shrugged my shoulders to mean, 'I thought so.' Jai chuckled at the exchange and Aakash gave me an irritated look.

'After about an hour of shopping, she finally picked up some stuff and we reached the billing counter,' Vinay said, 'and at the billing counter—'

'Even they didn't have the change,' I sputtered. Yes, I felt I knew where this was going.

'How the hell do you know that?' Vinay asked, bewildered.

'Just hazarding a guess,' I lied. I was not sure if I was actually presuming or if I was having a sense of déjà vu. The story seemed so familiar. Did I read it somewhere? If I did, then maybe Vinay had read the same story. But this was getting so damn predictable.

'You are right,' Vinay replied, 'even they did not have the change and I offered to pay for her purchases. So now she owed me three hundred bucks instead of sixty. We laughed at the situation and by now it was getting close to lunchtime. I asked her if she would mind having lunch with me. I told her that the lunch was purely my treat and she agreed. During lunch, I found her opening up to me even more. She talked to me about her troubled relationship with her father, who had issues.'

'What issues?' Aakash asked.

'Must have been an alcoholic,' I said.

'How did you know that?' Vinay asked, amazed.

How did I know that? Good question. I have no idea how I knew it. I still tried to think up something fast. 'There are only three issues a man could have that his family is aware of: financial, alcohol, and womanizing,' I said, hoping it sounded credible. 'Considering that she had just met you in the morning, I doubt she would have spoken about womanizing.

That leaves out financial issues and alcoholism. I think it was a lucky guess.'

I let out a silent sigh of relief as Vinay continued. 'By the time lunch was over, I was sure that this relationship was heading somewhere,' Vinay confided, 'and so I asked her if she would go to the fair with me in the afternoon.'

'You did? You devil,' Aakash said with adoration. 'And she came?'

'Yes, she did,' Vinay laughed. 'We drove down to the fair after lunch. I did not want the day to end. At the fair, just after we came out of the roller-coaster ride, I held her hand for an instant. Though I let go, I felt her grip my hand firmly, and after that, we kept holding hands for the rest of the evening. Her hands were soft like velvet and I felt a certain feeling of current passing down from her body to mine.'

'How much did the roller-coaster ride cost?' Jai asked. I thought that was a strange question at this point of time. However, I noticed that Vinay seemed to have been caught off guard by the question. Vinay had that strange look on his face when you are caught with your hands in the cookie jar.

'Fifty rupees per head,' he replied.

'It should be seventy,' I corrected.

Jai gave a surprised look and said, 'I didn't know you visited the fair this year.'

'I didn't,' I replied.

'Then how would you know?' Aakash questioned.

Another good question. Yeah. How would I know? But, I was pretty certain about it.

'Maybe I saw it on the Net,' I offered.

'The best one was the spooky house walk,' Vinay laughed, getting back to the topic. 'Has any one of you been to the spooky house walk?'

'No,' Aakash replied.

*'Have I been on the spooky house walk?'* I asked myself. For some reason, I felt I had been. But I couldn't be sure and so I preferred to keep my mouth shut.

'You walk along a dimly lit cave where you suddenly find skeletons tumbling and scary faces appearing out of nowhere,' Vinay explained. 'There is also this guy dressed as a zombie with blood splattering out of his skull. He chases you with an axe and makes you run for your life. The first time we took the walk, she was so scared that she held on to me the whole time and hid her face in my arms. I loved every minute of it.'

'You went a second time,' I said.

'What are you? A psychic?' Vinay asked, this time clearly irritated. 'How did you know we went the second time?'

'You said the first time she was so scared,' I replied. 'Obviously it meant that you went back.'

'Yes. When we went the first time, she was quite scared,' Vinay said. 'I told her it was all make-believe and that if she came with me the second time, she would have more fun. I just wanted the experience one more time, but she refused until I told her that we could get back at the zombie and scare the hell out of him if she came a second time. Her eyes lit up and she agreed. The second time, we went about scaring the people inside. I knew when a guy would pounce out of the window. We waited and before he startled us, we sneaked beside the window and screamed at the top of our lungs. You should have seen the poor guys face,' Vinay said, laughing.

'And then the zombie tried to sneak in behind us. We were expecting him, obviously. We snatched the axe away from him and ran behind him all the way out of the dark cave. He was so scared that we would hit him that he literally cowered at our feet, screaming.'

Aakash laughed like a schoolboy just visualizing the scenario.

'Poor guy was doing his job to feed his family,' I offered.

'Exactly what she told me when we were having dinner,' Vinay reflected. 'Yeah. Actually, somebody like us who has a lousy job to do.'

A couple of moments of silence intervened. I wondered if this story was going to end exactly like I knew it would. If it did, I wouldn't like it. Such a beautiful girl would be wasted on Vinay. I took another hard look at Vinay. I imagined looking at him from different angles and decided that he looked best when looked at from behind. Maybe beauty is skin-deep after all. Fair enough. Mentally, I began running a list of attributes that could have attracted the girl to Vinay. Either Vinay didn't have them, or the ones he had didn't seem remotely interesting, to me at least. The more I wondered, I realized that all through the story Vinay had not been his usual despicable self. He had projected himself as someone quite different.

That is when the realization hit me. Vinay had modeled himself on me all through the story. He had done everything I would have. He had said everything I would have. The bloody fraud. He would have never offered to pay for the photographs, I would have. He would have never offered to buy her lunch unless he was sure of what he was getting out of it. I would have. He would rather have opted for a pub or a movie to take a girl. I would have opted for the fair, where a girl would have found comfort in the crowds. No wonder I felt the story was so predictable. He had probably realized that being himself, he didn't stand a chance. The scumbag must have settled for someone more sober like me; I felt myself getting mad at him. It felt like he had stolen my identity.

Somehow I felt miserable thinking that the girl would probably have found me a more suitable suitor if only I had managed to reach her first.

'What happened next?' Aakash asked.

'Then we decided to have dinner together,' Vinay said with a mischievous smile. 'During dinner, she told me that she had never had so much fun ever before. She said that she felt she had known me not since the morning, but for an entire life. I said that I too felt so. We talked and laughed during dinner. After dinner, I drove her back to the hostel she was staying in. I did not feel like leaving and she asked me if I would walk with her to the nearby park. Once we reached the park we hardly talked and just held hands and lay down in the lawns, looking at the beautiful sky for a very long time. I do not remember how much time I lay there, just listening to her breathing. When it was finally time to leave, I suddenly felt this irresistible urge to kiss her. I turned my face towards her and realized that her lips were so close to mine, that all I had to do was reach for her lips. But I got cold feet. What if I was rushing things too much? What if I was getting too bold? And what if she did not like the whole idea? What if she refused to see me again? All these questions confused me and I did not want to mess up a beautiful relationship. I was about to withdraw my face when she brought her lips close to mine and kissed me. She held me for a long moment, our lips gently touching each other. I felt I could die that moment with her lips sealing mine. After we moved apart, she looked at me and said, 'A kiss is a lovely trick designed by nature to stop speech when words become superfluous.'

'Ingrid Bergman,' I said.

'Exactly,' Vinay said, 'that is what she told me.'

Jai gave me a look of surprise and admiration. 'I didn't know you would have known anything about the Swedish actress. Never knew you had an interest.'

The truth was I didn't. I had no idea Ingrid Bergman was Swedish or she had spoken those lines, for that matter. But I had heard this quote and it sort of stuck with me. I was not able to recall where I had heard it.

'I asked her what it meant,' Vinay continued, 'to which she asked me to go figure it out.'

I understood what it meant but seriously doubted if Vinay ever would. He was too hollow to understand it.

'Tell me something,' Jai turned to Vinay and asked. 'You told us everything except her name.'

'Ruth,' Vinay replied. 'She is a Christian.'

I looked in the direction of the girl. She was still sitting alone drinking coffee and reading a book. For an instant she again looked in my direction and smiled. I smiled back.

*'Ruth? No. That was not her name. It was something else.'*

'And where is she from?' Jai asked

'Dehradun,' Vinay answered.

'Who else is in the family?' Jai asked, almost as if he had Vinay in the witness stand and was interrogating him.

'Her dad is dead,' Vinay answered without batting an eyelid. 'Mom is a teacher.'

'Any brothers?' Jai asked. 'You know, it is dangerous to have brothers-in-law,' he joked. I was glad to see Jai slowly coming into his element. Outside the rain had reduced to a drizzle.

'Only a sister,' Vinay replied.

I wondered why I felt that Vinay was not speaking the truth. Was it because he didn't want to tell us the truth so that she was shielded from us or was it because he didn't know?

'Where does Ruth stay?' Aakash interrupted.

'Looks like you are digging too hard. You guys don't believe me?' Vinay questioned.

'Of course we do,' Jai sprang to our defense 'How could we not believe you. We saw her waving to you.'

'Now brace yourself,' Vinay said. 'I told you she has a sister, right?'

'Yes,' I nodded.

'The fact is she has an identical twin sister,' Vinay grandly announced.

I heard Aakash let out a huge gasp when the implications of the statement hit him.

'Can I meet her?' Aakash blurted out.

'Don't rush this, buddy,' Vinay said, raising his hands. 'If you need to meet her, you need a lot of things going for you.'

'Tell me. I am willing to put in the effort,' Aakash offered.

'Well, to start with, you need to be dynamic like me. Second, you need to dress smartly. She says she fell for these two qualities in me. Of course looking good and all that helps, but not always,' Vinay said.

I considered this statement for a moment. I was sure Vinay had none of the points he had mentioned so far. Dynamic? You could stick dynamite on his backside and he still wouldn't be anything close to it. Dress sense? His dress sense was so sloppy that no two pieces of clothing matched. If he ever ventured out in the rain, you could be sure a rainbow emerged from him.

'And what else?' I asked.

'Well, a lot more. But I have to go now,' he said and, looking out of the window and seeing the rain had stopped, got up to leave. 'For more information, log on to www.i-shall-buy-vinay-a-few-drinks.com.'

Vinay picked up his bag and dusted the lapels of his blazer. 'She is here to return the three hundred rupees,' he said as he winked at me and turned to leave. He headed straight for the exit.

Aakash did not want to be left far behind. He hurriedly drank up the remaining coffee from his cup and, collecting his belongings, rushed out. Maybe he wanted to meet up with Ruth personally and find out more about her sister.

I sat down reflecting on the story Vinay had told us. It had all seemed so familiar, so predictable. Was the story true? I would probably never find out. The story by itself had seemed so engaging and realistic. And the fact that he had done everything I would have done only made me feel bitter.

'What's the matter?' Jai asked me.

'Nothing,' I said, shaking my head as I looked at my watch. The date still showed 15th. I tried to fiddle around with the crown a couple of times. Nothing happened. I hit it on the table a couple of times, which attracted Jai's attention.

'What the hell are you doing?' Jai asked, irritated.

'Trying to reset the date,' I replied. 'It shows 15th, Wednesday.'

'Today is Wednesday the 15th,' Jai informed me.

'What? Really?' I asked. 'Oh crap. I thought it was Tuesday the 14th.'

'Something the matter with you?' Jai asked, seeing me upset. 'And where the hell were you yesterday? You didn't report back in the evening.'

'I had a job interview,' I said.

'That was the day before,' Jai said, 'unless you had another one yesterday too.'

'Nope,' I replied. 'That is the one.' *Where the hell was I yesterday?* I wondered.

'Something seems to be bothering you,' Jai interrupted my thoughts. 'What is it?'

'He just got me thinking,' I said. 'Vinay and that girl. I can't believe it.'

'Don't believe it,' Jai said. 'I bet my shirt that he was lying.'

'Why do you say so?' I asked, interested.

'Because that bum is lying,' Jai replied.

'Then why didn't you cut him off?' I asked.

'Because he lives in a make-believe world and draws inspiration from it. Why should I play spoilsport on his fantasies?' Jai replied.

'I see. And why do you think he was lying?' I asked.

'That's his second nature,' Jai replied, signaling the waiter for the bill.

'And what made you believe he was lying?' I continued.

'His body language and the way he said those things. The way he kept biting his upper lip and his exaggerated expressions,' Jai said.

'Oh, so now you are a body language expert?' I asked.

'First of all, if he really knew her, he would have walked towards her from this table. Right?' Jai asked.

'Okay?' I replied.

'At the least, she would have walked out of the restaurant after she saw him leaving. Right?' he asked.

I turned to look at where she was sitting. It was true; she was still sitting at the same chair. She hadn't left after all.

'You must be right,' I said. 'I hadn't thought of that.'

I started to relax a bit, and then a thought struck me. 'Wait a minute,' I said. 'She did wave to him, right?'

Jai nodded his head. 'Come to think of it, she could have waved to anyone of us. She waved in this direction. We are not sure if it was at him.'

'I wonder whom she waved at,' I said, 'and I also caught her smiling at us.'

'You seem to be quite interested in the kid,' Jai laughed. 'Don't blame you, she is definitely a looker.'

I could feel myself blushing

'How about getting to know her?' Jai asked.

'You serious?' I asked Jai.

'Of course,' Jai replied. 'What do we lose? After all, we never let go of the opportunity when it presents itself.'

I was still unsure of the whole idea though it sounded good. It must have been my fear of rejection which was making me hesitate.

'You think it is okay?' I asked. 'Just walk up to her and ask her if she knows Vinay?'

'Why bring Vinay into this?' Jai asked. 'She waved to us, maybe it was Vinay. Maybe it was me. So what?' Maybe she thought we were someone else. But she made the first move. How could it hurt?' Let us just walk up to her and say she looks familiar and find out her name,' Jai said, 'and if her name is not Grace, end of story.'

'Ruth,' I said with hesitation, 'not Grace.'

'Whatever,' Jai said dismissively.

'So we just walk up to her and tell her she looks familiar and ask her name. Doesn't that sound like a pickup line, Jai?' I said. Frankly, I would have loved to get one chance to speak to her.

'So it does,' Jai replied. 'So big deal. That is what you are trying to do anyway. You know any better pickup lines?'

'No,' I shrugged.

'Then that is exactly what we will do. Maybe it works. Maybe you can get to know more about her. Who knows, you may even get to exchange phone numbers. Haven't you heard that opportunities are limited? You see one, you grab it.'

I was still unsure of the whole thing. How do you walk up to a girl and tell her, 'Hey, I know you from somewhere.'

Jai got up from his chair and pulled me by the arm.

'Come on,' he said, 'don't worry, I will do the talking. Trust me.'

'Just a minute,' I said and hurriedly picked up my blazer and wore it.

'Are you going for an interview or are you going for an introduction?' Jai asked, perplexed.

'Might as well look presentable,' I smiled as we started walking towards her.

She was sitting a mere twenty feet away from us, but it seemed like the longest walk I had ever taken. I was feeling excited and nervous at the same time. I kept looking at her and as we approached her, I realized how much more beautiful she looked. Her face so familiar, as if I had known her for years, if not generations. It was no more a feeling. It was a strange realization. A voice inside my head kept telling me that her name was not Ruth. It was something else.

She looked up from the book she was reading and her eyes met mine. For an instant, I saw a smile of recognition and then she saw Jai with me. She looked confused, not knowing how to react. When we were a couple of steps away from her and she was sure that we were headed for her table, she got up, smiled, and extended her hand to Jai.

'Hi, I am Aryeah. You must be his colleague, Jai,' she said.

Jai, like me, was caught unawares. He had a bewildered look on his face. He hardly managed to blurt out a polite 'Hi' by the time she already turned to me. She extended her hand towards me and I grabbed for it. It did indeed feel like velvet.

I held on to her hand as if I was under a spell. And then I realized that she had slipped something into my hand: three hundred-rupee notes. I looked at her, not able to understand what was happening. Jai seemed as puzzled as me on this strange turn of events. I looked at the notes for what seemed to be a long time as she stood there smiling. She held up her hand as if waiting for me to give her something. I had no idea what she was expecting from me.

She looked at me and shrugged. 'Are you going to give it to me or not?'

As I stood there bewildered, she just reached out to put her hand in my blazer pocket and fished out a wad of paper slips. She sorted out a little brown envelope and returned the bunch back to me. She held out the envelope for me to see. On it was stamped the date 14th November 11.30 hrs.

She smiled and said, 'Now that I paid for them, the photographs do belong to me.'

I turned to look at Jai, who had a shocked look on his face. He was holding his palms to his cheeks and had his mouth open. I looked at the slips on my hand. One of them was a ticket from the fair. It said, 'Admit 2' and below was printed 'Rs 140/- only'.

And then it all came back to me like I was watching a movie backwards. The ride to the fair, the lunch together, the supermarket, the ride to the mall . . .

She then moved her lips close to my ear and whispered, 'If you are not too busy, can we go out like yesterday? I loved the Ingrid Bergman thingy.'

A smile escaped my lips involuntarily as I thought of the Ingrid Bergman thingy.